TIGHTROPE

EVE TOWNSEND: SERIAL KILLER HUNTER

BOOK ONE

MARK LUKENS

Tightrope—Copyright © 2020 by Mark Lukens

All Rights Reserved

No part of this book may be reprinted without written permission from the author.

This book is a work of fiction. Names, characters, places and incidents either are a product of the author's imagination or are used fictitiously. Any resemblance to actual persons, living or dead (or in any other form), business establishments, or locales is entirely coincidental.

747 PRESS

Cover design by: Extended Imagery

OTHER BOOKS BY MARK LUKENS

THE ANCIENT ENEMY SERIES
ANCIENT ENEMY
DARKWIND: ANCIENT ENEMY 2
HOPE'S END: ANCIENT ENEMY 3
EVIL SPIRITS: ANCIENT ENEMY 4

THE DARK DAYS POST-APOCALYPTIC SERIES
COLLAPSE: DARK DAYS BOOK 1
CHAOS: DARK DAYS BOOK 2
EXPOSURE: DARK DAYS BOOK 3
REFUGE: DARK DAYS BOOK 4
AFTERMATH: DARK DAYS BOOK 5
SURVIVORS: DARK DAYS BOOK 6
HELL TOWN: DARK DAYS BOOK 7
AVALON: DARK DAYS BOOK 8

THE EXORCIST'S APPRENTICE SERIES
THE EXORCIST'S APPRENTICE
POSSESSION: THE EXORCIST'S APPRENTICE 2

COLLECTIONS
A DARK COLLECTION: 12 SCARY STORIES
RAZORBLADE DREAMS: HORROR STORIES
FOUR DARK TALES

STANDALONE NOVELS
DESCENDANTS OF MAGIC (with Tony Circelli)
SIGHTINGS
DEVIL'S ISLAND
WHAT LIES BELOW
NIGHT TERRORS
THE SUMMONING
THE DARWIN EFFECT
GHOST TOWN
THE VAMPIRE GAME
FOLLOWED
SLEEP DISORDERS
STALKER

THE EVE TOWNSEND SERIES
TIGHTROPE: BOOK 1
BLOOD PLAY: BOOK 2
BOILING POINT: BOOK 3

Special thanks to my wife, Jet, who is my rock and always there for me. I'd also like to thank a few people who read previous versions of this book and offered advice and their feedback: Kelli, Valerie, Mike, and Mary Ann—your help is invaluable to me and very much appreciated. I thank all of you so much!

ONE

Crooked River, Washington

The killer waited outside the family's home, hidden in the night shadows.

Tonight . . . it was finally going to happen tonight.

He'd taken his time looking for just the right family, just the right home. This family wasn't wealthy like the Townsends had been, but they weren't hurting for money. This family, the Krugmans, lived in a two-thousand-square-foot home, modest in comparison to the twenty-five acres it had been built in the middle of. The next closest home was almost a quarter mile away, with a dense, primordial patch of woods as a buffer between the two properties.

The killer had done his research on the Krugman family and their home. They had no security alarm, no dogs, no guns registered in their names. The Krugmans were a family of four: Scott Krugman, his wife Molly, their sixteen-year-old son Philip, and their fourteen-year-old daughter Amber. The father worked as some kind of software coder in Seattle. He made enough money so Molly could be a stay-at-home mom.

It was late. The lights were out in the house, everything silent on this chilly October night. A full moon peeked through the swiftly-moving clouds every so often.

The killer left the cover of trees and crept to the house. He worked his way around the home, staying out of the splash of light from the front porch. He only had three hours to get this done.

A few minutes later he had picked the lock on the back door and was inside the home. He closed the door softly and locked it. He stood just to the left of the door in the shadows, dressed entirely in black, melting into the darkness, becoming part of it. He held his duffel bag by the straps. His hands were gloved. He wore a form-fitting cloth hood over his head with eyeholes and a small hole for his mouth.

Even though he felt the seconds ticking away, he made himself wait beside the back door—he would still have plenty of time to get the things done that he wanted. He listened to the sounds as he stood against the wall: the refrigerator chugging along, making a slight gurgling sound; a comforting whoosh of air as the heat kicked on; the subtle creaks and pops of a settling house.

He loved the waiting, the moments before this truly began. He wanted to revel in the anticipation, all of his weeks of planning culminating in this moment. He wanted to commit every detail to memory. He felt like a driver at the beginning of a race, part of a football team lined up for the kickoff, one of a group of swimmers frozen, ready to dive into the water at the crack of a starting gun. Yes, all of his weeks of planning were about to pay off in the next twenty minutes as he got the family prepared for the ritual he had planned.

He waited just a moment longer, the anticipation almost electric. He could be a very patient man when he wanted to be. He'd always been able to control his impulses, able to deprive himself of immediate pleasures so he could experience even greater pleasures in the future. In his experience, he found that most people didn't possess the skill of patience, of self-deprivation—they were too lazy to hone those skills, too self-centered, too eager to satisfy whims.

The killer set his duffel bag down on the dining room floor, near one of the wood chairs. He would use these chairs tonight. They looked sturdy enough. They looked perfect.

He crouched down next to his duffel bag and opened it, pulling out a tool belt, much like a construction worker would wear, but modified for his tools. He stood up and slipped the belt on, adjusting it and tightening it just the way he wanted. He pulled a penlight out of one of the pouches and turned it on, keeping one gloved hand cupped in front of the end to cut down on the light. He could probably do this in the dark if he had to, by feel alone. Another pocket of the tool belt held a case of syringes, each with a specific dose, one for each member of the family according to a rough but pretty accurate guess of their weight.

He was ready.

It was time.

He crept into Philip's bedroom first. Philip didn't even stir as the killer slid the needle into his arm and pushed the plunger down. His eyes fluttered open for just a moment, but then they closed again.

Amber struggled a little more, but the killer clamped his hand over her mouth and nose, forcing her head down into the pillow, until the drug sedated her and knocked her out.

It was the parents' room where the killer encountered some difficulties. He realized his mistake as soon as he'd injected Molly—he should have gone around the bed and injected the father first. He made a mental note for the next time.

Molly's eyes flew open. She didn't scream, but she struggled enough to wake her husband. She bucked so hard the needle almost snapped off in her arm.

Apparently, Scott Krugman was a pretty light sleeper. He sat up like a piston, eyes wide open in the darkness, caught in a groggy limbo between sleep and full consciousness.

"What . . ." Scott croaked.

The killer didn't have time to inject Scott, but he always had a backup plan. He took full advantage of the few seconds of shock that paralyzed Scott, pulling a claw hammer out of his tool belt like a gunfighter drawing a six-shooter. He launched himself across the bed at Scott, crawling right over Molly.

Scott stared at the hammer flying toward him in the darkness, staring at the blur of movement like he still wasn't entirely sure if he was trapped in a strange and frighteningly realistic nightmare.

The head of the hammer thunked against the side of Scott's head, making a dull and slightly wet sound. Scott collapsed and slumped over, slipping off his side of the bed and onto the floor.

Scott was out cold. Maybe dead. Hopefully not dead—the killer needed Scott alive; he would play a crucial role in what he had planned.

The killer went back to check on Molly. Her eyes were still half open, but beginning to close. He was pretty sure she'd seen him strike her husband with the hammer, and he loved that she'd seen it. She would see so much more soon.

"Shh," he cooed. "Go to sleep now."

He was tempted to close her eyes for her like they did to dying people in the movies. But he didn't. He needed to act quickly; the drugs were only going to work for about an hour or so, and that gave him plenty of time to prepare the family, but he couldn't waste time, either.

The killer hurried around the foot of the bed to Scott, the hammer still clutched in one hand, the plastic case with the last syringe in the other. Scott lay motionless on the floor, a thick line of blood dribbling down his face and onto the carpeting. But how long would Scott be out? He needed to inject Scott before he came back to consciousness. There was the possibility that the drug and the hammer blow together might prove to be a lethal combination, but he would have to take that risk.

In the next fifteen minutes the killer dragged the members of the Krugman family out to the living room. He pushed any furniture that was in the way toward the walls, giving him enough room to set up the four dining room chairs in a row. He was a little out of breath from dragging the family through the house, even though he'd been training for this. But there was no time to rest.

Twenty minutes later he had the family tied to the dining room chairs with hundreds of feet of rope—bright red rope. Arms were tied behind backs, ankles were bound together, ropes lashing flesh to wood, an intricate design, like humans snared in a gigantic spider's web.

It was done—he had them tied, their mouths gagged with strips of torn bedsheets.

The two children woke up first; Amber, then Philip. They struggled and screamed into their gags. They were terrified, panicking, struggling against their bonds.

"Don't struggle too much," the killer warned.

And in those few seconds as the ropes tightened around their necks, they knew why he had warned them not to struggle. Some of the ropes were connected to all of their necks in nooses, slip knots tightening with every slight movement.

Molly woke up next and he had to give her the same warning. As the red rope dug into the flesh of her neck, she understood immediately, like the kids had.

The killer loosened the nooses so Molly and her two children could breathe. But they would struggle again soon . . . when he started cutting.

He was beginning to worry about Scott, but then Scott finally woke up, panicking for just a second.

"If you're very, very still," the killer told the family as he slipped a gloved hand into his duffle bag on the floor, "you'll live through the night."

That was a lie. Maybe they knew it. Maybe they didn't. Maybe they wanted to believe it. They prayed and sobbed through their gags.

He pulled out a rolled sheet of canvas from his bag, unrolling it on the floor, revealing the row of knives, the sharp blades reflecting in the cozy lights from the kitchen. He took a moment to select just the right knife to begin with. He stood up and approached Scott.

The nooses pulled just a little tighter around their necks.

TWO

Crooked River, Washington—8:50 a.m.

Special Agent Lewis Parker and his partner Martinez pulled up the Krugman's house. A collection of cars and trucks were parked in the front yard: a state trooper's car, two sheriff's deputy vehicles, a coroner's van, a plain car that probably belonged to a King County detective. Everyone was going to claim jurisdiction here, but Agent Parker was going to have to inform them that this was the FBI's case now because this murder was tied to another one from ten years ago.

Tightrope was back.

As soon as Parker got the call and heard the details about the murders, it felt like a rope was tightening around his chest, several lengths wound over and over again, cinching tighter and tighter with every breath, like a gigantic snake constricting and waiting patiently until all the air was squeezed from his lungs.

Maybe it was a small panic attack. He'd never had a panic attack before, but he knew what the symptoms were. But panic wasn't the motivating emotion for him—it was guilt. Guilt because he hadn't been able to catch Tightrope when he had murdered part of the Townsend family, abducting the youngest daughter and leaving behind only one survivor in the house—Eve Townsend. Guilt because he and the FBI had never gotten anywhere close to catching Tightrope.

The Krugmans' home wasn't the mansion the Townsends had lived in ten years ago, but this crime scene had some of the similarities of the first setting: it was remote, the home right in the middle of acres of land, a location where Tightrope could take his time. But there was something else that felt the same as it had when he'd been at the Townsends' home years ago, a feeling of evil hanging the air like a fog that clung to everything. Most might not sense the vileness in the morning air, but Parker could. He never claimed to be a psychic—and that wasn't what this sensation was, not in the literal sense—but it was more like a cop's intuition, a kind of sixth sense cops developed over time. When you visited crime scene after crime scene, you could sense the violence, and sometimes the evil, coming from the place (and sometimes from the suspects themselves when you finally apprehended them, the evil radiating from them in waves).

Parker was brought back instantly to the night ten years ago at the Townsends' home as he put the car into park. He saw seventeen-year-old Eve Townsend again. Eve had run from the house after she regained consciousness, running outside and calling for her sister, trying to find the abductor and her family's killer, a man the media would later dub Tightrope because of the intricate webbing of red ropes he used to bind his victims. Eve had sobbed later when Parker and his partner at the time, Agent Janet Friedman, had visited her in her hospital room. Eve said she'd been too late to save Maddie, and she couldn't forgive herself for letting Tightrope take her little sister away.

Parker had promised Eve that he would find the man who had abducted her sister and killed the rest of her family. He had promised that he would *personally* bring that man to justice.

But he hadn't.

The Townsend murders became a huge news story. The murder of James Townsend, a well-known billionaire who had made his fortune with a startup biotech company, was big news. James Townsend wasn't quite as famous as Bill Gates or Steve Jobs, but he *was* famous, a maverick, and some even said a genius in his field. As the news media closed in, cameras on, lights flashing, Eve had implored the public for help, breaking down in front of the TV cameras. Some had compared the abduction of Eve's sister to the kidnapping of Charles Lindbergh's son. (*And we all know how that one turned out*, the news reporters' eyes said.) Some called the Townsend Tragedy the Crime of the Century, trying to build up ratings and internet clicks. The whole country—and a lot of the world—seemed to be searching for Eve's sister and the man who had taken her. Psychics tried to help, some with good hearts and intentions, others looking for their fifteen minutes. Thousands of leads came in, but they all led to dead ends.

After a year, the news media had moved on. The FBI and state police had no choice but to move on; there were other crimes, other murders and abductions that perhaps had some chance of being solved.

Parker and Eve kept in touch after that night, even becoming friends of sorts. Over the years Parker had watched a normal seventeen-year-old girl harden into something vengeful, a beautiful creature with a single-minded focus. Eve had gone to college, but she didn't stay long. She was the sole inheritor of the family fortune (unless Eve's sister was ever found). Some on social media pages proposed that Eve had been involved with the murder of her family and the disappearance of her sister—a few billion dollars was a lot of money, an irresistible amount to most. It was a popular theory.

A few years after college Eve tried out for the FBI. Parker had given her pointers on passing the tests. He even promised to put in a good word for her. But ultimately, she'd been turned down. She had aced the written and physical fitness tests, but she wasn't able to pass the psych evaluations, not to the FBI's standards, anyway.

Being turned down by the FBI had crushed Eve. If she couldn't find Tightrope then she wanted to go after others like him. She'd finally found her calling after years of wandering around in a fog. But the thing she wanted most in the world was beyond her reach.

"You okay?" Martinez asked.

Parker realized he'd been staring out the windshield for at least a full minute. He looked at Martinez, his fourth partner in the last ten years. He nodded. "Yeah."

Martinez knew the Tightrope case; hell, everyone in the Bureau did. He knew the memories Parker was struggling with.

"Ready to take a look inside?"

"Yeah," Parker said and got out.

They walked to the front porch. The front door was wide open. A sheriff's deputy stepped aside so they could enter.

Normally, this crime would fall under the jurisdiction of the sheriff's office, or even the Washington State police, but because this crime could be a link to an ongoing FBI case, Parker and Martinez had been called in. The details of this crime were very similar to the Tightrope case ten years ago.

Similar? No, it was almost exactly the same. Parker realized how similar as soon as he saw the bodies bound to the dining room chairs with the bright red ropes.

Déjà vu washed over Parker, along with the coppery scent of blood. The air was sticky with it.

"God," Martinez whispered, holding a handkerchief up to his nose and mouth.

A police photographer snapped a few more photos and backed out of the way so Parker and Martinez could get a closer look at the bodies. Two sheriff deputies hung back by the corner of the large living room, whispering to each other.

"It was like this before?" Martinez said. He hadn't been at the Townsend crime scene ten years ago, but he'd seen the files—he had studied the case while training at Quantico. All the recruits did.

But this wasn't *exactly* like the Townsend Tragedy. Ten years ago, at the Townsends' mansion, there were two empty chairs. This time all four chairs were occupied with the dead, their bodies rigid against the red ropes binding them, arms bound behind the backs of chairs, wrists and elbows wrapped in rope, more rope connecting the family members to each other, bound ankles to bound ankles, bound wrists to bound wrists, necks to necks. Webs of ropes. Seemingly miles of rope.

Dried blood matted the carpeting under the chairs, dark brown stains now. There were indentations in the carpet from where the chair legs had shifted as the family struggled, but the ropes holding all of them together kept the chairs from tipping over. The family's clothing had been cut away in large swaths between the ropes, pale flesh exposed, large patches of skin sliced away, holes gouged in their bodies, puddles of blood in their laps, dried on their legs. Ropes dug into their skin. Eyes bulged, glassy and lifeless. Mouths frozen open in screams underneath the strips of white bedsheets used as gags.

Martinez's phone buzzed on his hip. He walked away, talking into the phone in a low voice.

Parker studied the four bodies. He hadn't moved an inch when Martinez came back a moment later.

"Forensics is on the way," Martinez told him.

They wouldn't find anything, Parker almost said, but didn't. No evidence had ever been found the last time at the Townsends' home.

Maybe it would be different this time. Maybe Tightrope had slipped up. But Parker wouldn't bet on it. He was sure Tightrope was only going to get better at his craft.

THREE

An hour later the forensics team began their work inside the Krugmans' home. Parker needed to get out of the house for a little while. Martinez joined him outside. The coroner's van was still parked in the front yard, along with one of the sheriff's cars.

Parker searched for footprints and tire tracks as he walked past his car to the dirt driveway, which ran five hundred yards to the gate where a sheriff's car was stationed. Forensics would look out here eventually, but he felt like he needed to do something.

"You think it's him?" Martinez asked.

Parker stopped at the edge of the driveway. It had warmed up a little but it was still a chilly day. He shoved his hands into his pants pockets, gazing at the patch of woods in the distance beyond the other side of the driveway. "Seems like it."

Along with the guilt, Parker felt a sense of exhilaration, like he was finally getting a second chance at catching Tightrope. The science of forensics had gotten much better in the last ten years and there were more cameras everywhere now: surveillance cameras, security cameras, ATM cameras, traffic cameras. Everyone had a cell phone. Maybe they would spot Tightrope on one of those cameras at a gas station or at a stoplight, or at a store buying supplies. Maybe they would catch a glimpse of his vehicle, get the license plate. Something.

"Maybe it's a copycat," Martinez suggested.

Parker nodded. He'd already thought of that.

"I mean, he hasn't killed for ten years. Why would he start again now? Why wait ten years?"

"I don't know," Parker muttered, still staring at the woods.

"There hasn't been nothing like this in the last ten years," Martinez said, glancing back at the house. "Not like this."

"Maybe he changed his M.O. for a while." As soon as Parker said it, he felt it was unlikely. Killers like Tightrope usually had a certain way they liked to kill. And even though some killers changed their methods of murder, or the types of victims, there were still details that could link murders to a single killer, little idiosyncratic things they did, almost like signatures or fingerprints.

"Killers that change their M.O.s are usually opportunistic killers," Martinez said. "And I don't think Tightrope is an opportunistic killer. This . . . this was too organized. Obviously planned out."

Opportunistic killers prowled around looking for victims, happening on the right victim at the right place and time. They took the gifts given to them, or they traveled around until they spotted a certain type of victim they preferred, like a young blonde woman, or a homeless person, or children, or prostitutes. But Martinez was right, Tightrope planned things out meticulously. This family had been chosen for a reason.

But why?

It was the same question Parker had asked himself ten years ago at the Townsend crime scene: Why kill the Townsend family? Or at least *attempt* to kill them, because he hadn't gotten them all—he hadn't gotten Eve. If Tightrope had wanted to kill a family, why choose such a high-profile family like the Townsends, a family so hard to get to, a family with security alarms and cameras and a dog? Tightrope had killed the Townsends' dog before entering the house. He'd known about the dog, been ready for it. He'd disarmed the security system. Either he'd known the code or had bypassed it somehow. He'd parked his vehicle (some kind of truck, most likely a van or an SUV) on a dirt road that paralleled the one side of the Townsends' property, nearly a quarter mile from their home. He had taken Maddie Townsend with him, either alive or dead. Whether she was dead or unconscious at the time, he had carried her to his vehicle because there had only been his set of footprints. He had carried her all that way.

Tightrope had taken Maddie and killed her mother, father, and brother. But he'd left Maddie's older sister, Eve, behind. He had planned everything out so well, but somehow Eve had gotten loose—that's what she'd told Parker and his partner Friedman the next day in her hospital room. Eve had fought with Tightrope, but he'd kicked her in the head, knocking her out. He could have killed her after he had knocked her out—it would have been so easy for him to do it. But he hadn't. Why not? Was he too preoccupied with Maddie? Had he panicked and run?

No, Tightrope didn't seem like the kind of person who panicked. But he also didn't seem like the kind of person who made mistakes, leaving loose ends behind, leaving witnesses behind. That could only mean that he had left Eve alive purposely.

Tightrope's "mistake" of leaving Eve alive had led many at the FBI to suggest that the Townsends were Tightrope's first murders, and he had botched it by leaving Eve alive. Some posited that Tightrope had to choose which girl to take with him; he couldn't carry them both. Others felt that maybe Tightrope believed he had killed Eve and left her for dead. But he hadn't tortured Eve like he had her parents and her brother; he hadn't cut her like he had cut them. It was like he'd left the two daughters unmarked, saving them for something else.

Parker found it hard to believe the Townsends were Tightrope's first victims. The whole thing had been too well-planned. Parker believed, even though the Townsends would have been a challenge to get to, Tightrope had chosen them specifically. Maybe it had something to do with the biotech company James Townsend ran, something Tightrope felt that James had done wrong, a punishment meted out. The biotech company had crumbled less than a year after James Townsend's death, so maybe that was the ultimate objective. But if all he wanted to do was wreck James Townsends' company, then why hadn't Tightrope left a note behind, or some kind of manifesto like eco-terrorists who wanted to get their message out? And if it was only about James Townsend, why not pick him off with a high-powered rifle? Or blow his car up? Or kidnap him? Why break into his home to kill him, his family, and abduct his youngest daughter? To send a message to others in the same field as James Townsend?

Parker had chased all of those leads, but none of them had ever panned out.

Maybe Tightrope had gone after Maddie Townsend for a reason. But again, why not just abduct her when she was alone? Why go through all the trouble of breaking into the home and tying the family up in such an elaborate way? Why torture and kill the others? He had drugged them; they all had traces of the tranquilizer in their systems. After they were knocked out, why not just take Maddie and leave?

The questions bounced around in Parker's mind, old questions reawakened because of the Krugman murders.

"Why start again now? Parker whispered to himself.

"Because he can't help it," Martinez said. "It's an addiction for guys like him. They might stop for a while, but they can always relapse."

Parker's cell phone rang. He already knew who it was before he saw the name on the screen. He knew she was going to call eventually.

"Eve," Parker said into the phone as he walked farther down the driveway.

"It's him, isn't it?" Eve said.

"We don't know for sure." He didn't even need to ask her how she already knew about the murders of the Krugman family.

Eve was silent for a few seconds, and then: "Can we meet somewhere and talk?"

"Not right now."

"I know. What about this afternoon? Or tonight?"

"I'm going to be busy with this for a while."

"How about at the park? At sunset."

Parker couldn't say no. He had no one to go home to after the day was done. His wife had died two years ago from cancer. She had fought valiantly, but it had been a short battle. His children, Bobby and Mara, lived in different states on the other side of the country, Bobby in Hartford, Connecticut and Mara in Wilmington, North Carolina. Neither one had gone into law enforcement—neither one had the desire for it. They'd seen what their father and mother had gone through.

"Okay," Parker finally said. "I'll meet you there."

"At the bench by the hot dog stand," Eve told him. "I'll buy dinner."

"Hot dogs? How can I refuse?"

"Good. I'll see you then . . . and thank you."

"Of course."

Parker hung up. He knew the reason Eve wanted to see him was to pump him for information about this new case, but he couldn't say not to meeting, not with everything she'd gone through in her life.

FOUR

Eve Townsend wore jeans, a long-sleeved shirt, a hoodie sweatshirt, and a pair of sneakers. Her legs felt a little rubbery from her earlier workout. She trained regularly in martial arts and worked out three times a week with weights. She jogged twenty-five miles a week. Today she had exerted herself more than usual, needing to burn off steam after finding out Tightrope had come out of whatever hole he'd been hiding in to kill again.

Parker had called in the middle of the day and told her he could meet at the park an hour earlier than sunset, and now she waited for him. She watched people in the field: kids playing, mothers sitting together and watching their children, people walking their dogs. Fifteen people practiced at a Tai Chi class. Squeals of laughter and screams drifted over from the playground. She sat on the bench near the hot dog stand, the jogging trail not too far in front of her. Beyond the jogging trail was the Sound.

Every morning Eve scoured the internet for news stories about murders and abductions. Of course, she hoped to find news about Maddie, or at least some kind of clue. Benji, a computer expert friend of hers, had installed some software on her computer that monitored police scanners in major American cities, deciphering local codes and translating them into reports she could download or print out. She always checked the Seattle area first, then Portland and Vancouver. Then California cities. Then other cities, moving east across America.

This morning, while sipping tea, she'd seen the call come in for a family murdered outside the Seattle area. She called her source at the sheriff's department. He called back an hour later and told her exactly what had happened to the Krugman family.

Tightrope had killed them—she was sure of it.

Agent Parker strolled up the jogging path. She hadn't seen in him in months. He looked a little older today, haggard, like he'd lost some weight, but not in a good way. His hair was trimmed neatly and all gray, his skin wan in the dull afternoon light, the color drained from him.

She got up and hugged him when he got to the bench. "Thanks for coming to see me," she told him. She glanced over at Ernie's hot dog cart. "Dinner?"

"My favorite."

She smiled.

They walked up to the hot dog stand. Eve bought Parker a hot dog and a side of fries. She wasn't hungry and only got a bottle of water—her stomach was in knots. They went back to the bench. Parker ate his hot dog in a few bites.

"Is it him?" Eve asked when Parker was done with his hot dog and picking at the French fries.

"We don't know for sure. Waiting on forensics and the M.E.'s report."

"But things are . . . similar. Right?"

Parker sighed and nodded. "I guess you already know a lot of the details from whoever you've got at the sheriff's office."

"Not everything. I need to know more. I need to know what you saw, what you felt. What you think."

"Like I said, things were similar."

"*How* similar?"

"The family was tied to chairs. Dining room chairs."

"Red ropes?"

Parker nodded.

"All of them were killed? None taken?"

"None taken. All of them killed. A father, a mother, a daughter, and a son. Both were teenagers."

"How were they killed?"

"We're still waiting for the M.E.'s report. Should get it tomorrow morning."

"They were strangled. They strangled themselves when they struggled, didn't they?"

"Maybe. Seems that way, but I can't say for sure yet. There was a lot of blood, too. They might have bled to death or had a heart attack before they were strangled."

"The knots," Eve said. "The way they were tied, the ropes connecting to each other—"

"—Yes. All very similar."

Eve leaned back on the bench, realizing she'd been hunched forward, tense, leaning closer and closer to Parker.

Parker at the last of his fries, not seeming to really enjoy them, just chewing them up without tasting them. He crumpled the papers and napkins and got up, threw them away in a nearby trashcan. He came back to the bench, sipping his soda through a straw.

"It's him," Eve said, standing up.

"Could be a copycat."

Eve heard the sound of people approaching, kids squealing and laughing. They rushed up to Ernie's hot dog stand. "You want to walk for a bit?" she asked Parker.

He nodded.

They walked along the jogging trail. The water of the Sound was gray under the low clouds, a ferry floated far off in the distance, along with a few smaller boats and one yacht. The wind whipped at them. Eve shivered, wrapping her hoodie around her tighter, her hands stuffed down into her jacket pockets.

"You really think it's a copycat?" Eve asked. She couldn't hide her disappointment. Just like Parker hours earlier, she'd felt an exhilaration when she'd heard about the murder of the Krugman family, a chance to finally catch Tightrope, to possibly find her sister . . . or at least find out what had happened to her.

"I don't know."

"What does your gut tell you?"

He shrugged. "I can't say for sure. Seeing that family this morning . . .it brought it all back in an instant. I don't know if that's why it feels like it's him, because all those memories are coming back." He stopped and looked at Even, wincing. "I'm sorry. I know your memories are much worse than mine. I shouldn't have said that."

She gave a slight shake of her head, letting him know that he was forgiven.

They started walking again, both of them quiet for a long moment. A young man sped past them on a pair of inline skates. Two joggers approached from the other direction, their sneakers slapping the pavement as they ran.

"I just don't know why he would stop for ten years and then start again," Parker said. "It's been bugging me all day. I feel like I'm missing a piece of the puzzle."

"You know today's date?"

Parker nodded. "Exactly ten years to the day. But he killed the family last night."

"Could have been after midnight," she said. "So technically today."

Parker shrugged. "Maybe."

Eve moved away from Parker, walking to the metal railing that ran parallel with the jogging path and the Sound. She stared at the gray water, waiting for the joggers to pass them by. Parker approached and stood next to her.

"I want to help," she told Parker.

Parker sighed. "I wish I could let you."

"I could still help. I could be a consultant."

Parker stared out at the water, avoiding her eyes.

"I've got a degree in psychology. I've studied serial killers. You could use a consultant, couldn't you?"

"It's not up to me. You know that."

"But you could make a request."

"With your past . . . with you so close to all of this . . . you know what they're going to say."

Eve let out a long exhale—it had been what she expected Parker to say. But she had to try.

"I'll ask," he told her. "Okay?"

"Okay. Thanks. That's all I want. I just want to get this guy this time."

"Me too."

FIVE

Eve didn't go home after she left the park—she wasn't going home at all tonight. Every year, on the anniversary of the Townsend Tragedy, she stayed the night alone in that house, her old house, the house where her parents and brother had been murdered by Tightrope, the house where her sister had been taken. She already had her bag packed in the trunk of her car.

"Why don't you just sell the place?" her Aunt June had said so many times over the last few years. "It's kind of morbid to keep holding onto it."

After Eve's family was killed and Maddie was taken, Eve went to live with her Aunt June. Eve had been almost eighteen at the time, but still technically a minor. Aunt June had agreed to take her in. Of course, per her parents' will, Aunt June had received a very healthy monthly income to take care of Eve until she was twenty-one, at which time all assets held in a trust would go to Eve.

And there were a lot of assets. Even though Eve's father's company had fallen apart after his death, with stock prices plummeting, their family lawyer, Harold Shoemaker, had informed Eve and her aunt in the meeting after the funeral that James Townsend had cashed in a lot of his own stock at least a year before his murder, investing the money into land, single-family homes and commercial buildings, other stocks and bonds, and even a lot of cash in separate bank accounts.

Eve hadn't cared about the money during their meeting with Harold. And she didn't care much about it now—she looked at the money as a necessary tool to find Tightrope.

Her whole life since that night had been about catching Tightrope, and finding Maddie. She used to lie awake at night in her aunt's house, staring up at the ceiling, wondering where her sister was, wondering if she was alive, wondering if she was suffering. The worst pictures entered her mind and she couldn't do anything to stop them. Sleep held no peace because those same pictures haunted her dreams.

Aunt June wondered why Eve kept her old house, why she spent the night there on the anniversary of the Townsend Tragedy. Eve would never be able to explain it to her aunt, nor anyone else. The time spent at her old house allowed her to get close to the trauma again, to re-live it, and to perhaps see something she might have missed that night, some overlooked clue that could finally lead her to Tightrope.

Even though Aunt June didn't understand Eve's need to keep the old house, she finally came to respect her wishes and stopped harassing her about. Eve had left the family home just as it was ten years ago, all the possessions still inside, everything exactly where it had been that night. Maybe Aunt June had given up bugging her about selling the house because she thought it might eventually help her heal, but Eve suspected that Aunt June was more worried about staying on her good side and having some access to the family fortune. Aunt June hadn't been able to hide her shock that afternoon in Harold's office when she found out her sister and brother-in-law had left their entire fortune to their children, and nothing to any other family members—nothing to her.

As Eve drove toward the lake, thoughts of her family's funeral came back to her. Her father, mother, and brother were all buried at the same time, just one funeral service. The funeral had been held in a massive church, thousands of people attending, a swarm of reporters waiting outside. At the time all of it had been a blur to Eve; she'd felt lost in a fog of trauma, and she was truly grateful Aunt June had been there to hold her hand, to help guide her through that fog.

Two days after the funeral, Eve and her aunt had gone to see Harold Shoemaker at his office. And again, Aunt June had been there for her; she had agreed on the spot to take her into her home. Maybe her aunt's motives had been selfish all these years, but Eve couldn't hate her aunt; she was thankful her aunt had been there for her then, and she was still there for her now. Besides, she'd rewarded her aunt quite well over the last ten years.

Eve pulled into the entrance to the massive gates that opened up to their long driveway that led down to the home by the lake. She punched in a five-digit code on the box nestled among the shrubs by a small rock fountain and the gates swung open. The only other people who had the code to the gates were the landscaping crew that came once a month and a property manager who came to check on the house, making sure everything was okay.

And maybe Tightrope had the code. She'd never changed the code in case he decided to return one day . . . maybe tonight.

Yes, Eve came back once a year to re-live the trauma of that night, to hopefully find some kind of clue she had missed all these years, but there was another reason she came here on the anniversary of the Townsend Tragedy. She had a theory (and if she was being totally honest, a wish) that Tightrope would eventually return to the scene of the crime. She'd done a lot of research on serial killers and she'd learned that many of them liked to return to the murder scenes to re-live the experience, to see the horrors they had created, to recapture those feelings. Sometimes they would take things from the scene or take photos, similar to how some serial killers collected trophies from their victims, items they could take out and hold, to experience their crimes again. The percentage of serial killers who either revisited the scenes or kept trophies (or both) was pretty high, and she hoped Tightrope was one of them.

But was Tightrope really a serial killer? Parker had asked that question before and Eve had always wondered the same. Tightrope had only killed once that anyone knew of. Whether Tightrope could be called a serial killer had been debated ad nauseum on TV shows and documentaries, in books, newspaper and magazine articles, online posts. Tightrope just didn't fit into the mold of most serial killers.

But today Tightrope had struck again, killing another family.

Eve drove down the long driveway, passing massive fields of tall grass to the left and another field to the right, all of it fenced off. Stands of dark woods stood in the distance to the right. She pulled up to the front of the home, the driveway widening and circling around a massive concrete fountain adorned with bronze angels around the base, surrounded by small shrubs and flowers. She got out of her car and looked up at the two-story home. A small guest house was off to the left just beyond a seven-car garage that was nearly half the size of the house. The air was cold but thick with humidity, making it feel chillier. A heavy mist would move in tonight over the lake, creeping over the grounds as the temperature dropped.

The home could probably be called a mansion, but it wasn't an obscene tribute to wealth; it wasn't much larger than many of the other houses in this affluent rural area. There were six bedrooms and seven bathrooms. Her father's large office with an adjoining library was just off the foyer. A set of wide steps wound up to a balcony that led to halls and the bedrooms. Beyond the foyer was a sitting room with her mother's piano near one wall. Beyond those rooms was the living room, the family room, the formal dining room, the kitchen. A basement was below the home with a floorplan nearly as large as the ground floor. The basement had been partitioned off into large rooms. They'd had a game room down there with a pool table, ping pong table, video games, couches. It was all still there.

Eve set her bag down on the settee after she entered the house and punched in the code for the security alarm. She locked the front door. She hoped Tightrope would return tonight—she prayed for a chance to confront him—but she wasn't going to make it easy for him to get inside; he wasn't going to just walk right in.

After the alarm was back on and the front door was locked, Eve entered her dad's office, strolling through it. The waning afternoon light shined in through the closed blinds, the drapes open. She walked past a wall of books, the leather chairs, a massive wood desk with a cold fireplace beyond it. Framed photos lined the mantle. Everything was nearly the same as that night ten years ago, except her dad's computers had been seized by the FBI as evidence. She eventually got them back and now had them stored at her house. She'd pored over the files in those computers many times, but she'd never found the clues she'd been looking for.

Though large, the office had always seemed stuffy to her, even a little hazy, dark and cold. But she found warmth here now. She saw her father again behind his desk, reports and papers spread out everywhere, several laptops and tablets lit up, his earbuds in his ears as he talked to several people at once, sometimes barking orders at them.

After she left her father's office, she walked through the entire home. She walked through the bedrooms, her parents' room. Her mother's make-up and creams were still on the counter in the master bathroom, a thin layer of dust covering everything.

She visited her old bedroom after that. Most of her stuff was gone, packed up when she had moved in with her Aunt June.

Her brother's room was neat. She stared at the posters on his walls, the corners curling just a little. His closet overflowed with sports equipment and clothes. His desk took up one corner of the room. His blanket and bedsheets were disturbed, exactly like when Tightrope had taken him from the bed, dragging him downstairs to the family room to tie him to a dining room chair.

Finally, Eve was in Maddie's room. She went to the bed; the blanket and sheets pulled halfway off, just like her brother's bed. She picked up the stuffed rabbit from the floor, the one Maddie had named Ralph the Rabbit. Mom had told Maddie she was too old to sleep with stuffed animals, but Ralph the Rabbit was the one Maddie had always held onto.

Eve brought the stuffed animal to her nose, breathing in deeply. She swore she could still smell Maddie, but she knew it was just her imagination. She broke down and cried, a sob turning into a wail, and then a scream of rage and frustration.

A few minutes later she put Ralph the Rabbit back on Maddie's bed, its head resting on the pillows.

She went back downstairs. It was time to get things set up for tonight.

SIX

Eve left her car in the circular driveway, right in front of the house instead of parking it in one of the garages. Even though she wasn't going to leave a lot of the lights on inside the house tonight, she wanted her car right out in front of the home, right where Tightrope could see it if he came. An invitation to him.

She took a hot shower before it got dark outside, leaving her Glock on the toilet tank lid and the bathroom door locked. After she dried off, she changed into sweatpants, a thermal shirt, and a pair of thick socks. She put her sneakers back on and laced them up. She wanted to be ready in case he came.

As usual, a couch in the family room would be her bed for the night. She had her duffel bag by the couch. She slid the shotgun she'd brought with her underneath the couch. Her cell phone was on the small table, a bottle of water beside it, along with a hunting knife, two flashlights, and a small canister of pepper spray. Her backup handgun was stuffed under the seat cushion. She was as ready as she could be.

She munched on some dried fruit and nuts, sipping warm water from a bottle. She sat hunched forward on the couch, the house quiet and mostly dark. She could see the dining room from where she sat, the large dining room table and the chairs pushed in around it. After she finished her baggie of fruit and nuts, she stood up—it was time to get the chairs ready.

She set the dining room chairs up just as Tightrope had set them up ten years ago; these were the same chairs she and her family had been tied to, the wood still stained dark with their blood, the wood worn from the ropes, one of the seats of the chairs cracked from struggling, a split in the leg of another chair, spindles cracked and loose, two of them broken off completely.

Ghosts sat in these chairs now on each side of Eve, but she saw ghosts in every room of this house. She heard echoes of laughter and teasing. She saw Maddie chasing Mike after he had taken Ralph the Rabbit from her, Maddie squealing with laughter. She saw them throwing each other into the pool in the backyard. Now that pool was drained and covered with wood and wire mesh to keep anyone from falling in.

Eve sat in "her" chair between Mike and Maddie's chairs. She put her arms behind the back of the chair, clasping her hands together, like they'd been tied that night. She put her ankles together, drawing them up under the seat of her chair, imagining the intricate series of ropes tying all of them together, all of them to each other.

Maybe if she sat like this for a while and closed her eyes in the nearly-dark house, she could remember every second of that night. Maybe she could see something she had missed all those years ago, a word spoken by Tightrope, a glimpse of his face.

Her mind drifted back to that night ten years ago. She didn't want to remember, but she *needed* to. She needed to force herself back to that night when she had woken up tied to this chair.

And then she was there again.

The day had been normal enough. Dad had been at work, in downtown Seattle for most of the day. He'd been out of town for a few days, but Mom and everyone else was looking forward to him being back for a week or two. He was usually in good spirits when he came home from his business trips, but today he was different, something off about him, like he was distracted by something. But Eve knew he always had a lot of things on his mind.

They'd eaten a late dinner and then Mike was off to his room to play video games. Eve went upstairs to check her phone. She called her friend Becca and talked to her for thirty minutes, but then Maddie begged her to come downstairs and watch a movie with her and Mom.

Dad was in his office, but he caught the end of the movie, annoying them by asking questions about the movie the whole time (Mom said he did it on purpose).

A few hours later Eve went to bed, thinking about school and the upcoming Thanksgiving break. She had volleyball practice tomorrow and a test she needed to cram for. She'd taken advanced science courses, sure that she wanted to study some kind of science in college—wherever she planned to attend. Maybe she would get a degree in biology, or even genetics. Maybe she would work for Dad at his company; she though he would like that. As she drifted off to sleep, she thought about Robert, a boy she liked at school, but she'd been too nervous to approach him just yet.

And then her life changed before the sun came up the next morning.

She woke up groggy and uncomfortable, paralyzed but still too sleepy to panic just yet. The panic would come soon enough. She tried to move her arms, but she felt sharp pains in her shoulders, pressure on her wrists and elbows. She opened her eyes, blinking. They felt gummy. She tried to say something, but her mouth wasn't working right. Her tongue felt swollen. It was hard to swallow.

She saw her family all around her, tied to chairs. Maddie was to her left, Mike to her right, Dad and Mom just beyond Mike, their chairs back-to-back with at least a foot of space in between them. Some of her parents' clothing had been cut away, their skin stained with blood, their eyes wild, hair messy, bright red ropes tied tightly, binding them to the chairs, white strips of cloth stuffed into their mouths, wrapped around their heads.

Eve screamed into her gag. She looked down at her legs, at the red ropes wound around her knees and thighs, her ankles pulled under the seat of her chair, her legs immobile. She felt ropes around her torso; they seemed to tighten with each movement and breath she took, digging in deeper and squeezing the air from her lungs. And, like the rest of her family, there was a noose tied around her neck.

That wave of panic had come now, drowning her in suffocating terror. For just a moment she swore she couldn't breathe.

"You're awake," their tormentor said.

He was dressed entirely in black. He emerged from the shadows, materializing from the darkness. He seemed tall and thin, but powerful, with wide shoulders. His clothing was tight but not formfitting. He wore some kind of shiny gloves, leather, or maybe latex. He had a hood over his head, a mask with only small holes for his eyes and one for his mouth. In one gloved hand he held a bloodstained straight razor.

He's cutting us!

Mom and Dad struggled against the red ropes, but they barely budged in their chairs. As they moved their heads, the nooses tightened, red ropes digging into their flesh, their eyes bulging. Choking and clicking and grunting noises came from their throats, their bodies trembling.

"I told you . . ." Tightrope said as he moved in between Mom and Dad, loosening their nooses just a bit so they could breathe again. They both drew in greedy, wheezing breaths of air through their nostrils. "You have to be very still or the ropes will tighten."

Eve screamed into her gag, yelling at their tormentor, begging him to stop, to let them go.

Tightrope didn't respond to her muffled words around the cloth stuffed into her mouth, the cloth soaked now from her saliva. He understood what she wanted, but he didn't care.

Something seemed to have intrigued Tightrope. He approached her with the bloody straight razor open in his hand. He stood in front of her, bending down so they were nearly at eye-level. His eyes were dark behind the eyeholes of his black cloth mask, his teeth white in the mouth hole, his breath had the lingering odor of something sweet eaten recently.

"Do you want me to stop?" he asked. "Is that what you're trying to say?"

Eve started crying—she couldn't help it. She nodded as much as she could, as much as the noose around her neck would allow. Her nose ran and it was harder to breathe. Panic took over again, her body shaking under the lengths of rope wrapped tightly around her.

Tightrope's eyes flashed to Maddie in the next chair. He was in front of her in a flash of movement, appraising her.

Eve watched Tightrope for a moment, but then his appraisal seemed to be over. He went back to Mom and Dad. He stood in front of Mom and dug the corner of the straight razor into the wound in her shoulder, just under her collar bone, digging the thin steel into her, blood running down the front of her chest.

Dad growled into his gag as Mom thrashed, a squeal of pain escaping through the rag stuffed in her mouth. She tried so hard not to move, but as Tightrope dug the blade deeper into her flesh, she couldn't help it; she struggled as the blood soaked her shirt, dripping down and puddling on the wood floor beneath her. The chair legs thumped on the floor, the nooses around their necks tightening again.

And again, Tightrope loosened the nooses. He went to Mike whose noose had also tightened. Eve felt her own noose beginning to tighten, and that's when she realized that they were all connected to each other somehow in the webbing of ropes.

Tightrope stood in front of Mike, studying him like he was a blank canvas, deciding where to make his cuts. He started working on Mike's right eye. Mom, who could see the torture better than Dad, screamed again, a more forceful yell. She struggled again, nooses tightening again.

It was at that moment that Eve understood they were all going to die. Tightrope wasn't going to let them go. And it was at that moment she knew her mom had realized the same thing. Mom realized that it would be better to strangle to death than to be cut apart little by little, and it was better to strangle than to watch her own children tortured, their skin sliced open by deft little cuts from razorblades and knives.

But Tightrope wouldn't let them strangle; he kept loosening the nooses every so often.

Over the next fifteen minutes Tightrope worked his sharp instruments on Mom, Dad, and Mike. When the nooses got too tight again, he patiently loosened them. Tightrope sliced off Mom's ear. He carefully removed Dad's eyelids. He reopened wounds on their bodies, and sliced open new wounds. He cut Dad's kneecap open, revealing bright white bone before the blood washed over it and poured down his leg.

Over those fifteen minutes, Eve felt the ropes around her loosening just a bit, the ropes around her wrists behind the back of the chair loosening. At first, she couldn't believe it, thinking it was some twisted trick of her imagination, a cosmic joke to raise her hopes and then dash them down, but a few minutes later her hands were free.

She needed to move quickly—she really didn't have any kind of plan, just a primal need to escape her snare, an animalistic urge to flee from pain . . . and to protect her pack.

But she couldn't let Tightrope see that she'd gotten loose.

Her shoulder joints ached as she moved her arms around the chair to the ropes around her thighs and knees, her torso.

Maddie squealed next to Eve. She was going to give them away.

Eve glanced at Maddie's terrified face (but wasn't there a flicker of hope in her eyes?), trying to communicate with her eyes, trying to signal to her to be quiet.

Tightrope hadn't seemed to notice so far—he was still busy working on Dad.

Eve looked at her brother as she managed to wriggle out of her ropes. Mike's head was slumped forward, the front of him a gory mess. He was either passed out or dead. Every movement she made pulled at Mike's ropes, jerking his body slightly like a marionette pulling a puppet's strings.

Tightrope dug another knife into Dad. One of Tightrope's longer knives stuck out of Dad's chest. There was a sucking sound coming from the wound with each breath Dad struggled to take, the noose tight around his neck again.

Mom's noose was tight again too, her eyes bulging so badly it looked like they were going to pop out of her face, the rope buried so deeply into her neck it looked like a thin red line now.

TIGHTROPE

Could Mom see anything anymore? Her eyes were glassy and unfocused, but Eve swore there was still some life left in her; she swore Mom could see her escaping, and there was a glint of hope, not hope of her own survival, but of her daughter's—at least one of her children could escape this madness and pain.

Or maybe it had only been Eve's imagination—maybe there was nothing in Mom's eyes anymore, just dead eyes staring and seeing nothing.

Eve was finally free, pulling her legs out of the tangle of ropes at her ankles, wriggling out of the ropes around her lap and the chair. She was free, but she still didn't have a plan.

Tightrope still hadn't noticed that she'd gotten out of her ropes. He only saw that she was free when she stood up from the chair.

Eve stood on wobbly legs, blood coursing freely through her body again. Her hands felt numb, her feet like blocks of wood, pins and needles exploding under her skin like a colony of fire ants. Her joints ached from being bound in one position too long. Her head was too light, her muscles too weak, nothing seemed to be working right.

She had no chance at this.

Tightrope rushed her.

In that split second Eve surprised herself by not escaping; instead, she ran right at Tightrope as she tore the rag out of her mouth, finally able to breathe, to scream. She attacked Tightrope like she was an animal. She pulled at his mask, trying to tear it away from his head, trying to expose his face, the face of a monster, a demon from hell.

From behind Eve, Maddie screamed into her gag, maybe cheering her on. Eve couldn't be sure, but she knew now that her mother, father, and brother were all silent. All dead now.

A blind rage filled Eve, a whiteness washing over her mind. She just wanted to hurt Tightrope, to kill him for what he'd done to her family.

The battle with Tightrope was a blur, and then she was on the floor, the back of her head striking the wood hard. The world seemed to darken, everything swimming out of focus.

Then everything came back, a sharp and crystal-clear picture of Tightrope looming over her. His hood was gone—she must have torn it away at some point—but from this angle on the floor his face was hidden in shadows.

"Good night, sweetheart," he said in a low voice, a smile in those words.

He kicked her in the head, the toe of his black work boot colliding with the side of her head, near her ear. And then everything went black.

SEVEN

Eve woke up in the wooden chair. For a few seconds she panicked. It seemed like she was back in time ten years ago, tied to the chair along with her family, Tightrope waiting to finish what he had started.

But her family wasn't there in the other chairs. There were no red ropes, no blood.

She had fallen asleep in the chair as she tried to remember every detail of that night. She was alone in the house now, her family still gone.

Something was on the floor in front of her, a few feet away, a white object that almost seemed to glow in the semi-darkness of the living room.

For a moment Eve sat frozen in the wooden chair, her body tense as she listened to the house around her, the silence of it. She tore her eyes away from the object on the floor and looked around, still listening for any sounds . . . sounds of him.

Had he been in the house while she had dozed off?

She was on her feet in an instant. She picked up her flashlight from the floor and drew her Glock from the holster on her hip. She'd glanced at the couch, hoping the weapons she'd stashed there earlier—the shotgun tucked under the couch, her backup .380 under the couch cushion, the hunting knife on the table—were still there.

If he'd been here, he would have taken her weapons.

As she hurried to the couch, she panned the flashlight around. She checked the couch. The shotgun was still hidden under it, her .380 under the cushions, the knife and pepper spray on the table next to her bottle of water. Nothing had been disturbed.

She used her flashlight to search the home, leaving the lights off as she crept through the dark house. She began her search at the front door, making sure it was still locked.

It was.

The alarm was still on.

She peeked out the front windows. The porch lights illuminated the stone walkway in a yellowish glow. Her car was a dark monolith in the circular driveway, the milky light of the moon painting the roof and hood. The foggy fields in the distance were shrouded in darkness.

Everything was quiet outside, no movement anywhere.

It took Eve nearly twenty minutes to search the house, every room, every closet, every cabinet. She checked all the windows and any doors that led outside, making sure they were all still locked.

If he was really in the house, he could be doubling back during her search, slinking in the shadows, following her from room to room. But she felt reasonably sure he wasn't in the house.

But the object on the floor in front of the chairs . . .

Eve was back in the living room, back in front of "her" chair. She stared down at the object on the floor: Ralph the Rabbit. She crouched down and picked up the stuffed animal. She was almost afraid to touch it, afraid it was a figment of her imagination and also afraid it was real.

It *was* real. She felt the weight of it in her hands, smelled the faint scent that she imagined was Maddie.

If Tightrope wasn't in the house, if he hadn't brought Ralph the Rabbit down to torment her, did that mean she had gone up to her sister's room in some kind of fugue state? Had she been sleepwalking? Had she blacked out while trying too hard to re-live those terrible memories as she tried to catch a glimpse of Tightrope's face after she had pulled off his hood, trying to spot some clue she had missed, some clue that could help her find Tightrope . . . and Maddie.

She sat down on the chair with Ralph in one hand, her Glock in the other, the flashlight lying on the floor next to the chair, the beam of light shining across the floor. The wood creaked slightly as her weight settled onto the seat of the chair.

Holding Ralph brought her back to that night again. She'd had Ralph with her when the cops had shown up. She'd had Ralph with her when the FBI agents came later to her hospital room. The FBI had brought themselves onto the Townsend case, declaring the acts a form of terrorism, an umbrella term the agency used now to cherry-pick which crimes they wanted to investigate.

Eve looked down at the gun in her right hand and Ralph the Rabbit in her left. She leaned back in the chair and closed her eyes.

And then she was back in this room again, ten years ago, waking up on the floor.

Eve sat up on the floor, her head throbbing. She was confused for a moment about why she was on the floor, but then a wave of adrenaline rushed through her, like her subconscious mind knew the danger she was in.

She saw her parents, her brother, all three of them lifeless and slumped against the red ropes pinning them to their chairs. She saw her empty chair with the coils of rope on the floor around the legs, some of the rope still wrapped around the seat and the back of the chair, some of those ropes still connected to rope around Mike and his chair, other ropes from her chair still connected to Maddie's chair.

Maddie's chair was empty. She was gone.

"Maddie," Eve whispered.

For just a second hope erupted in Eve. Maybe Maddie had gotten away. Maybe when Eve had loosened her own ropes, she had loosened Maddie's ropes too. Maybe when she'd been fighting with Tightrope, Maddie had run.

But those hopes were crushed as soon as they had come. Eve knew in her bones that Tightrope had taken Maddie.

Eve was on her feet a second later, but she had to wait a moment for a wave of dizziness to pass.

"Maddie!"

There was no saving her parents or Mike, but maybe she could still save her little sister.

"Maddie, answer me!"

Eve wondered how long she'd been unconscious from Tightrope's kick to her head. A few seconds? A few minutes? Longer? It was still dark in the house, the kitchen lights still on, still night outside. Maybe she hadn't been out that long. Maybe Tightrope and Maddie hadn't gotten too far. Maybe she could still find them.

She rushed to the kitchen and grabbed a big knife out of the wood block on the counter. She ran through the house, searching the rooms, calling Maddie's name. She entered Maddie's bedroom, turning on the lights. Maddie's blanket and sheets were pulled halfway off the bed, her favorite stuffed animal, Ralph the Rabbit, on the floor. She picked up Ralph and ran out of the room, back downstairs.

Maddie wasn't in the house.

Eve grabbed the cordless phone and dialed 911.

"911. Is this a medical of police emergency?"

"Police! A man was in our house. He killed my mom and dad. My brother. He took my sister."

The 911 operator tried to slow things down, trying to keep Eve on the phone, but she dropped the phone on the countertop in the kitchen, then ran for the front door.

She was outside a moment later with the knife in one hand and Ralph in the other. She rushed out to the circular drive, looking around. Her father's truck was the only vehicle parked there. Her mother's SUV was probably in the garage. No other vehicles . . . whatever vehicle Tightrope had driven to her house wasn't there now.

Eve ran down the driveway, deeper into the night.

"Maddie!"

She stopped running when she was a third of the way down the driveway, breathing hard, looking around, trying to spot the lights of a car or a truck somewhere in the mist hugging the ground, trying to listen for the sound of an engine. But there was nothing, only the faint sound of police sirens in the distance, getting closer.

Minutes later Eve was back inside the house. She pressed the button to open the front gates at the road so the police could get down the driveway. She left the front door wide open. Cops rushed inside with guns drawn. She had returned the knife to the kitchen, but she still had Maddie's stuffed white rabbit in her hands.

Two of the cops coaxed Eve outside, getting her to sit down on the stone steps that led up to the front porch while other officers searched the home, turning on lights everywhere. She knew the bright lights inside were now shining down on her family tied to the chairs. Eve told the police officers that she had already checked the house—he wasn't there. He had gotten away with her sister. She felt like precious seconds were ticking away.

Eve was still limp with shock as she sat on the front steps of the wide porch in front of the house. One of the cops must have gotten a blanket for her because she had one draped over her shoulders. She was shivering in the chilly night air.

One of the cops, a big man with a flushed face and a thick mustache, asked her what had happened, while another younger cop took notes. The other officers were now outside, searching the property.

Eve told them what had happened, everything she could remember. An ambulance pulled up. She didn't want to go, but the paramedics convinced her that she needed to get her head checked out at the hospital—she might have a concussion, or worse. She let them take her away in the ambulance.

Later that day, two FBI agents showed up at her hospital room. Her Aunt June had been in the room for a while. She gave the agents permission to question Eve. The agents identified themselves as Special Agent Parker and Special Agent Friedman, flashing badges with a practiced flick of their wrists.

Eve sat up in bed. She tried to talk, but then she broke down into sobs. The female agent, Friedman, sat on the bed with her, arm around her shoulders. Eve broke down even more from the contact, all of her misery coming out in those sobs. But no, her misery couldn't all come out—it would never completely leave her; she knew that then.

Friedman let her cry while Agent Parker got her a bottle of water from the nurses. He'd been out in the hall talking with Aunt June for a few minutes, and then he was back. He stood in front of her, staring at her. He looked older, ancient to her as a teenager, but he exuded strength and confidence; this man would find her sister. She was sure of it. His hair was completely gray, combed back, trained into that style over the decades. His face was hard and lined, a glint in his light blue eyes. He looked angry, impatient to get the details so he could go after the sick animal who had done this.

"Eve," Parker said. "I know this is difficult, but we need to know exactly what happened last night at your home. We need you to tell us everything while it's still fresh in your mind. You understand that, don't you?"

Eve nodded, wiping at her eyes, still shaking a little.

"Be as detailed as you can," Parker said. "I know it's hard, but it will help us find the man that did this."

"Parker," Friedman whispered in a motherly tone, her arm still around Eve's shoulders. "Maybe this can wait for a few minutes."

Parker sighed, giving in.

No, Eve didn't want that—she didn't want Parker to give in, to wait; she wanted to tell him everything she knew so he could go after this man. She felt like puking. She felt shaky and weak. A bad headache was coming on. Aunt June had told her that the doctors hadn't found anything seriously wrong, just some bruising, but they wanted to keep her there for the day just to be sure.

She stared at Parker through tear-blurred eyes. "I can talk." Her voice was suddenly clear, her tears gone. She imagined herself feeding off Parker's strength, feeding off the anger she could sense from him. She was angry too.

"You sure?" Friedman asked, pulling her arm away, staring at her with eyebrows scrunched in concern. "Because we can wait."

"No. I want to talk."

Eve told Parker and Friedman everything that had happened. Parker jotted notes down in his small notepad at a furious pace. She expected his pen to snap at any moment. He asked a question every so often to clear up details, but mostly he was quiet, letting her talk, letting her get it all out.

"You'll catch him?" Eve asked Parker when she was done telling him everything she could remember. "You'll get my sister back?"

"Yes," Parker said without hesitation. "I promise you we'll find him." He didn't promise that he'd bring Maddie back alive, but he promised that he and the FBI would catch the killer who would soon be known as Tightrope.

It was a promise Agent Parker never kept.

Eve was back now, staring down at the stuffed toy rabbit and the gun in her hands. It was exactly ten years later, and Parker, as hard as he had tried, had never been able to find Tightrope. She hadn't found him, either. All leads led to dead ends. She had never stopped looking, though. And every year she came back here, hoping Tightrope would do the same.

But he hadn't been here tonight, had he?

She must have brought Maddie's stuffed rabbit down without remembering it, which was a creepy and alarming thought, to be so deep into her memories that she had moved around the house without remembering it.

Eve got up and went to the couch. She made her bed with the sheet and blanket. She lay down, her head on the pillow with her backup gun underneath it. The other weapons were within easy reach. She watched the semicircle of chairs arranged across the room just as Tightrope had arranged them on that night ten years ago, a weak light shining into the room from the kitchen.

She closed her eyes. She would sleep here tonight. She would sleep light in case he came. Then she would go back home tomorrow morning. She had come here to re-live those horrible moments in her life, hoping to see something new, something she had missed before, but nothing had come.

Nothing.

EIGHT

The next morning Agent Parker and Agent Martinez met with the medical examiner at the morgue. The M.E. had just finished his examination of the Krugman family. Normally Parker would wait for the M.E. to write up and send his report in, but Parker wanted to be here this morning. He wanted to move on this before Tightrope slipped away again, disappearing off the face of the earth like he'd done ten years ago.

Thankfully the Krugman children's bodies were already slid back into the huge metal drawers and only the father and the mother were still on the metal exam tables. The mother's body was covered, the father's body exposed, a Y-pattern of scars on his chest from the autopsy, the pale skin of the scar puckered with black stitching. The autopsy stitches had always reminded Parker of a zipper that could easily be opened up again. The skin of the victims looked so thin, such a fragile layer of protection from the horrors of the world.

Parker had seen plenty of dead bodies in exam rooms through the years, but these bodies affected him differently because Tightrope had done this—the killer Parker couldn't catch, the killer Parker couldn't even come close to catching. This family had died because of his failure.

"Cause of death?" Martinez asked the M.E.

"Seems to me they were strangled to death. The oldest boy may have died from blood loss, or his heart may have even stopped from shock. The others too. It's difficult to say for sure, but I'm going to list the official cause as strangulation."

Parker had been in this county hospital basement morgue a few times over the years, working on different cases. He'd spoken to this same M.E. before on those occasions—he was the same M.E. ten years ago when the Townsends had been brought in.

The M.E. was an older man, older than Parker. He had to be close to retirement by now. He was short and probably stocky at some time in the past, but much of the muscle he'd once had was turning soft and fleshy. His gray hair was thin, beginning to bald on top, but he still combed it to the side with a neat part like he'd probably done his whole life. His face was jowly, his basset-hound eyes emotionless, his skin pale. He looked washed out, like any joy in life had been drained out of him long ago. Parker supposed a job like this could do that to someone.

Parker and Martinez left the morgue, walking down a wide, well-lit hall to the bank of elevators.

"Pretty much like ten years ago?" Martinez asked when they got to the elevator.

Parker nodded. "Similar, but not exactly the same. He didn't take one of the victims this time."

"Or leave one of them alive," Martinez said.

Parker didn't respond. He watched the plastic triangle on the wall above the elevator doors, waiting for it to light up and a bell to ding.

"Maybe Tightrope has spent the last ten years perfecting the ritual," Martinez suggested. "Trying to get it right this time. Trying not to make any mistakes like he did before."

Parker still didn't believe taking Maddie Townsend had been a mistake. Maybe leaving Eve alive had been a mistake, but he was sure Tightrope had planned on taking Maddie right from the beginning, part of some plan of his.

But maybe he and Martinez were both right. Maybe Tightrope had meant to take Maddie, but Eve getting loose hadn't been part of his plan, and then he had panicked; he had kicked Eve in the head hard enough to knock her out. Maybe he believed he had killed her.

But why not make sure Eve was dead before leaving? He had been slicing up her parents and brother all night—it would have only taken him a few seconds to cut her throat. But he hadn't done that—he'd left her there alive.

And he must have knocked Maddie out, or he had drugged her again, to make it easier for him to carry her to where his van had been parked. He had carried her almost a mile, off the Townsends' property, through the woods, to the dirt road where he had parked his van. Maybe he had someone else with him, but there were only one set of prints found in the dirt in the woods, only one set of prints around the van.

Maybe he was in a hurry by the time he took Maddie. Maybe he had wasted too much time torturing Eve's family and he was rushed by the time Eve got loose. But that didn't make sense to Parker either. Tightrope had gained access into the Townsend home by either shutting off the alarm or shutting it down somehow. Maybe he'd gotten the code somehow. He'd gotten in through a locked door. He had killed their dog outside. He had obviously gone to great pains researching the Townsends before breaking into their home.

Another thing that had always bothered Parker was that Tightrope had tortured the father, mother, and brother, but he'd left Eve unmarked (and Maddie, according to Eve's story). Had Eve gotten loose before he could torture her and Maddie? Had he taken Maddie so he could have more time with her?

Parker had managed to put the Townsend case and its mysteries on the back burner of his mind these last few years, but now Tightrope was back and all of those mysteries (and failures) were plaguing him again. It was driving him crazy all over again.

The elevator doors opened up.

"Let's get back to the Krugman house," Parker said. "Let's see if Bruckner's found anything there."

*

A sheriff's car was parked at the end of the driveway of the Krugman's house. Parker stopped his car and flashed his ID and shield. Martinez did the same. The cop nodded and waved them through.

Parker drove down the driveway to the home. The layout of the land was somewhat similar to the Townsends' estate, but on a much smaller scale.

A collection of forensic vans and sheriff's cars were parked in front of the home. Parker parked well back from the other vehicles and got out. Martinez walked in silence with him to the front door.

The crime scene tape was broken, the door cracked open. Parker knocked and then entered, showing his badge to another sheriff's deputy. He entered the family room where the chairs and ropes were still exactly where they'd been yesterday, nothing moved.

Two forensics experts in dry, papery white suits, along with masks and gloves, were on their hands and knees, collecting samples into plastic baggies.

Bruckner watched his men. He wore no protective clothing except for a pair of blue nitrile gloves. He was tall and thin, a nervous man, always twitchy and jerky. He constantly adjusted his glasses, fiddling with them. His head was clean-shaven and there was always a film of perspiration on his upper lip.

"What have you got so far?" Parker asked Bruckner.

"Running blood samples now. Type and DNA. Checking them against medical records. See if we might have anything else except the family's blood here."

Bruckner didn't look hopeful about that. And Parker wasn't, either. Bruckner was another one who had worked on the Townsend case ten years ago and Parker felt the weight of guilt on him again, a failure who couldn't catch a killer. And now this had happened.

"What about the ropes?" Martinez asked.

"We're working on some samples," Bruckner answered.

Parker already knew what they were going to find: ordinary clothesline rope that could be bought online or at any department store or supermarket. The rope would be dyed with a generic red dye. The dye would only be slightly less difficult to buy than the rope.

The knots at the Townsend crime scene were another thing that had been studied, various complicated knots and the peculiar way of tying the rope, but the intricate way the ropes had connected the victims to each other, while also binding each individually, was of even more interest to Parker—an apparent signature of Tightrope. The killer was obviously an expert with the webbing of ropes he had created. A bondage aficionado? That was a hunch that had been explored before, but it had led them nowhere.

"Prints?" Martinez asked Bruckner.

"Just the family's so far."

Parker knew that's all they would find. Tightrope wore gloves and seemed to leave no hair or fibers of any kind. He was probably clean-shaven, his face, his head, maybe even his entire body.

"Footprints?" Martinez asked.

Parker already knew: a work boot, one that could be bought online or from a dozen of stores, newer boots, but not brand new, broken in.

Bruckner nodded. "Work boots. Size eleven. An older boot. Not the most expensive brand. Not the cheapest."

"Same brand Tightrope wore at the Townsends?" Martinez asked.

"Same size boot," Bruckner said. "Same type of boot, but a different brand."

"Tire tracks?" Martinez continued.

"A car," Bruckner said. "An older sedan probably. Newer tires."

That was different. Tightrope had used some kind of truck at the Townsends, most likely a van or SUV. But he had used a car this time. Maybe he hadn't brought a van because he hadn't planned on abducting any of the victims.

"We'll get something here," Bruckner promised. "He'll slip up. Make a mistake. They always do."

Parker didn't respond. He was getting a sick, sinking feeling in his stomach. Was Tightrope going to slip through his fingers again? Was he going to go back into hiding after this murder, disappear again for another ten years until he was ready to kill another family?

NINE

Eve eventually slept a few hours in her parents' home, but it was a restless and fitful sleep. She woke up every forty-five minutes, haunted by dreams. An hour before dawn, she jumped up from the couch with her Glock in her hand, aimed at the chairs still set up at the other end of the living room. She'd been sure she'd seen Tightrope standing among the chairs in the dim wash of light from the kitchen, a tall and lean shadow holding Ralph the Rabbit in his gloved hands, studying the toy.

But he wasn't there.

After two solid hours of sleep just after dawn, Eve got up and packed her small bag. She returned the chairs to the formal dining room, sliding them in around the massive table.

Even though she was sure all the windows and doors were locked, she checked them again. She went upstairs to put Ralph the Rabbit back on Maddie's bed. She stared down at the stuffed animal laying on the rumpled sheets and blanket.

Why had she come up here to get her sister's stuffed animal last night? Did it mean something? Was there something she was overlooking?

She picked up the stuffed white rabbit and took it with her downstairs. She stuffed it into her bag along with her backup handgun, half-eaten bag of snacks, her bottles of water, her pepper spray.

It was time to go. She grabbed her bag and the shotgun she'd brought with her and unlocked the front door. She went out onto the front porch and locked the door again. The alarm system was armed. She walked down the stone steps off the front porch, down the walkway to the circular drive where her car was parked, walking away from this museum of the dead, a scene of horror frozen in time.

After driving down the long, tree-lined driveway, she waited as the iron gates swung open slowly. She watched the woods off to her left for a moment as the gates opened, the fog dissipating some since the sun had come up, a few tendrils still hugging the trees. Tightrope had parked beyond those woods ten years ago. He had carried her sister across that field, through those woods, to his vehicle.

She drove through the open gates and waited for a moment, making sure they had shut again before turning onto the narrow road that wound through estates with mansions on them.

*

It took Eve almost an hour and a half to get back to her home, a modest four-bedroom, four-bath home that she had designed and built on fifty acres of land, most of it wooded.

She used her remote control in the car to open the garage door as she drove up the trail through the woods, the trees thinning out and opening to a plateau her home had built on. The woods crowded all around the house, the brush thick with ferns and shrubs, tree trunks coated with mildew and moss, the woods always dark and wet. It had drizzled recently and the paved drive reflected the headlights of her car. The tree branches above formed a canopy along the long driveway in several places.

Her home could be called modern-style, but without the usual walls of windows. She had some large windows in the front and the rear facing the courtyard in back, but those windows were bulletproof, tinted, and thick enough to repel parabolic microphones. A large smooth stucco wall ran along the front of the home, hiding the front door and creating a little courtyard there. Another set of walls enclosed the large pool area in back, the ground dropping off quickly just beyond the back of her house. It was a split-level home with a basement and part of the home underground. She had a panic room off the door to the basement, what looked like a bookcase concealing the stairs down to the basement.

Mountains rose in the distance beyond her home, but she couldn't see them unless she went to the far edge of her property, the farthest bend in a course through the woods she had created to resemble the course at Quantico, Virginia. She'd had the course designed four years ago when she had applied to the FBI, preparing herself for the physical training she would have to go through.

But it had all been for nothing. She'd been turned down. Not even Parker's endorsement had been enough.

She drove her car down into the massive garage and parked, clicking the remote again to close the garage door. The door slid down smoothly and silently, the overhead lights on. A tan SUV, her only other vehicle, was parked in the farthest bay of the garage, backed in.

Eve got out of her car and grabbed her duffel bag and shotgun from the truck. She punched in the five-digit code on the keypad and then entered her home through the laundry room.

Her shotgun went back into its spot behind the couch. She had other guns and weapons stashed around her house. She had a security system and weapons, but she knew this place wasn't a fortress. She didn't *want* it to be a fortress—if Tightrope ever wanted to pay her a visit, she didn't want it to be too difficult for him to get inside.

After a quick change into jogging pants and a T-shirt, she went into her gym. She worked out on the heavy bag for twenty minutes and then headed for her bathroom to take a cold shower.

She'd been training for years, training herself to fight, to shoot, to kill, all in preparation if she ever got the chance to face Tightrope, if he ever came to finish the job he hadn't completed that night ten years ago.

But her training hadn't started right after her family was killed and Maddie was taken. For a few years after that night, she had been in a fog. She had managed to finish high school (much of her work done online at home) and then attended college where she took prerequisite courses, not sure what she wanted to do with her life, unable to focus on anything. Nothing seemed to matter anymore now that her parents and brother were dead, now that her sister was still missing, not sure if she was dead or alive and suffering every day. Math and English Lit seemed meaningless in a world where these kinds of horrors could happen. Aunt June promised that she would get through this, that time would help to heal her wounds, but she was wrong—her wounds were still open and excruciating.

Throughout high school, Eve had seen her share of psychologists, psychiatrists, and therapists. But they didn't help, many of them just pushing anti-anxiety and anti-depression pills on her. They tried different methods of dealing with her pain, even hypnosis, but nothing seemed to work.

After Eve turned twenty-one and had full access to her trust fund and her family's fortune, she dropped out of college and stopped going to her latest therapist. She had started drinking and partying a little in college, and it got worse after collage. She had a few "good-time friends" who helped her drown herself in alcohol and drugs, chatting about meaningless things, but often it kept her from brooding on her past, or the present and her missing sister.

Eve started traveling the world. She bought a private jet on a whim, hiring a stoic pilot, Angel Vasquez, who never breathed a word about her wild parties in the air.

Soon she left her friends behind, traveling alone, going to countries more and more remote. She visited the Outback of Australia, the Cape of Good Hope in South Africa, the northern islands of Japan. She took a trip to Norway, traveling up to fishing villages in the north when it was still freezing in the summer. She sat on the edge of a cliff there, staring down into a fjord. She sobbed while she sat there alone, feeling like she was at the edge of the world, the fjord emptying into a gray and churning sea that seemed to go on forever.

That gray ocean water pulled at her. It would be so easy to jump, to end it all.

But she couldn't do it. If there was the slimmest hope that Maddie was still alive, then she couldn't give up. She screamed up at the gray sky above her.

She hated herself for crying, for feeling so helpless.

"What do you want?" she asked herself as she wiped at the tears. "You have everything in the world."

She *did* have everything most people would want, but she didn't have what she really wanted: Maddie . . . and Tightrope. She'd give it all away to find Maddie, to at least know what had happened to her, to bury her body if she needed to. She'd give her fortune away to find Tightrope, to make him pay, to kill him.

The idea struck her like a bolt of lightning.

She stood up there on the edge of that cliff, wiping her eyes, her blurry vision clearing. "I'll do it," she whispered to the jagged cliffs and churning waters below. "I'll find him. I'll make him tell me where Maddie is. Then I'll kill him."

Suddenly her life had purpose, a singular focus. Everything clicked into place. She would need weapons. She would need training. And then her whole life would be about finding Maddie and Tightrope.

TEN

Eve thought of that day in Norway seven years ago while she showered. She thought of how her life had changed so suddenly, how she'd begun the journey to what she was now. She left the cliff in Norway that day and went back to the small hotel she'd been staying in. She got a ride to a small airport outside of Oslo, where Angel landed the plane to pick her up.

She began training as soon as she got back home to her aunt's house. She took Krav Maga classes and hired a personal trainer for weights and cardio. She had the plans for her house designed and then the home built.

Over the next year, she would lose fifteen pounds of fat and gain that weight back again in muscle. She became an expert in several fighting styles, but it wasn't enough. She hired an ex-Special Forces solder who taught her how to kill, how to use dirty tricks, how to shoot with every kind of weapon, how to fight with a knife.

She had hired other professionals in her training. A stunt man taught her defensive driving. An ex-spy taught her how to blend into a crowd, how to watch people without being detected, how to follow people, how to tell if someone is lying just from their body language, how to assume new identities with just a few quick changes of accent, clothing style, makeup and hair; a master horse trainer who taught her how to ride; an ex-con who taught her how to pick any kind of lock and various kinds of handcuffs.

She learned about computers, but also met a man named Ben Holcomb (but he asked her to call him Benji) who handled the more complicated computer tasks for her with no questions asked.

She took college courses, getting a degree in criminal psychology. But her real studies were at home and online; the curriculum—serial killers, the true monsters of society. She read books and watched documentaries. She talked to victims of serial killers and family members of serial killers.

But it wasn't enough—she needed to talk to an actual serial killer.

She tried to convince the Department of Corrections in Washington (and a few other states) to allow her to interview serial killers, but even with her degree, and even with a good from Agent Parker, they always turned her down.

She kept learning, studying, searching.

Benji set up an app on her computer and phone that scoured the net for stories about killers, victims, abductions, unsolved murders and compiled the data into files she could pick from. Her ritual every morning was to go through the data, looking for Tightrope, for clues of where he might be.

She kept files on cases and killers, some still unsolved. Her office, with its bank of computer screens against one wall, filing cabinets and bookcases on the other walls, and maps and bulletin boards layered with internet printouts and newspaper articles looked more like a police war room than a home office.

After her shower, Eve got dressed and started the coffee machine in the kitchen. She still wasn't hungry, but some coffee would help. She fixed a cup and went to her office, turning on two of the computers and letting them boot up. After they were up and running, she checked her emails. She had eight different email addresses.

One email froze her in her tracks. It was from TR_2207. The subject read: It's been a long time, Eve.

She opened the email, her heart thudding. She read the short message and then read it again:

Eve, I just wanted you to know that I didn't kill the Krugman family. It was someone else, someone pretending to be me, mimicking my techniques. If you think I had anything to do with that, you're barking up the wrong tree. If you waste your time with me, you won't find out who is truly responsible for that family's murder.
Hope all is well, and say hi to Ralph for me.
T.R.
P.S. Keep your eye on the North Star ☺

Eve stared at her computer monitor as a chill ran across her skin on spider legs, her body trembling slightly.
T.R.
Tightrope.
P.S. Keep your eye on the North Star.
What was that supposed to mean?
She got up and paced around the large office, trying to calm down.
It wasn't him. That was all there was to it. She'd gotten emails from wackos through the years, people claiming to be serial killers, people claiming to know who Tightrope was, people claiming to know where her sister was. People claiming to actually be Tightrope. She could usually tell when the people writing to her were crackpots.
This didn't feel like that.
But it had to be.
Could this be the killer of the Krugman family contacting her, trying to throw her off the trail?
She sat back down at her computer and replied to the email.

Where's my sister?

She hit the SEND button.

TIGHTROPE

She only had to wait a minute and a half before the email was sent back to her as undeliverable

After trying to send her email two more times, she grabbed her cell phone and called Benji. He said he'd be right over.

She printed out the email Tightrope had sent to her and read it again, studying it.

Say hi to Ralph for me.

What did that mean? Was he trying to tell her that he'd been in the house last night, that he had gone upstairs and taken Ralph the Rabbit from Maddie's room and left it on the floor in front of her to prove that he'd been there, that he had watched her sleep in the dining room chair, that he'd been close enough to kill her, but hadn't done it?

Or maybe it was something else . . . something about the rabbit.

Eve jumped up from her chair and hurried to her kitchen. She grabbed a serrated kitchen knife and a pair of large scissors. She pulled Ralph the Rabbit out of her duffel bag that she'd left in her bedroom.

Maybe Tightrope had left something inside the stuffed animal, some kind of clue he wanted her to find.

Moments later Eve sat on the floor with stuffing all over the floor. Ralph was just a furry flattened skin now, his side ripped wide open.

There was nothing inside Ralph except the stuffing.

"I'm sorry," she whispered to what was left of Ralph. She had destroyed Maddie's favorite toy. She felt like bursting into tears. She would put the stuffing back, sew it up again, make it right.

ELEVEN

"It's probably some random email address he hijacked and bounced around the world a gazillion times," Benji said as he sat at the desk in front of Eve's computers.

Benji was tall and skinny. He had wild and curly dark hair that came down to his shoulders. He always had at least a day's worth of stubble on his jaw and sharp chin. His thin arms were decorated with tattoos. He wore a blue flannel over a black Pink Floyd T-shirt, the sleeves rolled up to his elbows. He had on baggy jeans and new white sneakers.

Eve paced behind Benji, her stomach in knots, her head spinning. Could it really be Tightrope? Could she be so close to contact with him? So close to the answers she needed? Why had Tightrope chosen her family to kill? Why had he let her live that night? Why had he taken Maddie? And where was Maddie now? Eve didn't dare believe that Maddie was still alive, but there were cases of girls who had been held captive for years, sometimes for decades. Sometimes they escaped or had been rescued. It was rare, but it was possible.

"You can't trace the email?" Eve asked.

"I'll try. It'll probably lead back to another personal account, a stagnant address from Russia or something."

"The email is TR_2207. TR for Tightrope. 2207, that's the address of my parents' house where he . . ." She let her words die away.

"It's probably a slave email riding along with a real IP address, the two of them kind of coexisting together. And as soon as the email is delivered, then the account automatically ends so you can't reply and it's harder to trace." Benji shook his head. "He probably has hundreds of them."

"But what about the email name? TR_2207?"

"He probably hacked into a deactivated email account and just renamed it."

"If he sends another email, will it have the same address?"

"Maybe. He's probably got hundreds of deactivated accounts ready to rename."

"But impossible to trace?"

"Maybe not. Like I said, it will probably lead to some other country." He shrugged. "I mean, after I trace it, you could fly to Russia or Germany, or whoever it is, and kick in some teenager's door who had no idea his account was hacked, or find out it's part of a network at some office building. Or maybe a house frau whose son or daughter set up an account for her years ago that she's never used. Or it could even be a dead person who never ended their account. There are millions of those kinds of addresses."

"Alright," Eve sighed. "I get it."

"Sorry I couldn't be more helpful."

"You'll still try to trace it, thought?"

"Of course."

"And see what you can find online about North Star."

"Got it."

"Thank you, Benji."

He was quiet for a moment, glancing back at the computer screen.

"What is it?" she said. "Spit it out."

"Shouldn't you be going to the police about this?"

"Are their computer experts better than you?"

"Probably not." He looked at the computer screen again with the email still there.

"I'll talk to them about it eventually," she told him. "But I want to see what you come up with first."

"You think it's really him?"

"I don't know."

"Tightrope, if that's really him, says in the email that he didn't kill that family. He means the Krugman family, doesn't he?"

Eve nodded. She knew Benji must've read the news about the family found slaughtered in their home. "I don't know what to believe just yet."

"He said, 'Say hi to Ralph for me.' What's that mean? If you don't want to tell me, I understand."

"Ralph was the name of my sister's stuffed animal. A white rabbit. She called it Ralph the Rabbit. She had it that night. She was sleeping with Ralph the Rabbit when he took her out of her bed and brought her downstairs to the chairs."

"Would anyone else know about Ralph?"

Eve shook her head.

"You think the stuffed animals has anything to do with—"

"I already thought of that. I cut it open. Nothing inside."

Benji was quiet for a moment, thinking. He shrugged like he had nothing left to offer. He stood up from the office chair. "I'll see what I can do." He collected his laptop and the other equipment he'd brought with him, stuffing them down into leather cases.

"Thanks, Benji."

"No problem. I want to help in any way I can."

*

After Benji left, Eve poured another cup of coffee. She went back into her office and sat down in front of the computer screens. There was no need to read Tightrope's email again, the words were burned into her mind.

Say hi to Ralph for me.

Why would he mention Ralph? Had he really been inside the house last night while she was sleeping in the chair? Had he crept upstairs just to get Ralph the Rabbit and bring it down to her? Just so she would know that he'd been there, that he'd been that close to her?

How would Tightrope have known that Ralph the Rabbit had been Maddie's favorite toy, her comfort at night while she slept? Had Maddie said something to Tightrope about Ralph after he had abducted her, begging for Ralph? Was it some kind of clue that Maddie was still alive? Or maybe Tightrope had seen her with the stuffed animal that night after she had woken up on the floor and searched the house, grabbing Ralph from Maddie's room, running outside with him. Had he been somewhere nearby, watching her?

Tears stung Eve's eyes, not just tears of sadness, but also tears of frustration and rage. She was frustrated because within the last twenty-four hours she felt she'd gotten so much closer to finding Tightrope than she had in the previous ten years, but she also felt further away than ever.

She checked her emails again.

Nothing from Tightrope.

She studied the printed email. Mentioning Ralph was definitely weird, but there were a few other things that stuck out to her. One was the words North Star, and symbol at the bottom of the email, the happy face emoji. She didn't know what North Star and a smiley face symbol were supposed to signify, but he had put them there for a reason.

A clue? To tease her? Daring her to figure it out? Had he known she'd been training so she could hunt him down? Was he helping her now?

The other thing that stuck out to her was his insistence that he hadn't killed the Krugman family, that a copycat had done it (which she and Parker had both already agreed was a possible theory). But why would he go out of his way to reach out to her now? Obviously, there was a lot of work involved if he had to set up fake accounts like Benji had said, hacking into other accounts and using them, or using deactivated accounts and renaming them. (She was sure Benji would find out soon enough which method Tightrope had used.) But why did Tightrope feel the need to tell her it wasn't him? Why was it so important to him? A sick sense of vanity? Maybe, but it felt like more than that . . . much more.

The third thing that bothered her was his use of the phrase "barking up the wrong tree." An archaic term, maybe, but Tightrope was probably an older man now. But the phrase seemed more intentional than just a phrase he used often.

Another clue?

If Tightrope was so adamant about not being involved with the killing of the Krugman family, then why go to such lengths to tell her that? Because he wanted her to know who had really killed that family—he was trying to point her in the direction of the real killer. If so, why not just come out and tell her who it was?

Because that was too simple, and this was all some sick twisted game to Tightrope.

"He wants me to figure out who the killer is," she muttered to herself.

She searched the app on her computer for recent murders and discovered bodies. She went back further: weeks, and then months, expanding her search farther and farther outside the Seattle area, into the northwest U.S. and parts of Canada. Two hikers were missing twenty miles east of Vancouver, British Columbia. A three-year-old child had been abducted in Portland, most likely taken by the child's father during a custody battle. A man was killed in a bar fight in Idaho, stabbed in the stomach—he bled to death as he tried to walk to the hospital. A young couple had been sentenced for killing their roommate because the man wouldn't move out—they had buried the body, panicked, dug it back up to bury it somewhere else and were pulled over by a State Trooper who noticed blood dripping out of the back of their truck and down onto the license plate.

There were shootings and car accidents. A young man's body had washed up in a creek in northern Utah. A prostitute was slain in northern California. A murder in Montana. A murder in Nevada. A shooting in northwestern Colorado.

Same old stuff she always found, but she kept looking.

Then she froze.

This might be something.

A man named Richard Michael Bonner was released from a psychiatric care center after spending the last nine years in the Cedar Haven Mental Health and Rehabilitation Center. He had confessed to killing three women ten years ago.

Cedar Haven. Cedar. A tree. *Barking up the wrong tree.*

Could that be it? Could Richard Bonner be the killer?

TWELVE

Eve looked up Richard Bonner's address; it was in the Seattle area. She also searched the history of his crimes before he'd been locked up in a mental institution. He had been accused ten years ago of killing three young women, and accused of the abduction of a fourth (who was never found). He slit the three women's throats, leaving their bodies naked and scrubbed cleaned by the edge of a creek, arranged artfully with sticks propping up their arms and fishing line sewed into their eyelids, holding them open, their dead and filmy eyes staring north, the direction he always faced the bodies.

A pair of campers had come across the first of the bodies at Blount Creek (which eventually became nicknamed "Blood Creek" by the locals). They had taken their kayaks down to the river and saw what seemed to be a naked woman sitting among the rocks on the shore. They called the police and the first victim, twenty-two-year-old grad student Brittany Wilks, was found.

Over the next three weeks two more bodies were discovered at different locations along Blount Creek, positioned the same way. Bonner hadn't tried to hide the bodies—he wanted them displayed; he wanted them found. And some suggested that he really wanted to be caught.

It didn't take long to arrest Richard Michael Bonner, aged twenty-nine at the time. The evidence that he had committed the murders of the three women was overwhelming, and he had admitted to the crimes readily. They tried to pin the disappearance of the fourth woman, Jennifer Watson, on him, but he adamantly insisted that he hadn't taken that woman. The police were baffled, wondering why he would admit to three murders but not take responsibility for the fourth woman's disappearance. Was there another serial killer working the same area at the same time? Some said that his refusal to admit to the abduction of Jennifer Watson lent credence to the insanity plea by his lawyers. His attorneys argued at trial that Bonner hadn't hidden his actions or even traces of his own DNA at the crime scenes because he hadn't cared if he was caught. They also argued that these ritualistic killings had a religious connotation to him in his own mind.

Bonner lived with his mother, who he claimed while on trial had abused him sexually, physically, and mentally when he was a child. The defense argued that Richard Bonner was a product of his upbringing, a tortured child who had become insane by the time he was an adult.

Ms. Bonner denied her son's allegations of sexual abuse, and she ended up as a key witness against her own son. She didn't have any direct knowledge that he had killed those three women, but she suspected that he'd done something wrong. She'd been the one to allow the police to search her home, including the basement where her son lived.

The jury found Bonner guilty by reason of insanity. The judge sentenced him to a mental facility in eastern Washington.

Eight months ago, Bonner's mother died suddenly in a fall in her home, falling down the stairs to the basement. She broke her neck and died instantly. The coroner believed she may have had a massive heart attack, and that's what had caused her fall.

Richard Bonner was allowed to attend his mother's funeral service, where he had openly grieved for her. Three months later a board of psychiatrists at the Cedar Haven Center found Bonner rehabilitated and able to re-enter society. Bonner was released with no probation, no supervised control, his criminal records hidden from police databases because of mental health privacy laws.

Now it seemed Bonner was living at his mom's house again. Back in the basement, most likely. Eve couldn't find any other addresses for him.

She sat back in her office chair, staring at the computer screen, which was frozen on an article about Bonner's arrest, a photo of him being escorted into a courthouse. She leaned forward and clicked the mouse to some other pages she had saved—one was of the Cedar Haven Center.

Tightrope said that if she went after him for the Krugman murders, she would be barking up the wrong tree.

Ten years. It had been ten years since Tightrope had killed her family and taken her sister. It had also been ten years since Richard Bonner had killed those three young women and left their bodies by the shores of Blount Creek. And now, ten years later, Tightrope had come out of the woodwork to kill again.

Or *someone* had.

Was it a coincidence that Richard Bonner had just gotten out of the Cedar Haven Center only a few months ago?

Eve didn't believe in coincidences, and a chilling thought was forming in her mind—Bonner could be Tightrope.

Her cell phone buzzed and she jumped. She picked it up, looked at the screen. It was Benji.

"You got something?" she asked him.

"Yeah."

"That was fast."

"It wasn't as difficult to trace the email as I thought it was going to be." He almost sounded disappointed at the lack of a challenge. "In fact, the email came from around here, right here in Seattle."

"Where?" She was getting a tingling feeling dancing across her skin—too many coincidences.

Benji paused like he was looking through some notes he had jotted down. "Uh . . . 6 . . . 2 . . ."

Eve wrote the first two numbers down, but then she stopped as she looked at the address she had written down only moments ago—Richard Bonner's address.

"Belongs to a guy named Richard Bonner," Benji said. "And get this, he just got out of a nut ward after doing nine years. He was convicted of killing three women and then got off on an insanity plea."

"Yeah. I found him already."

Benji couldn't hide his surprise. "You did?"

"Yeah. Barking up the wrong tree, that's what Tightrope said in the email. I started looking up recent criminal activity, any news. I kept going back further and further until I saw an article about Richard Bonner getting out of the Cedar Haven Center in eastern Washington."

"Cedar . . . like a tree," Benji said. "What the hell do you need me for?"

"I *do* need you," Eve said, but she couldn't help cracking a smile.

"So, this guy's been gone for nine years and then he gets out, and now the Tightrope murders begin again? And now Tightrope reached out to you from this guy Bonner's address? You think . . ."

"No," she said, cutting him off. "I don't think Bonner's Tightrope. I mean, it could be possible, I guess, but I don't think so."

"Wow, this is crazy."

"What about North Star? Did you find anything about that?"

"Yeah, I did. Well, maybe. Actually, the email was easier for me to trace. I found a few things about North Star online, a lot of businesses: North Star Plumbing, North Star Associates, North Star Production Studio. North Star—"

"Okay, I get it."

"There were blogs and screen names in chat rooms. But the strangest thing I found was on a black site on the dark web."

"What did you find?"

"I don't know. I couldn't get in."

"You couldn't get in?"

"You need a password," he said defensively. "It's just a black screen with one shining star at the top and a bar to enter the password. I tried three times with a password generator, but I got locked out."

"What do you think it is?"

"Some kind of secret website. Child porn maybe. Sex slaves. Selling illegal drugs or weapons. Could be anything like that."

"But it must mean something. Why would Tightrope want me to find that?"

"Maybe it has something to do with Bonner."

"But Bonner's been locked away for nine years. I doubt they let him have access to computers or the internet in there."

"Yeah."

"It means something," she said. "Some kind of clue. Like barking up the wrong tree was a clue."

"Yeah, but maybe it means something else. Maybe it doesn't have anything to do with this black website." Benji said and then grew silent for a moment.

Eve could tell something was bothering him. "What is it?"

"I reached out on some chatrooms and places on the dark web about North Star. Most didn't seem to know what it was and pretty much told me to fuck off. But there was one person who called himself, or herself, Wilding23, and he said, 'Leave it alone.' I asked him to elaborate, but he logged off and hasn't logged back on since."

"And you think this Wilding23 knows what North Star is?"

"Maybe. But probably not. Just some person pretending to possess some secret knowledge."

"Thank you, Benji. This has been a lot of help."

"What are you going to do now?"

"I'm going to have a talk with Richard Bonner."

"What are you going to do, go to his house?"

"I've got some ideas."

"You need to be careful with this guy."

"I will. Could you get me everything you can find on him? Any personal info that might help me."

"Yeah. I'll try to get it to you in the next few hours."
"Thanks, Benji."
"Anything for you, Eve."

THIRTEEN

The next morning Eve parked her car on the street in front of Richard Bonner's home, watching his house. The neighborhood was older, made up of homes built in the 40s and 50s, mostly two-story houses, close together, driveways crowded with vehicles. The homes weren't terribly large and many needed repairs, but the values had skyrocketed around this area over the last few years.

It was a usual gray and chilly fall morning, the air thick with humidity, the fog mostly dissipated now. It had drizzled a little on her drive to Bonner's house, but it wasn't raining now.

Benji had sent her everything he could find on Bonner in an encrypted email. (He had installed software on her computers and phones that automatically decrypted his emails for her.) He'd sent a mountain of stuff, much of which she'd looked up already: the murders of the three women, the fourth missing victim, Bonner's trial and insanity defense, his release from the Cedar Haven Center. But Benji had also dug up some personal information on Bonner: his DMV records, his credit and banking information, some of his medical records. Bonner had been issued a driver's license two months ago, with his case worker helping the process along. Bonner had no job, but he didn't really need one because his mother's life insurance policy had been paid out to him—he was the only beneficiary, and probate court had moved quickly, leaving Ms. Bonner's possession to her only son: her house and everything in it, her checking account with $14,305 in it, her car—a twelve-year-old Honda Accord. Bonner had been in no trouble since his release. He had joined no associations. He had opened no credit cards or any kind of credit in his own name, and (one of the strange things) he didn't have much of an online presence. He belonged to a few science fiction/fantasy fan groups and some of the major social media sites, but that was about it.

Eve looked at Bonner's two-story home down the street, it was built on a slight rise of land on the other side of the street. The front yard was tiny, with tasteful but overgrown landscaping. The front porch was clean and nearly empty. The white Honda sat in the driveway, backed in. The drapes were closed over all the windows facing the street.

She grabbed a burner phone and dialed Bonner's number. It rang three times and then he answered.

"Hello?" he said in a soft voice.

"Hi. Richard Bonner?"

"Yes." Still cautious. "Who's this?"

"My name's Rebecca Hayes. I work for a producer in Hollywood who specializes in documentaries. Many of his films are on Netflix, and one received two Oscar nominations three years ago."

"Who is he? This producer you work for. What's his name?"

"I can't tell you his name or anything about his films right now," Eve told him as she watched his house, waiting for him to peek out through the living room window curtains.

"What's this about?" He still sounded cautious, but also intrigued.

"Like I said, the producer specializes in documentaries, and he would like to tell your story on film. You *whole* story. *Your* side of things. He wants to make a film about your life and your struggles to re-enter society. He's a big believer that rehabilitation is possible, that someone who's had mental troubles shouldn't be treated like a criminal and punished the rest of their life for something they had no control over, for something they've been cured of."

Bonner was quiet for a moment, thinking, breathing into the phone. He hadn't peeked out through the curtains of his home yet.

"Does that sound like something you'd be interested in?"

"I'd like to know who the producer is and what films he's made."

"I can't disclose that until we all agree to make the film and you sign an NDA."

"I don't know . . ."

"My producer sent me up here to Washington to meet with you. I'm in town now. Of course, it's up to you if you want to consider this. We could meet for a few minutes, and I could tell you more about it."

"Do I get paid?"

"Oh yes. Of course. After the film gets made."

"How much?"

"Well, we'll have to negotiate that. Remember, we haven't decided to make the film yet. A lot of that decision depends on these interviews."

"You're going to interview me?"

"I wanted to ask you a few questions. You don't have to answer the ones you don't want to. You don't have to answer any of them if you don't want to."

Bonner was silent again for a long moment, and then he sighed heavily into the phone. "I'd like to have my story told. My side of things. My struggle."

"That's exactly what we want. When do you think we could meet? Is there any chance we could meet this morning? Maybe in an hour?"

"Yes, I guess that would be okay."

"We could meet at your home. Where you're comfortable."

Another long hesitation as Bonner thought it over. If he didn't want to meet at his house, then Eve was going to have to meet him somewhere else, make him comfortable enough to eventually meet him at his home.

"Mr. Bonner, I don't have a lot of time. My producer has plenty of other projects he's considering. I've looked up your address. I can be there in fifteen minutes if that's okay with you. The interview won't take long."

"Okay. Okay. Yeah, you can come over. You said you've got my address?"

"Your mother's house? Is that the correct address?"

"Yes. I'm here now."

"Good, Mr. Bonner. Great. I'll see you in fifteen minutes. Thank you so much for agreeing to this."

"Thank you, Rebecca. I'm looking forward to it."

Bonner hung up. Eve watched his house. She was far enough away that he wouldn't be able to make out her car. He never looked out through the living room curtains.

*

Fifteen minutes later Eve pulled up in front of Richard Bonner's home, parking on the street in front of the house.

She wondered if she should have talked to Agent Parker about what she was doing. She wondered if she should have told him about the email from Tightrope, the email that Benji had traced to Bonner's house.

But she couldn't talk to Parker just yet; she needed to learn more on her own first.

Benji had asked her yesterday if it was possible that Bonner could actually be Tightrope.

It was possible, but she didn't think so. Bonner's crimes and Tightrope's crimes were similar in a few ways, but there were far more differences in their methods.

The similarities: Both Bonner and Tightrope had killed their victims in elaborate ways, planning out their "ceremonies," getting things ready beforehand. And they both had abducted young women, Bonner his three victims that he had lured into his car (and possibly the fourth missing woman, Jennifer Watson), and Tightrope had taken Maddie.

But then there were the differences: Bonner, after luring his victims into his car, had killed them relatively quickly, whereas Tightrope had tortured his victims, drawing out their suffering.

Another difference was how they had displayed their victims. Both had created spectacular displays of them, but Bonner had done so after his victims were dead, and Tightrope while they were still alive.

Tightrope was very careful about not leaving a shred of evidence behind. Bonner had been sloppy—leaving footprints, fingerprints, hair, fibers; he'd also been caught on a security camera while shoving his second victim into the trunk of his car.

No, they were too different. Eve didn't believe Bonner was Tightrope. She'd possibly seen Tightrope's face that night when she tore off his hood, even though she couldn't remember his face now. But she had definitely heard his voice. And Bonner's voice on the phone today didn't sound like Tightrope's voice, or at least how she remembered him. But it might be different to hear his voice in person. And to look into his eyes.

She was fairly positive Bonner wasn't Tightrope even though Tightrope's email had come from this house. Maybe Tightrope had used Bonner's IP address to get her here. But that would mean Tightrope wanted her here at Bonner's house for a reason. Maybe to find something.

Find what?

Maybe Bonner was killing again. Maybe he was copycatting Tightrope's crimes. Maybe Tightrope, who had claimed in the email that he hadn't killed the Krugman family, was pointing her to the real killer—Bonner. Maybe Bonner wanted to kill again, but he couldn't kill the same way he had before, so he changed his methods. He'd had nine years to prepare, to fantasize about how he would kill again, and maybe he had decided to mimic Tightrope's methods so people would think Tightrope was back again.

But if Bonner wanted to kill again, why mimic such a famous killer? Why reenact such a famous crime? Wouldn't that put too big a spotlight on these crimes? Why kill a family instead of the young women he had been attracted to before?

And if Tightrope was telling the truth about not killing the Krugman family, then how did he know so quickly that Bonner was the Copycat Killer? Was Tightrope so vain that he wanted the world to know it wasn't him? Was it *that* important to him?

Of course, this could all be a big sick game that Tightrope was playing—clues that led nowhere. Just another way to torture her, just like she'd been tortured by these memories for the last ten years.

There was only one way to know, to get closer to the truth—she needed to go inside and meet Richard Bonner.

FOURTEEN

Richard Bonner opened his front door right after Eve rang the doorbell, almost like he'd been waiting right on the other side for her. He probably saw her pull up in front of his house, parking off the street. He'd probably been watching her while she sat in the car.

Watching her like a predator.

Eve could see the younger Richard Bonner in his older, fleshy face. He was at least twenty-five pounds heavier now and a lot of his hair was gone, the rest thinning. Fine wrinkles surrounded his dark brown eyes. But she could also see the handsome man he used to be, especially when he smiled and the wrinkles around his eyes crinkled. It was a warm smile, an easy smile, a charming smile. She saw how he could have lured those women into his car ten years ago.

"Rebecca Hayes?" he said.

"Yes," Eve answered as she shuffled the faux leather case in to her left hand so she could extend her right hand in greeting. She didn't want to shake Bonner's hand; she didn't want to touch his flesh, feel the monster's skin on her skin, but she had to sell her character to him.

He grasped her hand, his palm smooth and dry, his grip relaxed and gentle, almost like he was afraid of squeezing too hard and accidently hurting her. He gave her hand a quick pump and let go, not holding on too long.

Eve had dressed in a pair of baggy pants and a blouse with a bulky sweater over it, the shirt tails sticking out of the bottom of the sweater, the clothes concealing her athletic body. She wore a pair of oversized glasses that she fiddled with nervously. Her hair was tied back in a loose bun with a few strands hanging down onto her forehead. Along with her leather bag of notebooks, she carried a camera in a case slung over her shoulder, along with her purse.

"Can I help you with anything?" Bonner asked. "Take anything for you?"

"No thanks. I got it."

He took a step back. "Well, come on in."

Eve entered the foyer of the home, which was part of the living room, as Bonner shut the front door. He didn't lock it.

"Thanks," she said with a smile.

It still looked like Bonner's mother lived in the house; the décor was clean and orderly, a light coat of dust on everything and the slight musty smell of a house closed up too long.

Bonner seemed to notice her scrutinizing the living room. "My mom died almost six months ago."

"Yes, I know. And I'm so sorry about that."

"When I . . . I got out, I came back home. I left everything just the way she had it. I lived down in the basement since I was a teenager. When I was about fifteen, I asked my mom if I could make my bedroom in the basement. I wanted my own space, you see?"

Eve nodded.

"She let me move down there. I had my TV down there. My own bedroom. I even bought a little fridge and a microwave oven and put them down there. I didn't need to come upstairs for much." He glanced around. "Still don't."

Bonner's home was a museum to his dead mother, a place frozen in time. It reminded Eve of how she'd left her parents' home exactly the same over the last ten years. She fought a shudder as she thought about how she and this monster shared that in common.

"Do you want to come down to the basement and talk?" Bonner offered, already walking toward the kitchen.

Eve hesitated.

Bonner stopped and turned back around. He smiled again, a sheepish grin, like he'd just made some social faux pa. "Sorry. What was I thinking?"

"No," Eve said quickly, returning his smile. "No, we can talk wherever you want to."

"You're not . . . *uncomfortable* going down there with me?"

"Are you asking me if I'm scared?"

Bonner didn't answer. He stood there, patient, waiting for a reply.

"I'm a little nervous being here," Eve said. "I'll admit that. But my producer believes in rehabilitation, and so do I. We want to tell your story." She paused for just a moment, then added. "You *are* rehabilitated, right?"

It was Bonner's turn to hesitate, and for just a moment his face was slack, his dark eyes seemed to get darker and bigger, turning into black holes in his face, shrouded under his heavy and practically hairless brow. He smiled, his face lighting up. "Of course I am."

"People know I'm here," Eve sang out with a smile and lifted her cell phone in her hand. "And they're tracking me on my phone. If I don't call back every few hours, they'll call in the cavalry." She giggled like she was only joking.

"Really," Bonner said. "We could stay up here and talk. It's fine with me."

"No, I want to see your basement. Your home. I think it's important to help learn more about you."

"You're sure?"

"Absolutely."

"Okay."

Bonner led the way into the kitchen, then to the door that opened to the basement stairs. He flipped a light switch on the wall just inside the doorway, flooding the stairwell with light. He went down first. Eve followed.

Her heart raced as she followed Richard Bonner down the narrow, creaky steps. She was going into a basement with a killer. She had tried to set up visits with serial killers before to learn more about them, but she hadn't had much success with it. And here she was now with a true killer for the first time. Except it wasn't the first time—she'd been with a killer before . . . ten years ago.

The basement was large, as big as the floor plan of the first floor of Bonner's house, yet it still managed to feel claustrophobic with the bulky furniture, clutter, and the low ceiling, which was a grid of floor joists, pipes, and wires. The large room was murky, the only lights coming from a small lamp on a table next to the couch. Another light shined down from a doorway that looked like it led to a small bathroom. The small rectangular windows at the top of the walls on one side of the basement were blacked out with thick black paper or cardboard.

The room was full of furniture: a bed and two tables, a cedar chest at the foot of the bed, a sofa, two more tables, a recliner, a small table with two wood chairs shoved under it, a row of lower cabinets and a countertop where a microwave oven, hotplate, and a collection of canned and boxed food were lined up. A desk was pushed against the wall on the other side of the basement stairs, the crawlspace underneath the stairs stuffed with cardboard boxes and plastic tubs. A medium-sized flat-screen TV sat on a table near the bed with a video game system in front of it. The desk had an outdated computer monitor on top of it. The older computer tower sat on the floor next to the desk along with piles of papers, mail, and magazines. A bookcase overflowed with paperback books, comics, and magazines. More books and magazines were stacked on the floor.

The basement was a contrast to the rooms above, a cluttered mess comparted to the orderly and neat world up there.

Eve glanced at the posters covering the walls: Star Wars, Star Trek, Lord of the Rings, an X-Files poster with the words "I want to Believe" at the bottom of it.

"You like science fiction?" she asked Bonner.

"Yeah. And fantasy. Sword and sorcery. Medieval stuff. I like westerns, too. I like to read. I'd like to write a book someday."

Eve just nodded.

"I like stories about good versus evil. I like to see the good guys win because it doesn't happen a lot in real life. It *should* be like that, though. Good guys should win. Justice should prevail."

Eve nodded again, glancing around the large basement. It looked like a teenager's room, like Richard's development into an adult had stopped somewhere in those teenage years.

"You want to sit down?" he asked.

"Sure."

Bonner gestured at the couch and recliner, then at the small table with the chairs.

Eve chose the small table, pulling out one of the wooden chairs. For just a second the memories of being tied to a wooden chair flooded back, but she pushed them away. She couldn't crack now. Tightrope wanted her here in this house for some reason; he wanted her to find something, and she couldn't fail. Her hope was that these clues would eventually lead her back to him.

Bonner sat on the couch, not at the table next to her, like he could tell his close proximity was making her nervous. He wore a pair of baggy and stained shorts, a big T-shirt, socks and sandals on his feet even though it was a little chilly in his basement. But the cold air didn't seem to bother him.

Eve got busy pulling a notepad and a small battery-powered tape recorder out of her bag, setting them on the table next to her.

"Are you going to record this?" he asked.

"I can. Do you not want me to?"

Bonner shrugged. "Maybe not yet."

"Sure." She pushed the small recorder away just a little. "But if we decide to make this film, you'll have to go on camera. You know that, don't you?"

"Yeah. Of course."

"And that's something you're willing to do?"

"I just want to be treated fairly. Tell my story."

"That's exactly what we want to do."

Bonner looked away, his eyes darting to the "kitchen" area of his basement lair. "You want something to drink?"

"No, I'm fine. Thanks, though. But you can get something if you want to."

"No, I'm good, too." He sighed. "So, what now?"

"I just want to ask you a few questions and take some notes. Okay?"

"Okay."

Eve was ready to begin.

FIFTEEN

Bonner hunched forward on the couch a little, his elbows on his knees, like he was trying to look attentive, but it came off as nervous. He also looked bigger than before, but slow and sluggish. But Eve had the feeling that Bonner was capable of moving very quickly if he want to, like a crocodile at the edge of a watering hole, waiting patiently in the muck for the prey to get just a little closer.

"Some of these questions may seem a little personal," Eve told him. "I just want to warn you about that."

Bonner nodded, still hunched forward like he was about to pop up from the sofa at any moment.

Something about his eyes . . . about the way he's looking at me.

"Some of these questions we will ask again during filming, but we just want to get a good idea of your answers first."

He nodded again, his face still slack.

His expression was beginning to bother her.

"Do you remember the crimes you committed?" she asked, her pen poised above her small notepad.

"Yeah, I remember them."

"In detail?"

He nodded. "I remember the crimes I committed while not being in control of my own mind and emotions."

"Yes, of course."

"Yes, I remember them."

"And you'll be able to recount the . . . uh, the incidents we'll call them . . . in detail later when we film?"

"Yes."

"How did you lure the women into your car? I mean, what technique did you use?"

Bonner's face scrunched a little like he didn't understand the question, or understand why he was being asked the question. But then he answered: "Uh, two of them were prostitutes, so it was pretty easy to get them into my car. I offered them money, they got in. I gave them extra money so we could go to a motel room further away. They weren't too suspicious at first. I told them I was nervous, that this was my first time, you know, paying for it. I told them that my wife had been cheating on me and had left me and that I just needed to be with someone."

"You drove them all the way to the woods? To Blount Creek?"

"No. The first one, I pulled the car over and tazed her. She tried to fight back at the last second, but she was too dazed. Too weak by then. I pulled her out of the car and put her in a headlock until she passed out. I tied her hands and feet, threw her in the trunk. I was in a spot behind a building when I did that, a spot I had checked out several times to make sure there wouldn't be any witnesses around."

"And the some with the next one?" Eve looked down at a larger notebook she had opened with some of the articles she had printed out from the internet. "You grabbed the next one within a week of the first one."

"Yeah, I knew I had to work quickly before it became a big news story. I did the same thing to the next one, in the same place. It went a little easier the second time."

"What did you do when you got them to the creek?"

"I untied their ankles and made them walk into the woods. I told them I was going to make them clean. I also told them I would let them go if they would just do what I wanted them to do."

"And they believed you?"

He shrugged and frowned. "I don't know. I think they wanted to believe it, but I'm not sure if they did."

"And the third woman? The one you picked up from the bar."

"I couldn't go back to the same place I'd put the other girls in the trunk. So, I went to a bar I knew. I talked to this girl. She was pretty drunk. I slipped a roofie in her drink. By the time she was ready to leave with me, she was like a walking zombie." He snickered for a moment at the memory, and then his face went slack, like he knew he'd done something wrong. He cleared his throat, the smile gone, and continued. "I got her all the way into the woods without having to tie her up or put her in the trunk."

"Did you switch locations after the second person because there were cameras in the area?"

He shrugged again. "It just didn't feel right to me. I didn't know there were cameras there until later, when I was caught."

Benji had found the security camera footage that had been used in court and sent it to Eve. The footage was grainy, shot at night, but it showed Bonner stuffing a woman into the trunk of his car, and then tying her wrists behind her back, and then tying her ankles together. Bonner couldn't be made out clearly, but his car could.

"So, back to the woods where you took the victims. You said you wanted to clean them."

Bonner sighed and looked down at his hands, fidgeting with his fingers. It seemed to Eve to be a practiced gesture, a fake one. Perhaps he had perfected it while he worked with the psychiatrists at the Cedar Haven Center. Maybe it was his idea of showing remorse.

"I wanted to clean them," he finally said. "I felt like I was letting the bad stuff out, draining it out of them. I took off their short skirts, their tight shirts, their lacy underwear, their spiky shoes. I washed off all their makeup. I made them clean. Outside and inside."

"Like baptizing them?"

Bonner shrugged. "Maybe. I guess. I was just doing what the bad thoughts told me to do. I know that now."

Eve pretended to jot down a few notes. She looked up and saw that Bonner was watching her, his eyes never wavering.

"Are you sorry for the things you've done?" she asked him.

"Of course, I am," he snapped. "It wasn't me doing them. Not the *real* me. It's like there's this other person inside of me."

"Like a split personality?"

He stared at her. "Yes, I guess you could say that."

"I know you're rehabilitated now, Richard. I believe that you are. But do you still feel the urge to . . . to do the things you've done before?"

"No," Bonner answered a little too sharply. "I take medication now. The doctors said I had a kind of schizophrenia that was never diagnosed and treated. I can imagine how many others are in prison now, or even on death row, because they were never given the right diagnosis, the right medicines, the right therapy, or given the belief that they could get better."

"You don't believe that some people are just bad?" Eve asked. "Born evil? You think maybe some people don't have any reason for the evils they do? Maybe they just like doing it?"

Bonner didn't answer, still staring at Eve in a strange way, like he was trying to think of something, a word on the tip of his tongue.

"Have you heard about the Krugman family that was murdered recently?"

A smile played at the corner of Bonner's lips.

Something's wrong.

"Tightrope's back," Bonner sang out in a low voice.

"You think that's true? You think Tightrope killed that family?"

"I don't know. Maybe." His voice was lower now, like the growl of a dog. He was still staring at her like he was trying to figure something out.

Eve shoved her notebook, papers, and the small tape recorder she'd never turned on back into her bag. "I think that might be enough for today."

"I know you," Bonner whispered.

She stared at him.

He was smiling even wider now, like he knew a secret, a spark of recognition in his dark eyes.

"What?" Eve asked.

"I've seen you somewhere before."

"No," Eve said. "That's not possible. I'm from L.A. And I haven't been on TV or anything. Strictly behind camera for me."

Bonner's dark eyes lit up. "Tightrope," he whispered. "That's it. You're one of his victims, the one that survived. You're Eve Townsend."

SIXTEEN

Eve was busted. She thought about denying that she was Eve Townsend to Bonner, insisting that she just looked like her and that a lot of people made that same mistake, but she knew there would be no convincing him of that.

Bonner's slick smile was still smeared on his face. Eve realized that Bonner had been playing her all along—he'd never bought her phony story about being a producer's assistant. While she'd been playing that character, he'd been playing one of his own.

He was up in a flash, moving as quickly as she suspected he would, blocking her way to the basement stairs.

Eve jumped up from her chair, her bag in her hands, her purse looped over her shoulder, her cell phone shoved down into her pants pocket. Her body was tense; she was ready to defend herself. She had trained for years to fight, and she would fight, but only if she had to. Right now, it seemed best to play another character, that of a nervous and frightened woman.

"I wonder why Eve Townsend would come here to see me," Bonner said. His expression had changed, his smile no longer made him youthful and handsome, it made him look evil and deadly. "I wonder why she would pretend to be working for a movie producer."

Another realization dawned on Eve—she knew in that moment that he wasn't rehabilitated; the urge to kill was still inside of him, as strong as ever. He had waited nine years at the Cedar Haven Center, playing his own character to the doctors and staff, showing remorse, gaining their trust, giving them the answers they wanted to hear, taking his meds, biding his time until he was free again, until he could kill again.

"You don't want to do anything crazy," Eve warned.

"Are you calling me crazy?"

"Or anything *stupid*," she corrected.

"I invite you into my home and you *insult* me." He feigned hurt feelings.

"You need to move out of the way and let me leave."

"Why? Because if you don't call and check in with someone the cavalry will be called? Isn't that what you told me?"

Eve didn't answer.

Bonner somehow managed to frown yet keep the ghost of a smile on his face. "No one knows you're here, do they?"

Eve still didn't answer.

"You went out on your own. Came here on your own. Why? You think I had something to do with that family getting killed? Is that why you asked about them?"

Eve still didn't say anything. She let him talk. Maybe he would slip up and she would get the answers she'd come for.

Bonner stood in the same spot. There was no way around him, with all the furniture and clutter in the way. That's why he had sat where he had on the couch, positioning himself for this moment.

"Did you kill that family?" she asked him.

"You think I did?"

"Did you?"

"Maybe I did. But maybe it was Tightrope. Maybe he's back." Bonner's eyes lit up. "Do you think I'm Tightrope?"

Eve remained silent, her body still poised, ready to act.

"I thought you were playing detective, trying to trip me up, but maybe you think I'm Tightrope and you came for some revenge." He glanced down at the purse she carried. "Are you recording this? You won't be able to use it in court, you know."

"I'm not recording anything, but I have a gun." That was a lie—she hadn't brought a gun with her. She couldn't have one with her here. She knew the risks of being alone with Bonner, but if he attacked her (like he seemed about to do), she couldn't shoot him inside his own home—she would have to explain what she was doing here with a gun.

Bonner shook his head slowly. "No, I don't believe you have a gun. You would've grabbed it by now." He reached into the pocket of his baggy shorts and pulled out a large folded buck knife. He unfolded it, the blade clicking solidly into place.

Eve didn't move. She had trained with the ex-Special Forces soldier she had hired and he had taught her how to defend herself against an attacker with a knife. But training was one thing, seeing it in real life was another. And having a serial killer wielding the weapon, a man who wouldn't hesitate to kill, was another thing too.

"You want to know why I killed those three women? Is that it?"

She didn't answer.

"Because they were dirty whores, that's why. I killed them because I liked doing it. I washed them in the river to get rid of fingerprints, and any other evidence. But I guess I wasn't as careful as I should've been. But I'll be more careful this time, you can believe that."

Bonner took a step forward.

Eve dropped her bag, camera case, and purse. She moved to right one step, her knees slightly bent. Bonner was at least five inches taller than she was and a hundred pounds heavier. He was older, maybe slower, surely not as skilled in fighting as she was. But he did have a large knife in his hand.

"I used a knife like this to cut their throats. I watched them struggle, drowning in their own blood as it drained out of them. I listened to the blood gurgling in their lungs. I love that moment, the look in their eyes when they realize that they're dying, that no one's coming to save them, that it's really happening, only moments left to live, the seconds ticking away. They get this wild look in their eyes . . . they all do. Like an animal's eyes. It's hard to explain, like an acceptance of what's coming but disbelief at the same time. That's the look I like the best, the disbelief, like they'd never thought about dying, like it couldn't happen to them."

He took another step forward.

"You killed the Krugman family," Eve said. She had nothing to lose now. Why not lay her cards on the table? "You're copying Tightrope's crimes."

Bonner froze, alarm in his eyes. "I didn't do that. I didn't kill that family."

"You're saying Tightrope did?"

Bonner didn't answer.

Tightrope had emailed her, but he had made it look like the email had come from Bonner's house. Eve had suspected that Bonner was the copycat, but from the look on his face, she wasn't so sure now. He looked afraid . . . really afraid.

"You started killing again, didn't you?" Eve pressed. "You couldn't wait to start again. The three women you killed weren't enough."

"I didn't kill that family."

"And Jennifer Watson wasn't enough for you, either."

Bonner's face seemed to go white. "I . . . I didn't have anything to do with that."

"What did you do with Jennifer's body? How come you didn't wash her body in the river? Make it clean. What did you do with her?'

"I can't let you leave," he said, his eyes still bulging, his mouth slack. He licked his lips, making annoying sucking sounds.

"You're going to kill me? My car's right outside your house."

"I'll get rid of it."

"They'll catch you again."

"Not before I kill you. And others." He lunged at her, jabbing the knife forward.

The blade missed Eve by inches as she sidestepped, then spun and swept his leg with a kick to his knee. She spun around, landing a roundhouse kick that knocked him backward into the cedar chest at the foot of his bed. He collapsed onto the floor, dropping his knife, breathing hard, wheezing.

Eve was about to go for the knife, but Bonner grabbed it before she could make her move. She had rung his bell for a few seconds, but he was recovering quickly. He got to his feet, a little shaky, a little wary now that he knew she could fight. But there was a determined look in his eyes, like he relished the challenge.

In their tussle, Eve had ended up closer to the bottom of the stairs, switching sides in the fight. She could bolt for the stairs, but she wasn't sure she could make it to the top before he caught up to her. She'd be in a bad position, her back to him. He could stab at her legs, even cutting tendons or arteries. She'd be too vulnerable.

No, she needed to finish him off now—neutralize the threat.

"What are you going to do, kill me?" Bonner teased. "Beat me up? I'll call the cops. Tell them you came here to kill me, like some crazy vigilante. How are you going to explain that?"

"I've got lawyers. A lot of them."

Bonner was trying to rattle her, distract her so he could attack, but she wasn't going to let him do that. Instead, she decided to rattle him. She'd seen the look on his face when she had mentioned Tightrope, his insistence that he wasn't copycatting Tightrope's crimes.

He lunged at her again, swinging wildly with the knife.

She dodged to the side and landed a kick to his liver, dropping him to his knees immediately, then she kicked him square in the face while he was down, like she was punting a football. He was rocked back, his mouth slamming closed, teeth clacking together.

This time he managed to hold onto the knife. He popped back up on wobbly legs, dazed but not out, wincing from the pain in his side as he tried to catch his breath. Blood dribbled from the corner of his mouth. He might even have a cracked rib or two.

"I can do this all day," she told him.

"I'll get you eventually. I'll cut you wide open. I'm going to enjoy that look in your eyes as your life slips away. I'm going to fucking enjoy it so much."

"Someone *does* know I'm here," she said. "Tightrope knows. He sent me an email. He told me I'd find something here."

Bonner barked out a laugh, but it was a faked, forced laugh. The fear was back in his eyes. "That's not true."

"It was Tightrope. He knows things only Tightrope could know."

"You're a fucking liar!"

"Tightrope told me to follow the North Star."

Real fear crept into Bonner's face—he charged her with a scream.

She grabbed his knife arm, twisted, and flipped him over her shoulder. He landed with a crash down on the small table and set of chairs, smashing them apart.

Bonner had lost his knife again while landing on the table. Eve picked it up and held it to his throat, her face close to his. He wheezed through his broken nose.

"What is it?" she yelled at him. "What's the North Star?"

"I can't say anything," he yelled, beginning to cry.

"I'll cut your throat wide open, like you did to those women. Nobody will shed a tear for you."

"Do it," he said, blood spraying out of his mouth, a river of it flowing from his flattened nose. "Kill me."

"Tell me! Or I'll cut you in other places!"

"I can't. There's nothing you can do to me that would be worse than what they could do. You think my mother's death was an accident?"

For just a second blind rage overcame Eve. For just a second, she wasn't sure what she was going to do, if she was going to cut Bonner's throat, or stab him in his chest and stomach until her arm went numb.

She stood up. She had to get away from Bonner. She threw the knife across the room by the bed. It landed somewhere in the corner. She grabbed her purse and bags, and then went up the stairs.

Bonner didn't try to follow her.

SEVENTEEN

Eve called Agent Parker as she drove away from Bonner's home. She was still shaky from her fight with Bonner, but she had calmed down enough to make the call while waiting at a stoplight.

"Eve?" Parker said.

"Parker. I need to see you. I need to talk to you."

He sighed into the phone—his way of letting her know he was busy.

"It's important. I found out some things. I've got something to show you."

"What?"

"I don't want to talk about it on the phone." She thought he was going to argue that her "computer guy" probably had her phone as safe and hack-proof as possible, but he didn't.

"You okay?" he asked.

The tone of his voice touched her. "Yes. I mean, not really. When can we meet?"

"Where do you want to meet?"

"How about the park? Same place as before."

"Okay. I guess I could eat another hot dog. I'll meet you there in about an hour or so."

"Thanks, Parker."

"I'll call you if I'm running late."

They hung up and Eve turned left at the next light, heading toward the park. Her mind wandered as she drove, her body on autopilot. She was still rattled about Bonner, but it was more than that—it was everything. It was Tightrope reaching out to her, maybe killing again, or leading her to the copycat who was doing the killing. For ten years she'd been searching, nearly giving up hope, beginning to believe that Maddie was dead, believing that maybe even Tightrope was dead or incarcerated somewhere. But now he had come out of the shadows. Why? To torment her? And why now? Did it have something to do with Bonner getting out of Cedar Haven? Obviously, it did.

She was very early at the park. She parked her car and turned off the engine. Her bag and purse were down on the floorboard of the passenger seat, but she didn't need to bring those with her. She popped the trunk and got out, locking the doors with her key fob. She pulled a larger purse out of the trunk with the items inside that she planned to show Parker when he got to the park.

Moments later she walked down the wide, paved walking path that meandered lazily through the trees until it met up with the shoreline, straightening out a little at that point and paralleling the water.

It was a cold, gray day, but there were plenty of people on the trail: joggers, an older man walking by slowly with his dog, a few people on bicycles, moms pushing their babies in strollers, a businesswoman in a gray skirt suit and sneakers, yelling at someone on her cell phone while she powerwalked.

Eve reached the bench where she'd sat with Parker. No one was around. Ernie was at his hot dog stand three hundred yards away; he didn't have any customers right now. She sat down and waited for Parker.

*

Almost an hour later Parker marched toward her, dressed in his usual dark suit with an overcoat. His clothes looked rumpled, his shoulders slumped, his skin pale and saggy, his eyes glazed over. He looked exhausted.

She got up without a word and walked with him to Ernie's hot dog stand. Parker ordered the same thing he'd ordered the last time they were here: a hot dog with sauerkraut and mustard, and a side of fries. Eve didn't order any food. They both got large cups of coffee.

She let him eat. He wolfed down his food after they got back to the bench and sat down. When he was picking at the last of his fries, she asked, "You getting anywhere with the Krugman case?"

He smirked at her—she knew damn well he couldn't answer that question.

"No suspects?" she pressed.

"Is this what you dragged me all the way out here for?"

"You don't think it's Tightrope, do you?"

He shrugged, not giving in. He sipped his coffee.

"Come on," she said.

"What about you? You said you found some things out. You said you had something to show me."

"Give me something and I'll tell you what I know."

Parker looked away, sighing, acting like he was really thinking her offer over. But she knew he would give in—he wouldn't have come all the way out here if he wasn't interested in what she'd found out.

"An anonymous call came in about the Krugman murders," Parker finally said as he wiped at any crumbs on his pants legs. "But we haven't been able to trace the call. Probably from a burner." He looked at her. "Now it's your turn."

"I might have a suspect."

Parker's eyebrows shot up. He almost smiled . . . almost. The expression made him look a little younger, and a little healthier. "Who? Tightrope?"

"Maybe. Or a copycat."

His eyes narrowed like he realized he was being played.

Eve pulled out a folded piece of paper from her large purse and handed it to him.

"What's this?" he asked as he opened it.

"It's an email from Tightrope."

He froze, staring at her like he was trying to decide if she was bullshitting him.

"At least the author of the email claims to be Tightrope. But I think it's really him."

Parker read the email. It looked like he read it several more times, studying it. He looked at Eve. "You should have told me about this right away, Eve."

"I know. I'm telling you now. Showing it to you now."

He huffed out another sigh and looked back down at the paper in his hands, reading it again. "What's this about saying hi to Ralph?"

"Ralph was my sister's stuffed animal. A white rabbit. She called it Ralph the Rabbit."

Parker remembered the stuffed animal now. "You had it with you in the hospital room. Why would he mention that? Do you know what it means?"

"When we were here at the park the other day . . ." Her words trailed as she tried to find the words to explain what she wanted to say.

Parker nodded at her impatiently to go on.

"After we were at the park, after I left, I went to my parents' house for the night. I never told you this, but I go there every year on the date my parents and brother were killed and Maddie was taken. I spend the night there." She didn't want to tell him how she set up the dining room chairs again like they were that night, trying to re-create every detail of the horror, to re-live the experience, trying to remember some clue, something Tightrope might have said, a glimpse of his face after she'd torn the mask away. Parker didn't need to know *everything*.

"Why do you go there?" But it seemed like he already suspected the answer.

"I go there to try to remember."

"You go there hoping he'll come back some day."

Eve didn't deny it. "When I was there the other night, I had fallen asleep in the living room." Again, she didn't see the necessity of telling him that she had fallen asleep in the same dining room chair that Tightrope had tied her to. "When I woke up, Ralph the Rabbit was on the floor. The stuffed animal had been up in Maddie's room when I got there, but when I woke up, it was on the floor in front of me."

"Are you trying to say that Tightrope came into your house while you were there?"

"I'm just saying that Ralph the Rabbit was upstairs, and later, in the middle of the night when I woke up, he was on the floor in front of me."

"You're saying that Tightrope brought the rabbit down to you for some reason?"

"I don't know."

"Where's the stuffed animal now?"

"I've got it with me." She pulled out a large freezer bag. Ralph was inside with much of the stuffing she had pulled out of him.

"This is how you found him?" Parker asked. "Torn apart like this?"

"No. I did that."

He just stared at her.

"When I left the house, I took Ralph with me. I don't know why, but I felt like it meant something, Ralph being on the floor when I woke up, so I took it with me. When I got the email from Tightrope yesterday, when I read the part about saying hi to Ralph, I thought he might have hidden something inside Ralph. So, I cut Ralph open."

"Eve," Parker said, the word coming out in a rush of breath. "That wasn't a good idea. There could've been a bomb in there, for all you knew. Or poison. Hell, who knows what he could've put in there."

"There wasn't anything. Nothing I could find, anyway. But could you have your tech guys look at it?"

"We looked at it ten years ago. Along with a lot of other things from your house."

Eve remembered.

"Came back with nothing then. No other hair fibers. Nothing."

"Could you check it again? Maybe there's something this time."

Parker just nodded, but he didn't look too hopeful about it. He set the bag down beside him on the bench. "So, you think Tightrope may have been in the house and left the rabbit that he mentioned in the email to . . . what? To show you that he was there? That he's watching you? That he can get to you whenever he wants to?"

"Or to show me that Maddie's still alive."

Parker's face crumbled a little in misery for her. He had to look away for a moment.

"There's another possible explanation."

He looked back at her, waiting for her to continue.

"Maybe I blacked out and went upstairs to get the rabbit from Maddie's room."

"You have a history of blackouts?"

"No."

"You've walked in your sleep before?"

"No. Not that I know of."

"Were you drinking when you were there?"

"You know I don't drink anymore."

"Any drugs. Maybe a joint?"

She glared at him.

"I had to ask. Blacking out can mean a lot of things. Maybe you should see a doctor. Get an MRI or a CAT scan. It could be the stress. God knows you've been under tremendous stress, and the murder of the Krugman family, how they were killed the same way . . ." He let his words die away in the cold air, not needing to say more.

"I don't know what it was. I just know that I got this email from Tightrope the next day."

"If Tightrope was in the house with you while you were sleeping, while you were so vulnerable, why not kill you then?"

She shrugged. *Why not kill me ten years ago?* she almost said, but didn't. "Maybe he's playing games with me. Maybe he's been playing games for a while. I think one of the most important things about that email is that he mentions Ralph and asks me to say hi to him."

Parker glanced down at the paper in his hands with the email printed on it. "He signed it TR."

She nodded.

"What's this about 'follow the North Star'?"

"When I got the email, I called my computer guy."

Parker nodded for her to go on without a snide remark about her "computer guy." He knew she would never reveal Benji's identity to him, and he never bothered to try to find out on his own.

"I had him trace the email. He called me back a few hours later and said he'd found it, that it had been easier to find than he thought it would be."

"He traced it? Where's it from?"

"It appears to come from Richard Michael Bonner's house."

Parker's eyes shifted away as he tried to remember where he'd heard that name before.

"Richard Bonner just got released from the Cedar Haven Center a few months ago. He spent nine years there."

Parker's eyes lit up. "He killed three women. Left their bodies by a creek. Blood Creek." It was all coming back to him. "He got off on an insanity plea." He stared at her. "You're not saying Bonner is really Tightrope, are you?"

"No, but I think someone's trying to make it seem that way."

"Who? Tightrope?"

"I don't know."

"But you seem sure Bonner isn't Tightrope."

"I *know* he isn't."

"How can you be so sure?"

"Because I went to see Bonner just a few hours ago."

EIGHTEEN

"Eve . . . why would you go to Bonner's home?"

"Because I needed to hear his voice, look him in the eye," Eve said quickly, trying to diffuse Parker before he blew up. "I needed to know if he was really Tightrope."

"And he's not?"

"No. Not the same voice. I know Richard Bonner's not Tightrope, but Tightrope, if he's really the one who sent that email to me, wanted me at Bonner's house for some reason. He wanted me to find something."

"What?"

"Maybe Bonner's killing again, or maybe he knows where that missing woman, Jennifer Watson, is. Everybody was pretty sure he'd taken her like he had abducted the other three women. They were all taken around the same time. Maybe he hid her body in his house."

Parker nodded; he remembered the disappearance of Jennifer Watson—still an unsolved case. "The police searched his house when he was arrested."

"Then there's something else there at Bonner's house, maybe a clue where he buried Jennifer's body. There's got to be something else there, something Tightrope wants me to find."

Parker's eyebrows knitted in frustration. "You know you can't just go around meeting with—" he made air quotes with is fingers. "—suspects whenever you feel like it."

"I know the rules. But I'm not a cop. I don't have to follow those rules."

"Yeah, but you're giving this information to me now. How am I supposed to use information you got this way?"

Eve looked away, shaking her head a little. Here she was giving Parker a golden egg and he was worried about procedures. She could practically feel Parker wanting to tell her that this was exactly why she couldn't get into the FBI, because she believed she could do whatever the hell she wanted to without bothering with rules and regulations.

But Parker didn't say any of that. He didn't rub it in. Not yet, at least.

They were quiet for a moment.

"So, what happened when you met Bonner?"

"Oh, you want to know now? Won't we be breaking some kind of procedure?"

"Come on, Eve."

"Okay. I called him this morning. I told him I was working with a movie producer who wanted to make a documentary about his life, about his struggles to overcome his mental illness and re-enter society. I told him my name was Rebecca."

"And that fooled him?"

"I thought it did. But he knew all along that I was lying. It's like he knew who I was right away. Like he'd been waiting for me to contact him."

"So, you think someone tipped him off? You think he's in on it somehow?"

"I don't know. I just know he had me pegged as soon as he opened his front door and let me in. Maybe even before that, when I was on the phone with him. He's not as dumb as he pretends to be."

Parker looked down at the paper still in his hands, giving it a little slap. "Maybe Bonner sent the email to you, pretending to be Tightrope. He knew you would trace it to his house, that you would go to see him, that you couldn't resist."

"Could be possible, but I don't think so."

"Why's that?"

"There are things in that email that only Tightrope would know. Like about Ralph. Also, when I mentioned to Bonner that I'd gotten an email from Tightrope, he went white as a ghost. And he got even more nervous when I asked him about North Star. We were fighting, and when I said the words North Star, he just froze."

"Wait a minute . . . back up. You were *fighting* with Bonner? Jeez, Eve . . ."

"He attacked me. He said he was going to kill me. I had to defend myself."

"What did you do to him?"

"Definitely broke his nose. Maybe cracked some of his ribs."

"Damn, Eve. I can't believe you put yourself in that kind of situation."

"I fought him off easily enough. But listen, my computer guy tried to find information on North Star. All he could find was a website on the dark web. Just a black screen with the words North Star and a shining star at the top, and then a box to enter a password. Nothing else. No explanation about what kind of website it was. Nothing. But when I asked Bonner about North Star, he practically pissed himself. He said he couldn't tell me anything about *them*, like they're some kind of group. He said whatever I did couldn't be as bad as what *they* could do to him." She left out the part about holding Bonner's own knife to his throat while she interrogated him.

"You didn't think about leaving evidence behind at his house?" Parker snapped at her.

"I didn't leave any evidence."

"Fingerprints? Your fingerprints are in a government database now because you tried to get into the FBI."

She noticed his slight emphasis of the word "tried," but she didn't say anything about it. "I was careful. I wore clear latex paint on my fingertips."

"There's hair and clothing fibers."

She just shrugged.

Parker looked away, like he was trying to calm down for a minute, thinking. He still had the paper with the email printed on it clenched in one hand.

"Here's what I believe," Eve said. "I believe Tightrope came out of hiding to let me know he didn't kill the Krugman family. It seems important to him that he lets people know, or at least me, that he didn't do it, that there's a copycat out there mimicking his . . . his style of murder. And I don't think he likes it. He made it seem like his email had come from Bonner's house. That can't be a coincidence. He wanted me to find something there."

"Like what? A clue?"

"I don't know. Maybe."

"But you didn't find anything."

"It's a start. Bonner said some strange things about North Star, like I just told you. He also asked me if I really thought his mother's death was an accident. What if Bonner had his own mother killed for revenge because she had turned against him in the courtroom? Maybe Bonner had an accomplice in his murders, and that accomplice is now out there killing families like Tightrope did. Or maybe they're both working together."

Parker didn't say anything, staring at her with his blue/gray eyes.

"I think Bonner's killing again. I think he might have changed his M.O., making it look like it's another serial killer. One thing I know for sure after this morning is that Bonner is not rehabilitated—he still has the urge to kill, still likes it. He told me so. And I don't think he really cares if he gets caught again."

"What am I supposed to do with this information? I can't get a warrant with it."

"At least you know Bonner might be guilty. You've got some pieces of the puzzle. Can't you use the email? Trace it to Bonner's house. My guy said it wasn't hidden very well. Then you'll have enough of a reason to keep an eye on Bonner."

"Bonner will just destroy his computer. Get rid of it. And what if he lawyers up?"

"I'll get my own lawyers."

"What if Bonner says you came to his house with wild theories about him killing the Krugman family? What if he says you think he's Tightrope and you came for revenge? Attacked him. Broke his nose. His ribs."

"I'll say he contacted me first. From a burner phone. No record of the call."

"And you didn't go to the police about it?"

Eve didn't have an answer for him.

"No, Eve. Please don't do anything like that. If Bonner's really the copycat, if he's killing again, we can't let him get off on a technicality. Let me work on the email angle first. And you, no more contact with Bonner. Okay? Don't go watching him or parking in front of his house. Nothing. Okay, Eve?"

"Alright. But we need to get him before he kills again."

"We will." Parker glanced down at the paper still in his hands and then he looked at Eve again. "And what if this really is Tightrope that wrote to you?"

"Then I need to figure out why he waited so long to contact me." But what she was really thinking was that if it was actually Tightrope, then she needed to find him. She needed to make him tell her what he'd done to Maddie. And then she needed to kill him.

NINETEEN

After Eve left the park, she drove straight to her family lawyer's office in downtown Seattle.

"Thanks for seeing me on such short notice," Eve said after Harold's secretary led her into his office and closed the door on her way out.

Harold stood up and gestured at the plush leather chair and couch at the other side of his office, away from his desk. "Not a problem. I would clear my schedule for you in a heartbeat. You know that. Please have a seat."

Eve sat down on the couch and Harold took the chair.

"Can I get you anything to drink?" Harold asked. "Some coffee or tea?"

"No thanks."

"How's your Aunt June?"

"She's fine. I just had lunch with her a few weeks ago."

Harold nodded and leaned forward just a little in his chair, his smile fading away quickly. He was in his sixties, but in great physical shape, a long and lean body from years of running and cycling. He had a full head of silver hair and a kind face, with deep-set sparkling eyes, which were intently focused on her now. "I'm guessing this isn't a social call."

Eve felt the slight pang of guilt. She realized she should get in here to see Harold more often, making an appointment first, of course. Or maybe they could meet somewhere for dinner. And at the same time, she realized she should make a little more time for her aunt.

Harold, along with Agent Parker, had been one of her true friends since Tightrope had killed her family and taken her sister. Along with Aunt June, Harold had helped organize the funeral and then helped her with the trust her parents had left for her. He'd made things just a little easier in the hardest time of her life, and she loved him for that. She always would.

Since then, Harold had helped her manage her assets, much of which she had moved on to different money managers. He had recommended some of those managers and tax attorneys.

But more than that, Harold had always been there, ready to dispense advice. He'd given advice when she had gone through her wild and rebellious stage, traveling the world and running away from life, both literally and figuratively, jetting away, high on drugs and alcohol most of the time, shutting herself off emotionally to anyone who wanted to get close to her. But to their credit, both Harold and Agent Parker had never allowed themselves to be driven away. Of course, there was Aunt June, but she'd always had ulterior motives for being close to Eve, whether she wanted to admit them or even consciously acknowledge them. It was funny how the mind could play tricks on you—Eve knew that all too well.

"I might be in a bit of trouble," Eve said.

Harold frowned just a little. He didn't say anything, waiting patiently for her to continue. He'd always been a good listener.

Eve explained what had happened over the last week, trying to keep it short, knowing he most likely had clients waiting.

But Harold didn't seem rushed. He looked fascinated with her tale, and horrified in some places. Aunt June's reactions would have been some kind of theatrical expressions of emotions, but Harold seemed genuinely worried, and yet at the same time Eve saw the wheels of Harold's mind turning, strategies already forming.

She told him about the Krugman family's murder, the methods so similar to Tightrope's. She told him about her conversation with Agent Parker. She told him about spending the night in her parents' home, about finding Ralph on the floor in front of her chair, about feeling like someone—like Tightrope—was in the house.

And then she told Harold about the email she'd gotten from Tightrope, and how Benji (who she didn't name) had traced the email to Bonner's house. How she'd gone to see Bonner this morning, and how he had tried to attack her, how she'd fought back, and how frightened Bonner had gotten when she'd mentioned North Star.

And then she told him about her second meeting today with Parker at the park, his warning about how she might have left evidence behind at Bonner's house.

Harold sat very still when she was finished, exhaling a breath slowly, his hands resting on the arms of the leather chair, his legs crossed casually.

"I need a defense team," Eve told Harold. "I haven't been charged with anything yet, but I need them ready."

Harold held her stare. "But you're planning on doing something more, am I right? Something possibly . . . inappropriate?"

"I can't stay away from this. It's the closest I've ever gotten to Tightrope in ten years. It's the closest I've ever gotten to finding out about Maddie."

Harold nodded like he understood all too well her hardheadedness and her stubbornness, her obsessive pursuit of this thing that had consumed her life, changed her, turned her into this hunter she had become, a hunter willing to risk everything she had to find the killer and the secrets he possessed.

"Do you know someone?" Eve asked. "Someone you could recommend?"

Harold got up from the chair and walked to his massive desk at the other end of the spacious office. He opened a drawer and pulled out a business card. He walked back to the couch, handing the card to her.

She took the card, looking at it. The card was plain white with the words: Anthony Malone: Defense Attorney, and then a phone number and email address.

"I'll talk to him for you," Harold said. "Fill in some of the details in advance, get him ready. He's the best in the city. Best in the state. Hopefully you won't need him."

"Hopefully."

"Eve, will you do something for me?"

"Yes. Anything."

"Be careful with this."

"I'm always careful." She gave him a smile, but it felt false on her face.

"I know. But this feels . . . I mean it sounds like this could get very complicated. And dangerous."

"I have to know, Harold. I have to find him. I'm *going* to find him."

"I know you will."

"Thank you," Harold." Eve got up to leave, then she gave Harold a hug. She promised that they would get together soon when all of this was over.

He nodded, smiled, but it didn't seem like he believed it.

TWENTY

The killer slowed his car as he drove down the hill and around the bend on Slocum Road. The large patch of woods to his right opened up to a field of wild grasses and weeds with the Brady family's home set down in the middle of it, three hundred yards away from the road.

He slowed down to an idle and rolled past the beginning of the driveway to the Bradys' property. He parked his car on the side of the road, the engine still running. Even though it was dusk, he didn't have his headlights on.

It was cold. He wore a dark pair of pants, a black sweatshirt, and the black work boots he liked so much—they were as comfortable as sneakers but sturdier, with steel toes. They weren't a special brand and not overly expensive; they were shoes that could be purchased at a department store or online. He also wore thin leather gloves and a knit cap pulled down low to his eyebrows, both black like his clothes.

He had his phone with him as he got out of his car, the interior lights turned off so they wouldn't light up when he opened the door. He saw the faint wisps of his own breath in front of him as he exhaled, little wraiths escaping from inside of him, disappearing when they were let loose into the world.

No other cars were coming up or down the road. This area was remote, that's why he had selected it, that's why he had chosen the Brady family snuggled in their home down at the end of the long driveway.

The only other home within view was a quarter mile up the street, built up on a slight hill, the lights burning a cozy yellow against the gray dreary day as the inevitable darkness descended, inch by inch.

The Bradys' home also had cozy lights burning inside. Two cars were parked in the driveway where it ran up to the garage, another older car parked inside that garage—a project car for Mr. Brady on summer weekends, one he had been neglecting for quite a few months now.

The killer had done his research on the Brady family. Ken Brady, thirty-nine years old, worked as a manager at a busy restaurant in town. He worked long hours six days a week, and today happened to be his one day off. On the days he worked, he was usually at the restaurant at six a.m., and often he worked until six or seven in the evening. He wasn't a wealthy man, but he worked hard to provide a comfortable life for his family.

Ken's wife, Lucy, was thirty-seven years old. She worked part-time in a flower shop. The job brought in a little extra cash, which was good, but only working part-time gave her more time at home to be around her teenage kids and to attend their afterschool activities. Carson, fifteen years old, had baseball practice, and Makenzie, their fourteen-year-old daughter, had dance classes. Neither were prodigies by any stretch of the imagination—baseball and dance seemed to be excuses to hang out with their friends.

Yes, a typical family of four. A picture of Americana in the new century if the killer had ever seen one. The home the killer watched was purchased with inheritance money after Ken's mother passed away six years ago. Ken's mother and father had both died young, both from complications of heart disease, which didn't bode well for Ken; he had struck out with the genetic lottery, and the extra twenty-five pounds he was carrying around probably wouldn't help the matter much.

Not that it mattered. Ken's life was coming to an end much sooner than the lives of his mother and father. And he wouldn't die from something so mundane as a heart attack. No, Ken, and his family, would be remembered for a very long time. There would be whispers about the horrible things that had happened to the Brady family, especially Ken.

They will die in a spectacle no one will soon forget.

Mr. Brady sold their older home six years ago. He used that money, and the inheritance money, to buy this piece of land and this home way out here in the country, far away from the hustle and bustle of the city. He hadn't dropped all of their money into this place, though. They were still in debt for half of it. But Ken had been pretty good with their money. He had a nice retirement nest egg going and a 529 plan for his children's college.

But Carson and Mackenzie weren't going to attend a good college, and Mr. and Mrs. Brady weren't going to retire and take trips to Hawaii and Mexico. No, all of that was going to end tonight.

The killer stood on the strip of grass between his car and the edge of the road, the front of his car blocking him from the Bradys' home. He lifted his cell phone and took a photo of the home.

It was getting chillier, and there was a lot of moisture in the air. There would most definitely be fog later. And that was good.

He would come back in the dead of night, emerging from the fog like some kind of mythical monster.

He'd been here at the Bradys' home a few times already when no one was home. He had walked around the outside of the house, peeking in through the windows. He'd done research online, looking up the prior listing of the house, studying the photos posted there, memorizing the layout of the home, where each room was. There was no security system at the Brady house. No watchdog outside. And from what he could tell, Mr. and Mrs. Brady didn't own a gun—he hadn't found any registrations for them online. Of course, they might have bought an illegal firearm, but he doubted that. The Brady's weren't "gun people." And they certainly wouldn't have something illegal in their home, something that could jeopardize that nice big nest egg Ken was building and the property they had bought.

The Bradys were a perfect target for him, different than the Krugman family had been of course, yet similar in so many ways. And he wasn't going to kill them in quite the same way as he had killed the Krugmans—similar, yes, but also different. Something better. Something more spectacular. He'd already bought the equipment he needed; it was at his house. He just needed to go home and load it up into the trunk of his car for later tonight.

God, he couldn't wait.

TWENTY-ONE

"What's wrong?" Ken Brady asked his wife.

Lucy stood in front of the sink, staring out the window. A car was stopped on the side of the road, two hundred yards away at the end of their dirt drive that curved slightly down through the meadow of grasses and weeds. Dense woods flanked their property in the distance.

It was just getting dark. The car parked at the end of their property didn't have its headlights on—it was a dark shape in the deep blues and shadows of twilight. There was a streetlamp alongside the road at the other end of the driveway, but the car was parked just beyond the splash of light.

A wind had picked up and Lucy shivered as she watched the grass and weeds ripple like the surface of a dark lake.

But it wasn't just the thought of the cold wind that made her shiver, it was the dark vehicle and the man standing behind the front of it, like the top half of him was fused to the hood, all one creature, flesh melted to machine like a mechanical centaur.

"Lucy?"

And hadn't there been a small flash of light from the man, like the flash of a small camera on a cell phone?

Ken got up from the table in the kitchen where they ate a lot of their meals, rather than the formal dining room. His chair legs scraped across the floor. Carson and Makenzie stopped eating and watched him. They turned and looked at their mom frozen in front of the sink, staring out the window at the waning light of the day.

Lucy didn't turn around to look at her husband or children; she kept her eyes on that car and the man who seemed to be part of it. He was moving now, melting deeper into the car, and she realized he was getting inside of it, sitting down. No lights had come on inside the vehicle when he had opened the door to get in. That was weird, wasn't it? Maybe the dome light was burnt out, but it seemed more purposeful than that, like the man out there had either busted the interior lights or turned them off so he couldn't be spotted from their home.

Then he drove away, still not turning on the headlights even though it was almost dark now.

"Lucy?" Ken was right beside her, staring out the kitchen window, trying to see what had fascinated her so much. "What is it?"

The man and the car were gone. Ken had come to the window a few seconds too late.

"Nothing," she breathed out. She looked at her husband and smiled. It took effort to force the smile on her face. She wanted to tell him about the man and the car, the flash of light she'd seen from his phone, the unsettling feeling that had chilled her to the bone. But she didn't. She couldn't. Not right now, not with the kids sitting at the table. They were too quiet; she could feel them watching her. They weren't bickering or playing with their cell phones—they were watching her.

Ken was staring at her too. He could tell she wasn't being honest. He knew she'd seen something out the kitchen window that had stopped her in her tracks and completely absorbed her.

"Honey," he said in a low voice, almost a whisper. "What's wrong?"

"I . . . I thought I saw an animal out there."

"A bear?" Carson asked with equal parts fascination and fear.

Black and brown bears were known to be in the area, looking for scraps in trash cans, but she'd never seen one in their yard before. None of them had.

Lucy shook her head. "No, not a bear. Maybe a wolf." She shook her head again like the idea of a wolf prowling their front yard was just as ridiculous as a bear. "Probably just a stray dog."

That got Carson up from the table. He rushed to the sink on the other side of Lucy. She was now sandwiched in between her husband and her son as they peered out the window, searching the semidarkness for wolves and bears.

"Had to be dog," Lucy said more matter-of-factly.

"Maybe we should go out there and check," Carson suggested.

"No," Lucy answered a little too sharply. "No, you stay inside. It was a big dog. Could be dangerous. It'll move on."

Carson looked ready to argue, but he didn't. There had been something in the tone of Lucy's voice that had shocked him. He just nodded dumbly at her.

"It's just a dog," Makenzie said with a sigh to show how this conversation was really beginning to bore her.

Carson went back to the kitchen table and sat down next to Makenzie.

Ken hadn't moved away from the double sinks just yet. He hadn't said anything, but Lucy could feel him silently questioning her. They'd been married long enough that they picked up on each other's worries like they were psychic vibrations in the air. Lucy figured a lot of married couples developed this kind of sixth sense after years of being around each other all the time . . . if they paid enough attention to each other.

Lucy didn't want to meet her husband's eyes, so she busied herself in her work at the sink. She'd been rinsing off the dishes, getting them ready for the dishwasher, before the shadowy man at the end of their driveway had distracted her.

"You okay?" Ken whispered.

She nodded and smiled, glancing at Ken but not holding his stare. She hurried over to the refrigerator and opened it. Her mouth was so dry; she was suddenly so thirsty.

"It was just a dog," Lucy said as if someone had asked her again about what she'd seen outside the kitchen window. "A neighbor's dog, I bet. Probably got out through a fence."

"Or a wolf," Carson said.

Yeah, Lucy thought. *A wolf.* That's what the man and his car had seemed like, a sleek black wolf prowling and studying its prey from a distance, waiting for the right moment to come and attack.

What was wrong with her? The man in the car had definitely scared her. Maybe it was the news of the family that had been murdered nearly a week ago. They had only lived a few miles away. Tightrope had done it. Tightrope might be back, some said, the same killer who had murdered the Townsend family ten years ago. He had waited ten years, but he was back now.

She was just being silly, scaring herself like this. She was sure a lot of families around here were feeling like she was; they were as nervous as she was.

It had just been a man standing outside his car, that was all. Maybe he was a salesman or someone who worked for the county. Maybe he had the wrong house. There were plenty of reasonable explanations for why he had parked at the end of their driveway for a few minutes.

Yet she couldn't shake the creepy feeling. She couldn't shake the certainty that something was very wrong.

TWENTY-TWO

After dinner, Lucy and Ken went to the living room to watch a movie on Netflix. Ken asked the kids if they wanted to watch a movie with them, but they declined, Makenzie rolling her eyes at the horrifying thought of it. The kids locked themselves in their rooms to chat with their friends online or play video games, or whatever the hell they did in there. Ken liked to give them their space.

Ken sat beside Lucy on the couch. He was on his third beer now that the movie had started. He'd spent thirty minutes looking for a movie to watch. He kept asking her what she wanted to watch and she kept telling him she didn't care—just as long as it wasn't a scary movie. He finally picked one, but Lucy couldn't keep her attention on it; she couldn't stop thinking about the man she'd seen at the end of their driveway out the kitchen window earlier.

"It wasn't a dog," Lucy said.

Unlike Lucy, Ken's entire focus was on the movie. He looked at her. "What?"

"Earlier, when I was looking out the kitchen window, it wasn't a dog I saw out there."

Ken stared at her like he was trying to understand what she was saying.

Lucy picked up the remote control and pressed PAUSE, stopping the movie on the TV.

Ken knew she was serious.

Lucy glanced back at the hallway that led to the bedrooms, making sure neither of the kids was coming. Music thumped from one of their bedrooms. Maybe both of them.

She looked back at Ken. "It wasn't a dog."

"A wolf?"

"No. I saw a man out there."

Ken stiffened just a little, seeming to freeze for just a moment, his bottle of beer clutched in one hand. "A man?"

"He was standing by his car. It was parked on the side of the road near the end of our driveway."

"What was he doing?"

Lucy shrugged. "I don't know. Just standing there. It was getting dark. I couldn't really see him too well. He didn't have his headlights on. And where he'd parked, the streetlight didn't reach him."

Ken took a swig of beer, thinking it over.

"I didn't want to say anything earlier when Carson and Makenzie were there. I didn't want to scare them."

Ken nodded like he could understand that.

"But it really freaked me out."

"Yeah, I could tell. So, what was he doing? Just standing there? Like he was watching our house?"

"Yeah. Like he was watching the house. I mean I *know* he was. He just looked like a shadow in the dark, but I could tell he was watching us. And there was this little flash of light, like he'd taken a picture with a camera, or with his phone."

"What did he do after that?"

"He got in his car and drove away. Right before you came to the window."

Ken sighed. "Maybe he was someone looking for houses to buy."

"Our house isn't for sale."

"I know. Maybe he's searching for a house in the area. Or maybe he's looking for something similar. Taking pictures. Show his wife or something."

"Yeah, I thought of that."

"I bet you were thinking about something else," he said with a smile.

"I can't help it. It's on everyone's minds. I mean that family was killed only a few miles away."

"That doesn't mean some guy who pulled over in his car is the killer."

Lucy didn't say anything."

"Come on. You think a murderer is going to drive around taking pictures of people's houses? His victim scrapbook?"

"I don't know what maniacs do. And you don't, either."

"It's just some guy. Maybe he was at the wrong house or something. Didn't want to drive down our driveway and embarrass himself. Or maybe he thought we had dogs that were going to come running at him if he got out of his car in our yard."

Lucy had thought of rational explanations like the ones her husband had just proposed, but none of them seemed to fit. "When he got into his car, the interior lights didn't come on."

"Maybe the lights were broken or burnt out."

"He didn't have his headlights on, either. It was almost dark; he should've had his headlights on. He didn't have his four-way flashers on when he was parked on the side of the road like that."

Ken shrugged like none of it mattered.

"It was like he didn't want to be seen from our house." Yet at the same time, Lucy knew that he had *wanted* to be seen. He had waited there, waiting for her to look out the window, waiting for her to see him watching her. She knew deep down inside that he'd gotten off on that, on her seeing him, on her fear. But she couldn't tell Ken that—he would just laugh at her.

"Come on, babe," Ken said. "It was just some guy, that's all. Maybe he was lost. Checking his phone or something."

"We should get a gun."

"I don't think we need a gun. Not with the kids in the house. This neighborhood is safe."

"It *was* safe."

"That family getting killed was a one-time thing. A killer isn't going to come back to the same area like that. You'll see."

"Maybe we should get a dog, then."

"Yeah," he answered. "An attack dog. Or maybe three Dobermans patrolling the grounds."

Lucy didn't respond. She could tell Ken wasn't going to take this seriously. She wanted to tell him that she'd seen a man at the supermarket a few days ago who had creeped her out. He was tall and lean. He looked strong. He was completely bald or he had shaved his head. His skin was pale, his eyes light. She'd seen him a few times in the store, every time she went down a different aisle, almost like he was following her. The last time she saw him, he stared at her and smiled. There'd been something in those ice-blue eyes of his, a coldness like deep underwater or outer space, the detachment of a monster, almost like the reality he was seeing was different than what everyone else was seeing, like he was constantly fantasizing about terrible things.

She'd written the whole thing off as some pervert, or maybe just a strange-looking man trying to be friendly, or maybe just her own paranoia after that family was murdered. She thought she saw monsters everywhere. And maybe she was doing the same thing now, thinking every man she saw might be Tightrope, the killer they talked about on the news.

Ken got up to get another beer.

"Will you check the doors and windows?"

"I already—" He stopped, smirked, and nodded. "I'll check them again."

TWENTY-THREE

Agent Parker drove down the winding road to the Brady home, the visor pulled down against the morning glare of the sun shining in through the windshield. Martinez sat in the passenger seat, pointing at the sheriff's car at the end of the driveway after they rounded the bend. A sheriff's deputy stood by his car between the road and the driveway. Parker pulled into the driveway and stopped, rolling down his window and flashing his badge and ID. Martinez leaned over closer to Parker, making sure the deputy saw his credentials. The deputy nodded and gestured at them to continue down to the Bradys' home.

The driveway was paved for the first thirty yards and then it turned to dirt, a rutted trail through the field of weeds and wild grasses. A stand of woods lined the distance. The Bradys' home sat on a slight rise with a wall of trees a hundred yards beyond the back of the home. To the right, the top of a line of mountains was just visible above the tree tops.

A sense of déjà vu washed over Parker, like he'd been at this house before, driven down this same dirt driveway. But he'd never been here before; it was the similarity of this place and the Krugmans' property, and it was the similarity of both of those places to the Townsends' estate. All three homes were on large pieces of property. (Although these last two were nowhere near as large as the Townsends' property.) None of the victims had close neighbors. They all had woods around, almost like a wall of insulation. And all three of these homes were within a twenty-mile area. Maybe the killer, if it really was Tightrope again, was somewhat territorial.

"It hasn't even been a week," Martinez said. "This guy's really escalating."

This crime had come to the attention of the FBI the same way the Krugman murders had—an anonymous tip from a cell phone. The techs were trying to trace the call right now back at the office.

Parker drove up to the collection of vehicles in the front yard and parked. He and Martinez got out. Two officers waited by the front door of the house, another officer was down on the lawn, near the line of shrubs, bent over—it looked like he was trying his best not to throw up.

"Do it over by your car," Parker yelled at the man.

The deputy stood up, looked at Parker. His dark skin was ashy and pale, his eyes round with shock. He didn't respond, like he was afraid if he opened his mouth, he wouldn't be able to control the vomit. He hurried away to his squad car, bending over behind it, retching.

"It's bad in there," the taller of the two deputies on the front porch said in a deep, shaky voice.

The shorter and pudgier officer nodded in agreement.

Parker and Martinez slipped on blue nitrile gloves and entered the Bradys' home.

The smell assaulted Parker as soon as he was inside, and he stopped for just a moment in the foyer, hesitating for a second. The two officers on the porch were right, this was a bad one. The unmistakable scent of blood and gore hung in the cold air, an odor Parker had smelled too many times in his fifteen-year career.

A kitchen was off to their left, with a dining room beyond it, a former living room to the right. A set of steps in front of them in the foyer led upstairs. The foyer led back to a larger room—the family room. That's where the Brady family was.

The family room was large, taking up the whole back area of the house. The interior walls were done in brick, the floor brick, large windows looked out onto a wide wooden deck. The backyard sloped down sharply toward the dense woods. Potted plants and Adirondack chairs decorated the wood deck, a table between the chairs. Inside the family room there was a wet bar to the left of the wooden French doors Parker and Martinez had just walked through. A giant flat-screen TV was mounted on the wall to the left. A door on that side of the large room led out to the deck. A ping pong table would have been in the middle of the room beyond the wet bar, but it had been pushed back toward the wall of windows, along with any other furniture that was in the way of the arrangement of bodies in the middle of the room.

Ken Brady hung naked by his wrists on two red ropes attached to a metal bar. Another length of rope was tied to the metal bar (which looked like part of an exercise machine) and strung up to a pulley that had been bolted to the ceiling. The red rope ran up through the pulley and was pulled down tight to the footrail of the wet bar, the stools moved out of the way. Ken's bare feet hung five inches above the brick floor, a puddle of blood underneath him from the grotesque wounds in his body.

The rest of the Brady family lay in a heap on the floor eight feet away from Ken, a tangled mass of naked flesh and red ropes: wrists bound, ankles bound, nooses tightened around necks, all the ropes somehow connected. The dead family's glassy eyes bulged, their skin alabaster pale, white rags wadded up and stuffed into their mouths, held there with more lengths of red rope, tied cruelly tight.

"My God," Martinez whispered. "Yeah, I'd say he's escalating."

Similar, Parker thought. Similar to the Krugmans. Similar to the Townsends. But different.

The torture of Ken Brady, the father, was more brutal this time. He'd been disemboweled, a small hole cut in his lower abdomen, his entrails pulled out like a magician pulling scarves out from the cuffs of a coat sleeve.

There were other wounds on the man's body, deep cuts on his arms and legs, but no arteries had been nicked. A few of his toes had been snipped off, mostly likely with a pair of garden shears. The killer had made this man suffer before he died, but there was no noose around the man's neck, no quicker death for him, like it had been for the rest of the family.

"He made them watch," Martinez said, glancing back and forth between the hanging man and the collection of bodies tied together on the floor. He held a handkerchief up to his mouth and nose, his eyes watery.

Parker knew Martinez was visualizing his thoughts as he worked things out, stating the obvious like he needed to say it aloud to understand the brutality of it, trying to imagine the tortures and murders as they had happened, bringing it all to life in his mind.

"They were standing before," Martinez added. "In a line, probably. All of them tied together with the ropes. He made them watch while he tortured the father."

Parker could hear the anger in Martinez's voice. He studied the mass of dead flesh that used to be the rest of the Brady family, moving toward them a little closer.

"He likes to torture," Martinez continued. "But what he really gets off on is seeing how long the rest of the family will last before willingly strangling themselves and each other. How much they will watch, endure, before they'll end it all." He shook his head. "Sick motherfucker."

Parker still hadn't spoken.

"At some point they fell on the floor," Martinez said. "One of them dragged the rest down and their nooses tightened. All of them." He was quiet for a moment, thinking, then he nodded like he'd just come to an absolute conclusion. "The mother did it. She took herself and her kids out. She figured it was better to go out that way than watch one of her kids go through what her husband was going through. Or let them watch her hung up like a slab of meat and cut open."

Parker walked back to Ken Brady's body, staying clear of the pool of blood and mound of intestines coiled up on the floor in front of his dangling purple feet. Part of the intestines was still connected to the hole in his belly. A metal hook lay on the floor near the guts, obviously a tool the killer had used to poke around inside the man's belly, hook the entrails, pull them out.

Ken Brady's head hung down, his mouth stuffed with a white rag like the rest of his family, red ropes tied around his head to keep the rag stuffed deep into his mouth. His hands were purple like his legs and feet, his arms so white in comparison. The wrists and shoulders looked swollen, like they'd been broken or dislocated; either the killer had done it by yanking so hard on the ropes when he had pulled Ken up on the pulley, or Ken had dislocated his own joints in his struggles as the killer carved him up.

"Ropes are attached from his wrists to the metal bar," Parker said.

Martinez walked over to Parker, still holding his handkerchief up to his face. It wasn't just the smell of the blood and eviscerated intestines—Ken Brady had evacuated his bowels, most likely before the killer had pulled out the intestines. The whole family had shit and pissed themselves.

"Looks like some kind of bar from an exercise machine," Martinez said. "Like you'd use for lat pulldowns. Or maybe seated rows. See the handles at the ends?"

Parker nodded. "Could be from here. They might have an exercise machine in the garage or somewhere."

Martinez didn't say anything. There would be plenty of time later to search the house.

"He tied his wrists to each end of the bar, at the handles," Parker said. "To keep his arms apart. But he didn't tie his wrists directly to the metal bar. He used another short length of rope to tie around each wrist and then to the bar, to maximize the pain."

Parker walked over to the rope stretched down to the footrail of the bar. On the rope was a metal hand-cranked winch, sometimes called a come-along by shade tree mechanics who used the device and a chain to hoist car engines up.

"A winch," Martinez said. "Looks pretty common. Could've gotten that winch and the exercise bar anywhere."

Palmer nodded in agreement.

"He might have bought this shit three years ago at a garage sale."

"The way he tied the ropes," Parker said. "The cuts on the arms and legs, the disemboweling. Ken Brady was already in agony from hanging on possibly dislocated wrists and shoulders. But he kept hurting him, torturing him even more. It's about the agony, the spectacle of it."

"He's a sick fuck, that's what it's about," Martinez grumbled into the handkerchief.

"It's like he's trying to make this murder bigger, one-upping the others. Upstaging the last crimes."

"You still think this is a copycat?"

Parker thought about his conversation with Eve and the evidence he'd gotten that he couldn't share with Martinez. He had shown some of the evidence to Martinez, the email that Eve had gotten from Tightrope, the email that the tech guys were tracing along with the anonymous phone call that had pointed them here to this house, but he'd left many other things out: Bonner and Eve's visit with Bonner, the things Bonner had said to Eve, their fight in the basement.

Parker's phone rang. "Agent Parker," he said into his phone, glancing at Martinez. "Thanks." He hung up and slipped his phone back on his belt.

"What is it?"

"We need to go. They got a trace on the phone call."

TWENTY-FOUR

Parker sped down the street, weaving in and out of traffic.

"The others are on their way," Martinez said after getting off his phone. "Warrant's on the way with them. Uh . . . could you slow down just a little?"

Parker didn't answer. He didn't slow down.

Martinez studied his phone rather than look at the traffic they were speeding past. "This guy's got a pretty hefty list of priors: burglary, assault, resisting arrest. Did a couple of stints in County for drug possession. Most recent arrest was three years ago." He looked up from his phone. "Turn left up here."

Parker eased his foot down on the brake pedal, slowing just enough to turn onto the side street, the rear of the car sliding a little on the wet pavement.

"Holy hell, Parker," Martinez yelled, holding on to the armrest of the door.

Two-story homes whipped by them out the windows.

Martinez checked the map on his phone. "Up here. On the right."

A black SUV had caught up to Parker from behind, and another black SUV was sliding to a stop ahead in front of Mitchell Everett's rented home.

Parker skidded to a stop and cut the engine. He grabbed his blue windbreaker from the back, FBI on the back of it in big yellow letters. Martinez was slipping into his own windbreaker.

Their guns already in their hands, the other agents met Parker and Martinez at the front door. One of the agents carried a handheld battering ram. Two other agents were dressed in riot gear and held automatic rifles.

Parker and Martinez took the lead, posting at each side of the front door, the other agents situated on the porch steps, one of them back by the closest SUV. Parker pounded on the front door with the edge of his fist.

"Who is it?" a woman's voice screeched from behind the door.

Parker heard the fear in the woman's voice—she had already looked out the window and knew damn well who was out there. "FBI," he yelled. "Open up, ma'am. We have a warrant for the arrest of Mitchell Everett and to search this property."

No answer from the woman, but there were muffled voices from behind the door, a heated conversation between the woman and a man. Panicked voices. Confused voices.

Parker glanced at two of the agents with the rifles and gestured for them to go around to the back of the home, then he pounded on the front door again. "Open up or we'll break the door down!"

"Okay," a man's voice said. "Hold on just a second. I'm opening the door. Don't shoot, okay!"

A second later, the locks clicked and the front door swung open. The woman stood at the other side of the room, beside a long breakfast bar that separated the living room from the kitchen. Mitchell Everett stood in the doorway with his hands raised halfway up, his eyes wide with shock and fear. He was shirtless, only wearing a pair of jogging pants and white socks. His arms and torso were lean muscle and tattoos. A gold necklace with a cross hung from his neck. His hair was sleep-spiked, like he'd just woken up.

"Mitchell Everett?"

He nodded numbly.

Parker and Martinez rushed inside the house. Martinez tackled Mitchell to the floor, flipping him over onto his stomach and wrenching his arms behind his back to cuff his wrists together.

"Don't hurt him," the woman squealed with her hands up to her mouth.

As Martinez read Mitchell Everett his rights, Parker nodded at the next two agents inside the house, gesturing at them to search the home.

"Anyone else in the house, ma'am?" one of the agents asked the woman.

"No. Just us."

"Dogs?"

"No. No . . . no pets. It's just us. What is this?"

The agent approached the woman and handed her the copy of the warrant, then he looked back at the other agent, nodding at the stairs.

The woman held the folded sheets of paper in her hand like it was a snake that might bite her. Tears welled up in her eyes. She wore a pair of shorts and a tight T-shirt, her hair messed up like she'd just woken up, too. "What's going on? I don't understand what's going on."

"You live here, ma'am?" Parker asked.

She looked at him, focusing on him, on his calm voice, a haven of tranquility in this blur of madness. She nodded.

"You have ID you can show me?"

She nodded again. "It's in my purse over there on the table." She looked afraid to make a move.

"Please get it for me, ma'am."

She did as Parker asked. "Why are you arresting Mitch?"

"We're not arresting him right now, just detaining him."

"For what?"

"Your ID, please," Parker said and glanced around at the small home. The other two agents were upstairs, stomping around up there. Martinez had Mitch up on his feet. The place was a little messy and cluttered, but it wasn't a drug den or a pigsty, just a normal, lived-in home.

The woman opened a wallet and plucked out her driver's license with trembling fingers. She handed it to Parker.

"Debra Costa?"

"Debbie," she corrected.

"You work?"

"Yeah. I wait tables at Mickey's downtown. Mitch works there with me. He does dishes, but he's working his way up to line cook. We work the night shift. We were sleeping just now." She let her words die away. "What's this about?"

"We need to ask Mr. Mitchell Everett a few questions." He turned to Martinez who still held Mitch by one elbow, like the man was going to bolt. "Mitchell Everett?"

"Mitch," he said.

"You have ID?"

"It's upstairs in my wallet on the dresser."

Parker nodded. The other agents would find it and bring it down.

"We need to detain you while we make sure everything's safe," Parker explained to Mitch.

"It's safe," he answered and looked at the steps that led upstairs. "They can look all they want. I don't have anything up there I shouldn't have. I'm clean now. You can drug test me if you want to."

"Found God, did you?" Martinez asked with a sneer, glaring down at the cross hanging from Mitch's neck. "Is that it?"

"Yes, actually," he snapped. "That's it. I've changed. Debbie helped me change my life. God helped me. People can change, you know."

"We need to talk to you," Parker said. "Is there somewhere else we can go? Somewhere a little more private?" He glanced back at Debbie.

Another agent entered the home with a German shepherd on a leash.

"That dog's not going to have an accident in here, is he?" Debbie asked.

"Debbie's allergic to dogs," Mitch said.

"She can wait outside on the front porch," Martinez said.

Mitch looked at Debbie and nodded. She hurried outside, giving Mitch a strange look as she left.

Parker recognized the look from Debbie—she believed in her boyfriend, perhaps even loved him, but at this moment she doubted his innocence.

"This is all a big mistake," Mitch told Debbie as she rushed by.

She nodded, already crying, but she didn't look entirely convinced.

"How about the garage?" Mitch said. "We can talk out there."

Martinez led the way, opening the door in the kitchen that opened up to the attached, two-car garage. Three wooden steps led down to the concrete floor. There were no vehicles in the garage, the walls stacked up with boxes, tubs, shelves, exercise equipment, a workout station, two mountain bikes and a kayak.

"You like to work out?" Martinez asked.

"The body is a temple," Mitch answered.

Parker looked at the four-station exercise machine. Stacks of flat weights were attached to cables and pulleys. There was a pulldown bar hanging from the top of the machine that looked similar to the bar Ken Brady was still hanging from in his house.

"You got another kind of pulldown bar?" Martinez asked Mitch, following Parker's gaze. "The kind with handles on each end?"

"No. This is all we have," Mitch said, gesturing with a movement of his head at the exercise machine, the weight bench, and the scattered bars and dumbbells on the floor under the bench. "I've been trying to get healthy," Mitch continued. "Debbie helped me a lot. I don't want her to see this. Whatever *this* is."

"Agent Martinez has read you your rights," Parker said, forcing Mitch's attention back onto him. "And you understand your rights?"

Mitch nodded. "And I know what getting my rights read means—that I'm getting arrested."

"We want to ask you some questions," Parker said. "But you have the right to remain silent. You have the right to contact an attorney."

"Or we could do this downtown, right?" Mitch said. He sighed. "I understand my rights. Just ask your questions. Tell me what this is about. Please."

The door to the garage opened and one of the other agents poked his head in. "House is clean so far. Here's his ID."

Martinez took the wallet from the agent and opened it, glancing down at the driver's license, then at Mitch.

The agent left, closing the door behind him.

"It's him," Martinez said. "Mitchell Everett."

Parker looked at Mitch. "A family was murdered."

Confusion washed over Mitch's face. "That family? The one Tightrope killed? Why would you ask me about that? I was working that night last week."

"What about last night?" Martinez asked. "Were you working last night?"

"What? Yeah. Me and Debbie both. Why?" And then it seemed to dawn on Mitch. "There was another one? Another murder?"

Parker and Martinez didn't respond. This was the part where they waited for a suspect to trip over his own words.

"Why would you ask me about something like that? Is that what's going on here? Are you serious? That's . . . that's just crazy."

Parker and Martinez remained silent.

"I was working last night. I just told you that."

"What about after work?" Martinez asked. "This morning?"

"We came home from work. Both of us. Me and Debbie. You can ask her. We never went anywhere. Why are you asking me this? Maybe I need a lawyer appointed to me."

Parker took a risk with the next question: "An anonymous call came in this morning about a family that was murdered last night. Photos of the murdered family were posted onto the internet from that phone."

Mitch didn't say anything. He shook his head like he didn't understand what was happening.

"The call came from your cell phone."

"Oh God," Mitch whispered, still shaking his head like he was trying to shake himself awake from a bad dream. "My phone was stolen a few days ago."

"How many is a few?"

"Uh . . . uh, two. Not yesterday. The day before. Someone took it out of my car when I was at a store. A jiffy store."

Parker pulled his small notebook and pen out from his shirt pocket. "When did this happen? What time?"

"I don't know the exact time. Maybe 2:30? It was my day off. I ran up to the corner store to get some milk."

"Milk?" Martinez asked sarcastically.

"Yeah, milk. For our protein shakes."

"How did someone take your phone?"

"I left it in my car."

"You don't lock your car doors?" Martinez asked.

"No. I left them unlocked."

"Why would you do that?"

"The locks don't work right. The little button on the thingy on the keys doesn't work. And if I lock the doors, it's a pain in the ass to unlock them again. I have to put the key in the door and keep jiggling until they'll finally unlock. I don't know what's wrong with it, and I'm sure it's probably expensive to fix, so I just don't lock them anymore."

"Your doors were unlocked, but you left your phone in the car?"

"Yeah. I was just running in for some milk. I don't carry my phone everywhere I go like some people."

"Anything else taken from your car?" Parker asked.

"No. Not that I know of. I keep some change in that little cubbyhole thing under the dash. Maybe he grabbed some of the change, too. I don't know. I didn't count it."

"*He?*" Martinez said. "How do you know it was a *he*?"

"I *don't* know. I just figured it was. Probably a kid."

"So, you didn't see who took your phone."

"No. I didn't even notice it was gone until I got back home. I thought I left it here. I looked for a while. I had Debbie call my phone number a few times."

"You didn't go back to the store?"

"Yeah. I asked the guy working there if someone had found a cell phone or turned one in. I gave him Debbie's number in case he found it. I figured then that someone had taken it out of my car."

Parker and Martinez were silent again.

"That's the truth," Mitch insisted. "Whoever took my phone . . . I didn't do anything. If you're trying to pin murders on me, then I want a lawyer. I don't want to say anything else."

"Just try to relax," Parker said. "Did you report your phone stolen?"

"What? Like to the police? No. Why would I? They're not going to do anything about it."

"Did you call your cell service provider?"

"Yeah. I called them."

"They can't track your phone?" Martinez asked.

"I didn't have one of those kinds of phones or an app like that. It's an older phone. It takes photos and connects to the internet—slowly. I told them about it, told them I needed to get a new phone, anyway."

"And you have a new phone now?"

"Not yet. I'm waiting until I get paid."

"Where's the car your phone was stolen from?" Parker asked.

"In the driveway. You can look in the car if you want to."

Parker planned on it. He looked at Martinez.

Martinez didn't look too happy about running the errand, but he went into the house to tell the other agents to start looking at the car.

After Martinez left, Parker stared at Mitch. "I'm not going to get any trouble out of you, am I?"

"No. I didn't do anything wrong."

Parker used his handcuff key to unlock the cuffs. "We're going to be here for a few hours. A forensics team is going to take a look at your car, see if we can find prints from the guy who stole your phone. That person may be a suspect in the murders of two families."

"Tightrope," Mitch whispered, speaking the name of the bogeyman. He rubbed his wrists like the metal from the cuffs had irritated them.

Parker didn't respond to Mitch. The truth was that he wasn't sure if it was really Tightrope or not, but he hoped they would find some kind of evidence inside Mitch's car. But he wasn't going to get his hopes up yet. Everything that had to do with Tightrope seemed to lead to a dead end.

TWENTY-FIVE

The forensics team was at work on Mitch's car. They erected a tent over it, not happy about working in the drizzling rain. Any evidence on the outside of the car would probably be gone now, the lead tech informed Parker, but they would collect whatever they could find inside the car and take it back to the lab.

"We could get the car towed there," Martinez suggested. "We've got enough cause."

But Parker wasn't sure they had enough. For a warrant, yeah. But enough to tow Mitch's car to the field office? He didn't think so.

Martinez figured Mitch had something to do with all of this—he thought it was too much of a coincidence that someone just happened to steal Mitch's cell phone and used it to film and post photos of the Bradys' house and their dead bodies on the internet, and then make the anonymous call this morning. All from the same phone.

But Parker wondered if it could be a coincidence. What if the killer, the copycat, just waited around a convenience store, somewhere he had staked out, maybe even targeting Mitch specifically for some reason, maybe seeing that Mitch went there regularly? Or Mitch might have seen the killer hanging out at the convenience store and not even realized it.

"How much longer is this going to go on?" Mitch asked, walking up to Parker and Martinez, who waited inside their car. Mitch was dressed in jeans and a sweatshirt.

"Until it's done," Martinez snapped at him.

"I need to get ready for work soon," Debbie said from right behind Mitch, her arms folded over her chest like she was cold. "I *can* go to work, right?" she added.

"We'll be done pretty soon," Parker assured them.

Mitch seemed like he was about to argue, but then he sighed, shaking his head. "Aw hell, take all night if you want to. Debbie will give me a ride to work. I'll be there an hour early and she'll have to wait around later tonight until I'm done, but keep my car as long as you want to."

"Sorry for any inconvenience," Martinez said, not hiding his sarcasm.

"I can't get fired from this job," Mitch said. He looked like he'd been about to walk away, but then decided to pound the point home a little more. "You know how long it took me to find this job with my record?"

Parker nodded, but there was no sympathy in Martinez's eyes.

"If you need to go soon," Parker told them, "just go ahead and lock your house up. We don't need to get back in there right now. But we might need to talk to you some more over the next few days."

"Don't leave town?" Mitch said. "Is that what you're trying to say?"

"Yeah, something like that."

"Yeah," Mitch repeated, the word coming out in a weary sigh. He and Debbie went back into the house.

Parker looked across the street at neighbors gathered on front porches and front lawns, some peeking out their front windows, some filming unabashedly with their cell phones. Drivers and passengers gawked as they crept by in cars and SUVs.

The other agents were gone. The forensic crew was just finishing up, packing equipment and samples into their van. The leader of the team came over to inform Parker that they were leaving.

TIGHTROPE

Parker and Martinez waited in their car as the forensic team's van pulled away. They were the only ones left and Parker could feel the weight of Mitch's eyes on them from the windows of the house.

"We should go check that store where Mitch's phone was stolen," Parker said, starting the car.

"Where he *says* it was stolen," Martinez said.

Parker drove a few blocks to the store and parked at the edge of the parking area. He and Martinez entered the store, triggering a little electronic beep. It wasn't a chain store, just a local gas station and convenience store. Only one customer was in the store buying a pack of cigarettes. The customer gave Parker and Martinez a quick, guilty look from under the brim of his baseball cap pulled down low, and then he bolted out of the store.

Parker and Martinez stepped up to the counter and flashed their badges.

The store clerk nodded like he had already figured out they were cops.

"A man got his cell phone stolen a few days ago from his car in your parking lot," Parker said. "We were wondering if a phone had been turned in."

"No. The man was here two days ago. He was asking about his phone. I told him I would call him if someone brought it back."

That meant Mitch was telling the truth about his phone being stolen, or at least he had asked the clerk about a stolen phone.

"You were working here that day?"

"Yes. I'm part owner of the store. I'm here every day. Hard to find dependable help."

Parker nodded. "What kind of surveillance cameras do you have? Are they on tape or digital?"

"Digital," the man said as if Parker had asked him if he used a car or a horse and buggy to get to work.

"When do you delete the files?"

"Once a week."

"So, you would still have something from two days ago?"

"Sure."

"Would we be able to see the footage?"

The store owner hesitated, clamming up for a moment.

"We could get a warrant here," Martinez threatened.

"But we don't have to go through all that," Parker added quickly. "You could just show us some video from two days ago. You know, about the time the guy came in asking about the cell phone."

"Just one second," the owner said. He ducked into a doorway behind him for a moment then came back out with an older woman. He spoke to her in another language for a moment, then she positioned herself behind the counter, flashing Parker and Martinez a wary look.

Moments later Parker and Martinez were back in the man's cluttered office. He sat down at his desk and started clicking through files on his laptop. "The FBI is involved with a stolen cell phone?" he asked, his voice cracking just a bit.

"We take all crimes seriously," Martinez said.

"We may have to come back with a warrant for the video you have," Parker said. "Most likely later today."

The man nodded. "I have the video here, at about that time." He turned the computer around so Parker and Martinez could both see it.

"Could you fast-forward it a little?" Parker asked.

The man pressed some buttons on his keyboard and moved his mouse around. The footage sped up a little.

Parker watched cars pulling in and out of the parking lot. The point of view of the camera was from the far end of the parking lot and got most of the parking area and the gas pumps in the shot. The footage was grainy and a little blurry.

"Stop it right there," Parker said. "Back it up a little and then play it, please."

The man did as Parker instructed.

"See that?" Parker whispered to Martinez as he watched Mitch's car pull up in front of the store, a few spaces down from the front doors. Mitch wore a long-sleeved shirt, jeans, and a knit cap. He hurried from his car to the store and went inside.

A moment later a man wearing a hoodie walked from the direction of the camera toward Mitch's car, his back to the camera the whole time. He wore a dark hoodie sweatshirt and dark baggy pants. He walked casually to the passenger door of Mitch's car and opened it, bent down inside for only a few seconds, and then he left, closing the door and walking away from the car and the camera, walking past the front doors of the store and then around the far corner.

"He's wearing gloves," Martinez said. "Chilly day, but cold enough for gloves? He doesn't look like he's in a hurry, either. Like he knows Everett isn't coming back out right away with his milk for his protein shakes. It also looks like he *knew* a cell phone was going to be in that car waiting for him. He hasn't been checking other cars for shit earlier in the video. This was the first one. Lucky guess?"

Martinez was right, Parker thought. This looked a little too planned out, but he was still having a hard time believing Mitch was involved with this. Mitch was a petty criminal and he hadn't been busted in three years. Maybe he had gone clean. Then why throw everything away to work with a monster like Tightrope? Or a copycat? It just didn't make any sense.

"You ever see this guy around before?" Parker asked the store owner, pointing to the man in the dark hoodie after the tape was backed up and paused for a moment.

The older man shrugged. "All those guys in their hoodies look the same to me."

"Can't see his face," Martinez said. "He knew to stay out of the camera." Martinez leaned down toward the laptop screen, then snapped his fingers at the store owner. "Hey, rewind the video a little."

The store owner rewound the video.

"What is it?" Parker asked.

"Wait . . ." Martinez said, watching the man stroll to the passenger door of Mitch's car. "Stop it right there," he told the store owner.

The video was frozen.

"See that?" Martinez said with a wicked smile. "You can see the man's reflection in the car window. A little bit, anyway. Just his chin, a little of his mouth."

"Yeah," Parker said. "I see it. Good call. He looks white."

"Or maybe Hispanic," Martinez said. "Maybe young or middle-aged. The tech guys could enhance the video."

"The guy knew exactly where the camera was," Parker said again.

"That guy was waiting in the shadows by the wall," Martinez said. "Waiting where the camera wouldn't film him. And then Mitch comes. Why did Mitch park so far away from the doors when there wasn't any other customers parked there? Look." He jabbed a finger at the computer screen. "There isn't anyone else around, but he parks closer to the camera, farther away from the windows of the store."

Parker didn't answer.

"Mitch parked where that guy told him to, where the guy *wanted* him to. So that guy could take the phone out of his car."

Parker still wasn't sure about that—something just didn't feel right about it. He looked at the store owner. "Can we get a copy of this footage?"

"Sure. I download it to a thumb drive. Or I can forward the file to your email."

"Thanks," Parker said. "Yeah, forward it to this email." He pulled out a business card and handed it to him. "That would be a big help." He was glad the store owner wasn't demanding that they come back with a warrant.

TWENTY-SIX

Three hours later Parker and Martinez were back at the field office. Forensics was already working on any prints they found in Mitch's car, comparing the prints they had of Mitch on file from his many previous arrests. They were also looking at hair and clothing fibers they had vacuumed up and bagged from the seats and floors of the car. The computer techs were working on the CCTV footage from the file the store owner had given them of Mitch's cell phone getting stolen. They said they would try to enhance the video and use facial recognition software to hopefully get an ID on the man in the hoodie from the faint reflection in the passenger window, but so far there had been no results.

The techs sent the surveillance video from the store to Parker's computer at his desk so he could look at it again. He had watched it over and over for the last hour, then froze the video on the perp just before he opened Mitch's passenger door, the faint reflection of his face visible in the glass of the door window.

"I think we need to go and lean on Everett some more," Martinez said from his desk, right on the other side of Parker's desk. Martinez was leaned back in his chair, his feet up on the desktop.

"You still think he's involved?"

"Gotta be."

"You think he stayed clean for three years, then decides to work with a mass murderer?"

Martinez shrugged. "It's the only thing we've got right now."

Parker shook his head and looked at the frozen video on his computer screen again.

"Come on," Martinez said. "This is too convenient. I'm not saying Everett helped with the murders, or even knew the guy was going to kill someone. But maybe this guy just wanted to sell his phone to him."

"Why not go somewhere else to sell it? Go to his house? Why set it up to look like it was stolen?"

"I don't know. Maybe so he would seem innocent, so he'd be too far away from this."

"He could've sold his phone to anyone."

"Maybe this guy offered him a lot of money. A thousand dollars. Two thousand. Remember, our boy Everett's a dishwasher. It's not like he's raking in the dough."

"But his girlfriend's family is well off," Parker said. He had run a check on Debbie Costa a little while ago, and her family. All clean as a whistle, and rather wealthy. "Why would he risk something criminal for even two thousand dollars? I have a feeling if his girlfriend catches him doing anything illegal, she's out of there. He looks scared to lose her."

"Maybe the thrill of it. A leopard doesn't—"

"Change his spots, I know," Parker finished for him.

"I'm just saying. It's too weird, man."

"Everything about this is weird."

There was a soft knock at Parker's office door. Angie, one of the computer techs, pushed the door open just a bit. "Special Agent Parker?"

"Yeah, come on in, Angie."

Angie was a pretty girl in a plain, sheepish way. She beamed like she was honored that Parker had remembered her name. She held a printout in her hand. "We got a trace on the email that was sent to Eve Townsend."

"Okay. Good." He couldn't let on that he already knew where the email had been sent from.

Angie handed the paper to Parker.

Martinez was quiet, his face set in a frown. He'd made it clear earlier that he didn't think it was smart keeping in contact with someone like Eve Townsend—he also felt like Parker was going "behind his back" talking to Eve. He understood the relationship Parker and Eve shared; he just didn't like it.

"Where'd it trace to?" Martinez asked Angie. "Russia?"

"No," she said, adjusting her large glasses. "Right here in Seattle."

Martinez sat up at his desk, his feet hitting the floor, his eyebrows shooting up in surprise.

"Richard Bonner," Parker said, reading the paper. He read Bonner's address out loud.

Angie was already back at the door, about to leave.

"Thank you, Angie," Parker said. "I think this is going to help a lot."

Angie smiled, her face reddening, and then she was out the door, pulling it almost all the way shut like it had been before.

"Richard Bonner," Martinez said. "Why do I know that name?"

"He was convicted of killing three women ten years ago," Parker said, already pulling Bonner's name and information up on his computer screen, swiveling the monitor so Martinez could see it. "There was a fourth woman missing around the same time. Jennifer Watson. Everyone assumed Bonner had killed her too, but he never admitted to it. They only had the evidence on him for the murders of the three women he left at the creek."

"Yeah. Prostitutes, right?"

"Two were. The first two. The third one he picked up at a bar. And Jennifer Watson wasn't a prostitute, either."

"He left them at that creek," Martinez said. "Blood Creek."

"Blount Creek. Yes. They were washed and clean."

"He got an insanity deal," Martinez said. "Yeah. I remember now. I don't know how the fuck the jurors and the judge ever bought that shit. He wasn't crazy, just a stone-cold killer."

"And now he's out. Released a few months ago. Not long after his mother died. He lives at her house now. He lived there before. In the basement. Always had." He tapped the paper on his desk that Angie had just given him. "And now it looks like he sent an email to Eve Townsend."

"Saying that he's Tightrope," Martinez stared at Parker for a moment. "You think Bonner is Tightrope?"

Parker didn't answer.

Martinez walked away, pacing for a moment. "I mean, shit. You said he was locked up ten years ago. And he got out three months ago. Tightrope took ten years off, and now he's started killing again. That's quite a coincidence."

"If Bonner's really Tightrope, and he killed these two families, then maybe he's the one who stole Mitch's phone."

"The video," Martinez said. "Pull it back up." He grabbed his tablet, searching for an image of Richard Bonner.

Parker had the video back on his computer screen, the image still frozen on the reflection of the man's face in Mitch's passenger window.

Martinez came back with his tablet cradled in his hands. "Says here that Bonner's six foot tall. He looks heavier now. Balding."

They studied the computer monitor and Martinez's tablet.

"That guy might be six foot," Martinez said. "We can get the tech guys on it. Measure the height of Mitch's car, calculate the height of the man. But the guy in the video, he looks thinner than Bonner does now."

"His clothes are baggy," Parker said.

"Not *that* baggy."

"We'll have the tech guys figure it out."

Martinez shook his head, frustrated, sure that they had a connection.

"Some things don't make sense about Bonner being Tightrope," Parker said.

Martinez set his tablet down on the desk, pacing again.

"Why kill the Townsend family like he did?" Parker continued. "But then be so sloppy with the Blood Creek killings? If he's the same person, then he was doing these crimes at roughly the same time period. Why do them so differently? Why leave so much evidence at the Blood Creek murders and not a trace at the Townsends?"

"I don't know. The guy's crazy."

Parker knew Bonner wasn't Tightrope—he *couldn't* be. Eve had already gone to Bonner's house yesterday; she would've known whether Bonner was Tightrope or not, whether it was the same voice she'd heard that night ten years ago. She would've known him by his height, his weight, maybe even his eyes. But that knowledge gave him an idea. "Maybe we should see if Eve Townsend would want to come in here and see Bonner. We probably got enough to bring the guy in. She could watch us question him. She saw Tightrope the night her family was killed. She heard his voice. She would know if Bonner was Tightrope."

Martinez shook his head. "She was a kid then. And it was ten years ago. She might not be remembering things correctly now."

"She was seventeen at the time, and I'm sure she remembers every detail of that night."

Martinez stared at Parker. He seemed suspicious, and Parker thought he was going to say something about his relationship with Eve, how he had tried to help her get into the FBI. But Martinez didn't say anything.

"It's still worth a shot," Parker finally said. "Bringing her in here."

"Yeah," Martinez said. "We need to bring this guy in, anyway. Search his house."

"We're going to need to get another warrant. And you know what that means."

"Yeah, I know," Martinez sighed. "We gotta go see Sharko."

TWENTY-SEVEN

Moments later Parker and Martinez were in their supervisor's office: Neil DeMarco, Assistant Special-Agent-In-Charge. Martinez called DeMarco Sharko because he was convinced the man looked like a shark. DeMarco was a large, imposing man with pale skin and blond hair that was turning pure white. He had lifeless black eyes under heavily hooded eyebrows, and a mouth full of jagged and crooked teeth—way too many teeth for his mouth, Martinez had said. DeMarco carried himself like a man who didn't give a shit what people thought of him, and that's because he *didn't* give a shit what people thought about him.

It took a few minutes for Parker and Martinez to explain to Demarco why they urgently needed another warrant, Parker doing most of the talking.

Parker showed DeMarco the email to Eve Townsend from Tightrope, the one that had been traced to Richard Bonner's home.

TIGHTROPE

"Richard Bonner," DeMarco said, shaking his head in amazement after Parker caught him up to speed on who Bonner was and where he'd been for the last ten years. "I'll be fucked."

"We need that warrant, sir," Martinez said, not bothering to beat around the bush anymore.

DeMarco stared at Martinez for a full thirty seconds, his dull shark's eyes leveled at him. "Well, the last warrant I got you two didn't work out so well, did it?" He shuffled some papers around his desk, finding what he was looking for. "I already got some lady named Debra Costa filing a complaint for police brutality. Apparently, her family's got a few dollars laying around and they already have a lawyer ready to clamp down on my ass."

"We had to follow up on the cell phone, sir," Martinez said. "The photos of the Bradys' house, of their bodies, it was from Everett's phone."

"Did you have to . . ." DeMarco looked down at the paper clenched in his large, beefy hands. ". . . throw Mr. Everett to the floor, wrench his hands behind his back and cuff him."

Parker glanced at Martinez. "We might have gotten a little overzealous."

"I didn't hurt him," Martinez said.

"He went to the hospital," DeMarco growled. "He's there getting treatment for his injuries."

"He told us he needed to get to work," Martinez said. "He looked fine for the few hours we were at his house and forensics was going over his car. He never called the ambulance then or complained about anything."

DeMarco turned his attention back to Parker. "Honestly, I don't know if this is enough for a warrant." He picked up the papers with the email from Tightrope to Eve and the trace to Richard Bonner on them, rattling them a little in one hand. "Just because Bonner sent an email to a victim of a high-profile crime doesn't mean he's *fucking* Tightrope. He's *fucking* crazy, in case either of you forgot that." DeMarco's voice was getting louder. "He's fantasizing that he's Tightrope, picking on someone rich and famous. I'm sure it's not difficult to find this . . . this Eve Townsend's email. I'm sure it's been plastered on hotline posts asking for any scrap of information on Tightrope like a fucking missing cat poster, an email I would be willing to guess that this Eve Townsend put there herself. I'm sure other loonies have emailed her over the years claiming to be Tightrope, or claiming to know where her little sister is. Hell, we had our share over the years of people claiming to be Tightrope."

Parker remembered the people coming out of the woodwork the first few years after the Townsend Tragedy, but they all led to dead ends. Always dead ends.

DeMarco shook his head, suddenly calm again. "Sorry. I need more."

"Bonner just got out of Cedar Haven three months ago," Parker told DeMarco. "Notice the reference to barking up the wrong tree in the email? Tree? Cedar tree?"

DeMarco stared at Parker like he was as crazy as Bonner, his shark's eyes never wavering.

Parker didn't look away. "And the reference in the email to Ralph. When Eve gave me the email, she told me Ralph the Rabbit was one of her sister's favorite stuffed animals. That's knowledge the general public wouldn't ever know. That's something only the killer would know."

DeMarco sighed again, looking away, thinking for a moment.

"Even if Bonner is playing around, fantasizing," Martinez said, "he's dangerous. He's killed before. Those fantasizes of his could lead to something. He could act on them eventually. Like he did before."

DeMarco glared at Martinez.

"Martinez is right, sir," Parker said in a soft voice. "At the very least we should bring Bonner in for questioning. Maybe Ms. Townsend could listen in while we question him, see if she recognizes his voice or anything about him. At least we could absolutely rule him out as Tightrope."

"It was ten years ago," DeMarco said. "You think she would recognize the voice if she heard it again?"

Parker looked at Martinez who couldn't hide his smirk—he'd just wondered the same thing. Parker looked back at DeMarco. "Yes, sir. I believe she would."

DeMarco nodded. "Okay. Let me get on the phone with a judge that doesn't hate me. I'll see what I can do. Maybe we can get a warrant by tomorrow morning."

"Thank you, sir," Parker said.

TWENTY-EIGHT

Eve spent most of the day stalking Richard Bonner. She started early in the morning, driving by his house a few times. At dawn there were no lights on in his house, no front porch light. His mother's car was still backed into the driveway, right in the same spot as before.

When Eve drove by again just after noon, the car hadn't been moved. The drapes over his windows were still closed.

She used a burner phone Benji had given her to call Bonner several times. He never answered. Each call led to Bonner's mother's voice on the answering machine, directing the caller to leave a message in her rough, smoker's voice.

Besides stalking Bonner, Eve checked the email app on her phone about a million times, but Tightrope hadn't sent another email. She felt helpless as she drove around, checking her phone; she felt dependent on the next clue from Tightrope, waiting like a teenager for her high-school crush to text her.

She went back home just before dark, after one last drive past Bonner's home. Still no lights on in the house, no porch lights, and his car still hadn't been moved. She changed into workout clothes and worked on the punching bag in her gym, trying to force some of the anger and frustration into that bag.

After her workout, she felt a little better.

Only a little.

She made a protein and veggie shake, drank it while checking her email accounts again.

Nothing.

She grabbed her gun and took it with her to the bathroom. She always had a gun with her in the bathroom, the door always locked—she'd done this for the last eight years, but she needed to be even more diligent now, even more alert. Bonner might be coming for her. Or Tightrope. Or the copycat, whoever he was.

She stepped into her massive shower and turned the water on. She stripped out of her sweaty clothes and stepped under the rainwater shower head that hung down from the ceiling.

Her muscles felt a little spongy from her workout, her nerves tingling, her bones thrumming from the punches and kicks to the heavy bag. And even though the exercise had made her feel a little better, she still felt restless. She needed to do something.

She had driven by Bonner's house at least eight times today. It seemed like he hadn't left the house.

Or maybe he wasn't there.

Had he run?

If he had run, if he was gone, then she might never find the answers she needed. There was something at Bonner's house, something Tightrope wanted her to find.

A clue?

A clue to what?

A clue to find the missing girl, Jennifer Watson? Everyone thought Bonner had killed her and hidden her body.

A clue that would lead her to Maddie?

A clue that would eventually lead her to Tightrope?

Bonner was killing again; Eve was sure of that. And if he wasn't killing, if he wasn't the copycat, then he would start killing again soon—he had said as much when he had attacked her in his basement yesterday. Maybe he'd just been trying to scare her, having fun with her, but she'd seen the murderous intent in his eyes. He still wanted to hunt and kill; the craving hadn't gone away during his nine years at Cedar Haven.

She had to stop Bonner from killing. She couldn't let him start again. She couldn't let another young woman die.

Maybe she could talk to Parker again, try to convince him that Bonner needed to be locked up again, but Parker had certain protocols he had to follow, rules of law that had to be abided by.

But she didn't have to follow those rules.

As she stood under the steaming water, she realized that she'd already made up her mind to go back to Bonner's house tonight. She had to. Something was there. Bonner was hiding something—the truth—and she needed to get it out of him somehow.

But she'd tried that before. She had held a knife to his throat and he'd still been too scared to talk to her, to tell her the truth.

His words echoed in her mind: *There's nothing you can do to me that would be worse than what they could do.*

What was he so afraid of? Tightrope? North Star? Were they connected? They had to be, otherwise, why would Tightrope mention North Star in the email?

Yes, Bonner had been paralyzed with fear once she'd mentioned North Star, once she told him that Tightrope had sent her an email. He'd been ready to let her cut his throat.

Was he afraid to run?

Maybe.

Maybe not.

She couldn't let him get away, not when she was so close.

Eve shut off the water and got out of the shower, toweling off. She went to her bedroom and dressed in a pair of running leggings and a dark sweatshirt. She grabbed a pair of running sneakers from the shelf of shoes in her closet.

She had an idea of how she could get to Bonner tonight.

TWENTY-NINE

An hour later Eve parked her car seven blocks away from Bonner's neighborhood. She parked at the far side of a parking lot in front of a large plaza that housed an all-night supermarket on one end and a few other businesses on the other end that were probably about to close at this hour of the night.

She got out and locked her car. She wore a leather fanny pack under her sweatshirt with her backup weapon, a Smith & Wesson .380, inside. She also had a small flashlight, her burner cell phone (which was turned off at the moment), a canister of pepper spray, and a slim black leather wallet with her ID, a concealed carry badge, and some money all tucked together inside. Stuffed down into her thick socks were two pairs of black nitrile gloves, a silencer specially fitted for her handgun, and a lock-pick kit. She wore a dark knit cap with her hair tied up in a bun. She had earbuds in even though her phone wasn't turned on. She was just a fitness fanatic out for an early evening run.

After stretching a little, she took off jogging from the parking lot.

It took her less than fifteen minutes to get to Bonner's street. No one was on the sidewalk or out on their front porches on this cloudy, chilly night. Lights burned in the windows of the old two-story houses as she jogged by, cars parked in the driveways, other vehicles parked alongside the road. The occasional car drove past her on the street, masking the slapping sound of her sneakers on the concrete for just a moment.

Streetlights lit up the sidewalk every so often, the splash of light weak and leaving most of the sidewalk and front yards hidden in shadows.

As she got closer to Bonner's house, she saw that his porch light still wasn't on. Neither were any of the lights inside his home. The white Honda was still backed into the driveway in the same place as before. There wasn't even the faintest of lights coming from the blacked-out basement windows.

After a quick glance around, Eve slipped behind a truck parked on the street right next door to Bonner's house. She hid in the shadows for a moment, pretending to re-tie the laces of her sneaker, but she watched Bonner's house. No cars were coming down the street; no one else around that she could see.

This was her chance.

She used the darkness between the streetlights to creep up to the corner of Bonner's front yard, creeping alongside a tall row of hedges that marked the property line between his house and the next one.

A moment later she was behind Bonner's car. She made herself wait ten minutes. A few cars and trucks drove by on the street. No one walked by on the sidewalk.

She turned her attention to Bonner's house as she waited in the shadows behind his car. His house was still dark. She planned on going around to the back door, but there was always a chance that he would have some kind of motion-sensor light that turned on when it detected movement.

But she had to try.

No lights came on as she crept to the back door. The shadows were still heavy here, the backyard fenced in and secluded. She pulled the pair of gloves out of her sock and slipped them on, then she got the lock-pick kit out.

This was her last chance to turn around and leave. What if Bonner knew she was here? Like he'd known her producer's assistant story was a play to get into his house right from the beginning, maybe he knew she would come back and he was waiting for her. Maybe he was much smarter than she was giving him credit for. Maybe he had waited all day for her, as patient as a predator, waiting for her to slip back inside his lair, waiting until she was too far inside to get back out.

She was taking a big chance, but she had to know. She couldn't get this close to Tightrope, this close to the answers she needed, to let it go.

The back door lock was a simple one and she picked it in seconds. She opened the door and slipped inside, closing it softly, but not locking it yet. She needed to wait a few minutes to make sure an alarm system wasn't going to sound off. She didn't remember seeing a keypad by the front door when she was here before, but she still needed to be careful.

And those few minutes of waiting gave her a chance to listen to the sounds of the house: the whoosh of the heat coming on and blowing through the vents, the refrigerator gurgling, a clock ticking—maybe from the dining room, the occasional pop and creak of the house. She heard the cars driving by on the street, music blaring and thumping from one vehicle.

She didn't think Bonner would be up here in this part of the house if he was waiting for her. No, he would be down in his basement, waiting for her. She checked the upstairs of the house first, creeping from room to room. She had stuffed her lock-pick kit back down into her sock and now she had her .380 in her hand, the suppressor attached to the weapon, a flashlight in her other hand. She hadn't turned on the flashlight yet; her eyes had adjusted to the darkness well enough now.

The house was clear: the closets, the bedrooms, everywhere was clear—Bonner wasn't up here. That left only the basement, and if he was down there waiting for her, it was going to be difficult to get down there without him seeing her. He would have a hell of an advantage.

He could have a gun. He could shoot her. But she was going to have to take that chance. There was still a fifty percent chance he wasn't even here, that he had run.

She was at the door to the basement in the kitchen, gently testing the doorhandle with her gloved hand.

Unlocked.

She inhaled a breath, held it, and eased the door open. The hinges didn't creak; the door opened soundlessly to complete darkness down the stairwell. She wished now that she would have brought night vision goggles with her. Maybe Bonner had a pair strapped over his eyes, waiting in the dark for her to come down with a smile on his face.

One option was to rush down the steps with her gun in her hand and her flashlight shining. She couldn't try to navigate the basement steps in near-total darkness. She couldn't take the chance he was watching her. She would have no choice but to use her flashlight, and she would be lit up like a shooting star as she came down the steps.

She chose a second option. She flipped the light switch on the wall that turned on the light in the ceiling of the stairwell, and another light down at the bottom of the stairs. It was too late to turn back now—she had turned on the lights. She was all the way in this now.

Eve rushed down the basement steps to the bottom, her gun in her hand and aimed toward the interior of the vast basement. When she got to the bottom of the stairs, she froze.

Bonner was in the basement.

THIRTY

It took everything Eve had not to pull the trigger of her gun. Not only was she fighting automatic self-preservation, but there was a split-second thought that she had to keep Bonner alive. She couldn't get answers out of him if he was dead.

She had braced herself as best she could for a barrage of gunfire, a hail of bullets slamming into her, knocking her back into the stairwell wall. She had stayed low, using part of the stair railing and knee wall of the stairwell to hide behind, not that the wood was going to slow the bullets down too much.

But those bullets never came.

Something was wrong.

The smell from the basement hit her . . . a familiar smell, a noxious odor that she could never get out of her memory after experiencing it ten years ago—the smell of blood, of gore, of torture, the metallic heaviness of it in the stale air of the basement.

She aimed her flashlight into the murkiness, her hand trembling, the beam of light shifting as she tried to focus it on Bonner, who was seated in a wooden chair in front of the cedar chest at the foot of his bed. It was one of the same wooden chairs she'd sat on when she'd been here yesterday.

Bonner wore only a pair of boxer shorts and a white tank top that was too tight for his overweight body. The front of his shirt and his lap were soaked with blood that looked like a black oil slick in the flashlight's beam. His legs were apart, his bare feet seemingly stuck in the puddle of blood on the floor. His head hung low, his balding head and thinning hair reflecting the light. His fleshy arms dangled loosely at his sides.

Even though Bonner was obviously dead, Eve remained where she was at the bottom of the steps. She breathed quickly but tried to be quiet, listening for any other noises in the basement. She panned her flashlight beam around the large basement room, the beam sweeping across the bookcases, the desk, his bed, the door of the bathroom that was halfway open, the kitchen area with the dishes and boxes of food cluttered on it.

No one.

Besides the smell of blood, there was the smell of shit and urine. And the beginning of rot and decay? Or was that just her imagination? She guessed Bonner had been dead for a while. At least since this morning. Had he been murdered? Had he killed himself? Obviously, his throat had been slashed—she could tell that from where she stood, even with his head hung down. The hunting knife used to cut his throat lay in the blood on the floor, stuck in the muck.

To her right was a bank of light switches to turn on more lights in the basement, but she didn't dare turn on any more lights. She was fairly sure the lights couldn't be seen outside through the heavy black paper taped to the small basement windows, but she wasn't going to take that chance.

She realized how bad of a situation she'd found herself in. She had broken into a man's home who had most likely been murdered. Even though it had probably been made to look like a suicide, she was certain someone had killed Richard Bonner.

Tightrope? The copycat pretending to be Tightrope?

Was this a setup? If Tightrope had killed Bonner, then maybe he had suspected she would come here tonight. If Tightrope had killed Bonner, then why? Why get her to come here, get her interested in some secret that Bonner possessed and then kill him?

Or had Bonner done this to himself? Had he been so scared of Tightrope—and North Star--that he felt he had no place to run, no place to hide?

There's nothing you can do to me that would be worse than what they could do. She could almost hear the dead man's words from yesterday when she'd had his own buck knife pressed against his throat.

There was something on Bonner's lap, seated right on top of the splash of gore. She didn't want to enter the basement, but she needed to get a little closer.

Eve took a step into the basement, then another, creeping closer, her hands and arms trembling as she tried to hold her gun and flashlight steady.

Then she stopped.

A rose lay on Bonner's lap, a single red rose cut from a bush. It still looked somewhat fresh. There was no blood on the rose so it had to have been laid there after Bonner had bled out. Someone else had laid the rose there.

A rose. It meant something.

Her nerve endings were tingling. She needed to get out of this house. She backed up to the basement steps, hurrying back up to the top. She shut off the lights to the basement and closed the door gently. She had already shut her flashlight off and she stood in the dark, waiting for her eyes to adjust to it again. In those few seconds she felt helpless, certain that whoever had killed Bonner was waiting for her, moving silently toward her through the darkness, a monster who'd been waiting for her to come back up from the basement.

It took all of her willpower not to turn her flashlight back on again—she couldn't take the chance that someone outside might see the flash of light from inside Bonner's house. She remembered her martial arts training—her body tense, knees slightly bent, ready for an attack. She trusted her training.

The seconds crept by. As her eyes adjusted, she began to make out the details of the kitchen: the appliances, the cabinets, the squares of glass in the window of the back door with the thin curtains over them—a beacon for her to walk toward.

She hurried through the house, sure that a hand would reach out and grab her, drag her deeper into the darkness, maybe back down to the basement. She was at the back door. She opened it and slipped out into the night, locking the doorknob and then gently closing it. She waited, crouched down by the back door for a moment. She listened to any sounds coming from the backyard, or beyond it. The cold air was refreshing after the oppressive heat inside Bonner's house.

As she waited, she slipped off her black gloves and stuffed them down into her socks, where she'd stashed her lock-pick kit. She was breathing quickly, her exhales misting up in front of her like little wraiths. But her breathing was slowing down now, her heartbeat getting back to a normal rhythm.

A moment later she was behind Bonner's white Honda, making herself wait again for at least a full minute, glancing around, listening. She waited for a car to drive by on the street and then she bolted for the hedges, running alongside them, using their shadows to hide her as she made her way back down to the sidewalk.

No one was on the sidewalk, no one on their front porches. Cozy lights still burned in people's homes on this damp, chilly night.

She slipped out from the hedges and onto the sidewalk, jogging, her sneakers pounding the sidewalk as she ran. She ran faster and faster, hurrying back to the parking lot seven blocks away where she'd left her car.

THIRTY-ONE

Agent Parker and Agent Martinez waited in the kitchen of Richard Bonner's house while the M.E., a photographer, and tech guys did their work down in the basement. DeMarco was down there too.

DeMarco had come through with a warrant for Parker and Martinez, somehow convincing a judge to issue one at 6:30 a.m. for the search of Richard Bonner's home, car, and any other property he had or owned. Parker and Martinez had rushed to Bonner's house as fast as they could. They had knocked, yelled at Bonner to open up. Agents had surrounded the house. Eventually, an agent with a small battering ram had busted Bonner's front door in. Parker, along with the other agents, had rushed in with their weapons drawn, flashlights guiding their way through the murky rooms, yelling Bonner's name, identifying themselves as FBI.

They found Bonner in the basement, where apparently he lived, his body rigid in a wood chair, blood caking the front of his undershirt and the lap of his boxer shorts, puddled on the floor beneath him, a deep gash across his throat.

Richard Bonner was dead. He'd been dead for a while.

Two hours had now passed since Parker and Martinez had entered Bonner's home. Agent Evans had led a cadaver dog through the house an hour ago, but she found nothing, no sign of other dead bodies in the basement, the house, the garage, or Bonner's car.

A coroner's van was parked in front of the home, waiting for the M.E. to finish his initial onsite examination. Other deputy and city police cars were parked up and down the street, detouring traffic and hurrying gawkers along. Neighbors huddled on their front porches, a few in their front yards and driveways. The forensics team had arrived an hour ago, dressed in their white bunny suits and gloves, with their black plastic evidence cases and battery-powered handheld vacuums and plastic baggies.

Parker watched a tech at the back door, right off the kitchen. The tech, sensing he was being watched, looked back at Parker. "This lock was picked."

Parker didn't say anything to the tech. He thought of Eve. She'd been at Bonner's house a few days ago, but she told him that Bonner had let her in, that she had posed as a producer's assistant.

Had she lied to him? Had she picked the lock? Had she come back a second time?

A stomping sound came from the basement stairwell, someone hurrying up the steps. DeMarco emerged from the doorway, eyeing Parker. He didn't look happy. DeMarco never looked happy these days.

"Need to talk to you," DeMarco grunted at Parker.

Parker's stomach turned. He wondered if they'd found evidence of Eve being down in the basement, of her tussle with Bonner when he'd been alive.

If she was telling the truth.

Martinez started walking with Parker toward DeMarco.

"Just you," DeMarco told Parker without even looking at Martinez.

"Okay," Martinez said. "Fine."

Parker glanced back at Martinez before following DeMarco through the living room, then down a hall to the master bedroom where Bonner's mother, Gloria, used to sleep when she was alive.

"Close the door," DeMarco ordered.

Parker closed the door. He stayed by the door, watching as DeMarco paced to the middle of the room and then stopped. DeMarco turned and looked at him, his nearly-black eyeballs set deep in his pale face.

"Suicide," DeMarco finally said after a few seconds of staring at him. "That's what the M.E. thinks."

"Suicide?"

"Yeah, suicide. M.E. said the way the throat was cut, the prints on the knife handle. That's what he said. Suicide. We got a warrant to bust into a guy's home for a suicide."

"This could be murder."

"I just told you what the M.E. said," DeMarco snapped, but there wasn't much force behind his words. He sighed like he was trying to get his sudden anger under control. "Look around, Parker. Nothing was taken. The house wasn't trashed. This wasn't a robbery, a break-in gone bad. Bonner sat down in that chair down there in that basement and slit his own throat. End of story."

"A tech just told me that the back door lock was picked. And you saw Bonner's face. Someone roughed him up pretty good."

DeMarco nodded. "M.E. said those wounds were earlier, probably from as far back as a few days ago. Those wounds hadn't occurred at the same time his throat was slashed."

"They might have something to do with this."

"So Bonner got in a fight two or three days ago. Maybe he got mugged. But it doesn't have anything to do with him killing himself."

"Seems weird," Parker said. "Someone beats this guy up and then he slices his own throat? Most people shoot themselves when they commit suicide. Or they overdose on pills. Or they hang themselves. Jump off a bridge. How many people have you ever seen cut their own throat?"

"He was crazy. Maybe he finally felt guilty about the women he murdered. He cut their throats, so maybe he did to himself what he'd done to them to . . . you know, to atone for his sins or some shit like that."

"For some reason, I don't think Bonner felt guilty."

"Then maybe he was afraid of getting caught. He sent the email to Eve Townsend, claiming to be Tightrope. We know that now. Maybe he knew he'd fucked up and that he was going to get caught and he didn't want to go back to the looney bin. Or maybe he didn't want to face new charges and actually go to prison this time."

Parker remembered Eve telling him that Bonner wasn't afraid of getting caught or being locked up again. She said Bonner wanted to kill again, that he was *going* to kill again. Had someone come in here to stop Bonner before he could kill again? Had someone picked a lock, got in here, knocked Bonner out, slit his throat, pressed his bloodstained hands on the knife handle?

Could Eve have done this? She'd told him she'd been here two days ago and that she had fought with Bonner. Had she come back last night to stop Bonner from killing again?

"What about the rose on Bonner's lap?" Parker asked.

DeMarco shrugged. "I don't know. Who the hell knows? The guy was crazy. Maybe the rose was like his suicide note, his message to the world, something only his fucked-up mind would understand."

The rose meant something; Parker was sure of that—but he didn't push his luck with DeMarco right then.

"Look, Parker. I know this is some strange shit, and you might want to make more out of it than is really there, but sometimes life gives you a present wrapped up neat with a little bow on top. And when that happens, you just have to accept the gift."

Parker stared at him, saying nothing.

"Tightrope killed Eve Townsend's family ten years ago and took her sister. Then he didn't kill again for ten years. Bonner got caught killing three women at Blount Creek, and everyone was pretty damn sure he also killed that fourth woman no one ever found. Somehow Bonner got an insanity deal and goes away for ten years. No Tightrope in those ten years.

Then Bonner gets out a few months ago and the Tightrope killings start up again. Bonner was Tightrope all along. He even sent a friggin' email to Eve Townsend."

"An email telling her that he wasn't the killer, that there was a copycat."

"So what? Maybe Bonner was trying to throw her off the trail. Or us. Everyone. Like I said before, Bonner wasn't playing with a full deck."

Parker was quiet again. He knew Bonner wasn't Tightrope—Eve had told him so.

"Let's not keep pursuing this," DeMarco said.

"What do you mean?"

"It's over. For now, it's over. So let's not keep pursuing the copycat business. The North Star bullshit. And everything else Bonner was babbling about in that email."

"We looked into North Star. There's a website on the Dark Web, a website that requires a password."

DeMarco shrugged again, an exaggerated shrug as he frowned, his dark eyes steady on Parker. "So what? There's a website. Might have been something Bonner found while cruising the web. Might not have anything to do with this. Might just be a coincidence."

Parker didn't believe in coincidences, and he knew DeMarco didn't either.

DeMarco stepped closer to Parker, his dark eyes laser-locked onto Parker's, his hand on Parker's shoulder in what was supposed to be a friendly gesture, but Parker felt DeMarco's fingers squeezing, digging into his flesh.

"Let it go," DeMarco said, his voice lower. "Stop chasing this. Stop chasing North Star. You've got a great career going. I think you're going to move up, get that position in D.C. you've been gunning for. I can feel it."

Was that a threat?

"Like I said," DeMarco continued, "presents and bows. Neat little gifts all wrapped up for us." He removed his hand from Parker's shoulder and walked to the bedroom door. "Bonner was Tightrope," he said over his shoulder. "And now he killed himself. We've got enough here for that."

Parker watched DeMarco open the door, about to leave the room.

DeMarco froze with the door halfway open. Something resembling a smile crawled onto his face, but his smile of shark's teeth didn't touch his coal-black eyes. "We've got other cases to work on. I think this one's over now."

Until Tightrope kills again, Parker thought.

THIRTY-TWO

The killer's work had paid off—the first two families he had killed had gotten him noticed. They had noticed him. *He* had noticed him.

Soon he will see that I'm not his protégé. I'm not a student . . . not anymore. Now I'm his equal. And I'll be part of the plan.

The killer watched the family while they shopped inside a department store. The father wasn't with the family—he was working. He was always working, so now Tracy and her two daughters were on their own for the day. The girls were excited about picking out backpacks, boots, and other supplies for their trip into the national park tomorrow. The younger of the daughters, Amber, only seven years old, held up a pair of red rubber boots, begging her mother to buy them for her.

He pretended to be inspecting a rack of flannel shirts while he watched Tracy and the girls. He smiled slightly, looking back down at a red shirt, pulling the arms out wide as if seeing if it would fit him.

It was all coming together now. The pieces were falling into place perfectly. First, the Krugman family, and then the Brady family. He'd had quite a time with them, but the new family he had his eye on, the Kelso family, their spectacle would top the others. This family had been chosen for him, and the killer had no intention of letting them down . . . letting *him* down.

"Can I help you, sir?"

The saleswoman startled the killer—he hadn't heard her sneak up behind him. He jumped before he could stop himself. He turned around and looked at her. He had let himself get too distracted with the Kelso family; he hadn't been paying enough attention to his surroundings. He hadn't been careful enough, and he needed to be very careful. This had to work—nothing could go wrong. It had to be perfect.

The saleswoman was tall and big-boned; she reminded the killer of a frontier woman from the 1870s, her pale skin ruddy, her fingers like thick sausages, her blond hair tied back in some kind of bun. And there was no mistaking the look of suspicion in her light blue eyes.

"No thanks," the killer said, flashing a smile. Usually, his smile disarmed people immediately. Usually, he could lay on the charm. It didn't hurt that he was a young, good-looking man with a lean and athletic body.

But his charms didn't seem to be working on this woman.

"We've got some clothes on clearance over there," the saleswoman said, hitching a thick thumb back at a circular rack of clothing with a big yellow CLEARANCE sign sitting on top of the particleboard platform in the middle of the rack.

"Thanks," the killer said, struggling to keep the smile on his face.

She's trying to trip me up. Or maybe move me along.

The woman grinned; it was a mean little grin, the kind a schoolyard bully might have. "Just looking, is that it?"

She knew. She must've seen me watching Tracy Kelso and her daughters.

He hadn't been careful enough, and she'd seen him. It was little things like this that people remembered, little slipups that led to bigger mistakes.

But he couldn't let the situation get any worse.

"Yeah," he answered. "Just looking." His smile slipped a bit—he felt it. She saw it. "I don't think I'm finding what I'm looking for here, though."

"Oh." The woman's face crumbled in mock concern. "I'm sorry to hear that."

But she wasn't sorry—she was happy she had interrupted him.

"Thanks for the help," he told her.

"Not a problem." She wasn't moving on to other customers. She stood there, waiting for him to make a move.

The killer walked away. It was all he could do. He felt the woman's eyes on him; he could feel her memorizing every detail about him: his height, his weight, his age, his eye color, his smooth, cleanly shaved head under his ball cap.

But he couldn't blame the saleswoman. People around here were understandably paranoid. And they had every right to be. A killer prowled the darkness, a killer who preyed on entire families, a killer who slipped into the house and tortured and killed. Their sense of safety had been shattered. No one was safe as long as Tightrope prowled the night—lightning could strike from the sky on a clear night.

The killer enjoyed how the world thought Tightrope was back. He loved picturing the families in this city, in these counties, hiding away at night inside their homes, making sure doors and windows were locked, making sure their errands were completed before the sun went down.

He left the department store.

He had somewhere else to go.

There was a chance the frontier woman salesperson was talking to her manager right now, or to security, or even the police. But there wasn't anything they could do. He hadn't done anything wrong. He was allowed to come into this store and look around. He hadn't bought anything so there was no record of him purchasing anything, no information on him. Of course, there were cameras in the store, in the parking lot, but by the time they figured out who he was—if they could—things would be finished, the plan already in place. He would be with *them* by then, protected by *them*. He would be safe.

And what if the worst happened and he got caught? He'd be as famous as Dahmer or Bundy or Manson. However, if he was never caught, then he might be even more famous like others who had killed and then stopped for some inexplicable reason, killers who had become bogeymen, monstrous legends who seemed almost supernatural: The Torso Killer of Cleveland, the Zodiac Killer, Tightrope, and perhaps the most famous of them all—Jack the Ripper.

He would win, either way.

The killer pulled his dark ball cap down a little lower. He had parked at the edge of the parking lot. He had smeared some mud on his license plates, just enough to make a few of the numbers and letters hard to read on any security cameras. He would wipe the mud off when he was a few miles away from the mall. He couldn't get pulled over for mud on his license plate—that would be a pretty stupid mistake. He always had to be careful. So careful.

He drove across town toward the Sound, to a park. He'd been given a message, and there was a clue in that message about a person who would be at the park—a very important person. He could already guess who it was, but he didn't dare believe it.

After parking, the killer strolled the walking trail past fields, past little exercise stations, past people walking their dogs, past a huge wooden playground contraption meant to look like a castle with turrets on top. Children played there under the watchful eyes of mothers.

So watchful these days.

A little boy slid down the slide a little too fast and took a tumble. The boy stood up and froze for just a moment, like he was taking an injury inventory—making sure everything on his body was okay, deciding whether he should cry or get back to playing.

"You okay?" the killer asked the boy as he stepped up to him, flashing him a smile that could melt hearts.

The boy looked up with his big brown eyes. He nodded.

"You took quite a spill, but you're okay. Right? You're a tough guy, aren't you?"

He nodded, the beginning of a smile forming.

"Bobby!" the mother called, running up to them.

"He's okay, ma'am," the killer said, still smiling. "He fell off the slide."

"Yeah, Mom. I'm okay. I'm a tough guy."

The killer nodded in agreement, giving the boy a wink the mother didn't catch.

"Thanks," the mother said, but it sure as hell didn't sound very sincere.

The killer just nodded again and moved on. He'd seen that same suspicion in the mother's eyes, the same look he'd seen in the saleswoman's eyes. He knew he didn't look suspicious. It wasn't his fault, and it wasn't their fault.

It's just the times we live in.

He moved on down the walking trail, two female joggers running past him, breathing hard, their ponytails bobbing back and forth. He glanced at them, appreciating them for a few seconds, and then he stopped at a water fountain for a quick drink.

At that moment he saw her across the field, sitting on a park bench with an older man in a rumpled dark suit and tie. The man might as well have had a neon sign hovering above his head flashing the word COP.

The killer took a chance, moving a little closer to the two of them. Not close enough to hear their conversation, but close enough to get a better look.

Eve Townsend. It was really Eve Townsend, the one who had gotten away from Tightrope. Unfinished business. An unsettled score.

So, it was Eve they wanted him to see. Why? Was she going to be a target soon? Part of the plan? He couldn't see the whole plan yet, but he knew she was part of it, connected to all of this somehow.

He watched Eve talk to the cop for a little while, and then he moved down the trail, strolling leisurely back to his car. He couldn't afford to be spotted. Not yet. Not until he was done with the Kelsos. He still had to be so careful.

THIRTY-THREE

"Thanks for meeting me," Eve told Parker as he joined her on the walking trail in the park, heading for the park bench with the field of grass beyond it that rose gently up toward the stand of trees.

They sat down on the bench. Parker was stiff and nervous.

She waited for him to speak.

"Richard Bonner's dead."

Eve didn't respond. She just stared at him, her expression blank.

Parker's face morphed into something between shock and anger. "You knew, didn't you? You already *knew*."

Eve didn't bother denying it.

Parker looked away, over at a playground in the distance that looked like a small castle. Squeals of laughter came from the kids climbing ladders, running across wooden bridges, shooting down slides.

He looked back at her. "Christ, Eve. You know I could take you in right now as a suspect, don't you?"

Eve was sure he wouldn't.

Well, pretty sure.

"I need to ask you a question," he said. "I need you to be honest with me. Absolutely honest. I can't help you if you're not honest with me."

Eve nodded, waiting.

"You didn't do it, did you?" Parker asked in a low voice, almost a whisper. "You didn't kill Bonner, did you? Even for the right reasons."

"No."

Relief washed over Parker's face. He seemed suddenly drained. But then he stiffened again, like he was bracing himself as another thought occurred to him. "Did you go into his house again?"

Eve looked away. She couldn't help it—she didn't want to meet his eyes. She felt like she was disappointing her father.

"Christ, Eve," Parker said again, breathing the words out.

"I needed to know." Eve kept her voice low, her tone calm. She looked at Parker again, locking eyes with him. "Tightrope sent me that email from Bonner's house for a reason. There's something there."

"So, after I told you not to go into his house again, you went anyway."

Eve didn't answer.

"You picked the lock on the back door?"

Eve still didn't answer. Why bother? He already knew.

"That solves one mystery," he grumbled.

"I don't know if Bonner killed himself, or if he was murdered—" Eve began.

"M.E. said he killed himself."

"I don't think so."

Parker didn't answer, but Eve could tell that he didn't think Bonner killed himself, either. She continued: "The rose on Bonner's lap. Why the rose? It means something."

"Or nothing. Bonner just got out of the insane asylum."

"It means something," Eve insisted. "We need to figure out what it is."

"I told you to stay out of this."

"I can't," Eve snapped. "Tightrope contacted me for a reason. He's doing all of this for a reason. I need to know what it is."

"To get closer to finding him? Is that what you think?"

Eve didn't say anything.

"Maybe he's doing all of this to frame you. You ever think of that? And so far, he's doing a pretty good job."

She looked away again, toward the field and the playground.

"He's playing a big game with you." His voice was softer. "He's getting off on this. Still torturing you after all these years. Or maybe his copycat is. Maybe this isn't even Tightrope you're dealing with, but the copycat. Maybe Tightrope's not even here anymore. Maybe he died or maybe he's in prison somewhere, or in another country, and this psycho came out of the woodwork pretending to be Tightrope."

Eve didn't want to think about that. Her worst fear was that Tightrope had died and any chance of finding Maddie or what happened to her had died with him. She would search the rest of her life, never knowing he had died, driving herself crazy looking for someone who wasn't there anymore.

No. She refused to believe that. Tightrope had to still be alive. The email she'd gotten was from Tightrope, not the copycat—she was sure of it.

"I'm sorry, Eve. I had to say it. Had to put it out there."

Eve nodded, but she didn't look at Parker, still staring at the field.

They were quiet for a moment.

"DeMarco thinks Bonner might be Tightrope, or maybe the copycat. Regardless, he thinks Bonner killed the Krugman family and the Brady family. He thinks Bonner sent the email to you, pretending to be Tightrope, fantasizing that he was. And then when Bonner thought we were getting close to him, he offed himself rather than getting caught and sent to prison."

"But Bonner's not Tightrope. You know that."

Parker stared at her.

"I saw Bonner," Eve continued. "Talked to him. Saw his eyes. He's not Tightrope. I'm sure of that. I remember Tightrope and Bonner wasn't him."

"I'm just telling you what DeMarco believes. He thinks this case is wrapped up with a neat little bow on top."

"But it's not. You know that." She felt a shiver dance along her skin, tiptoeing down her spine. It felt like she was being watched. She looked behind her at the field again.

Parker looked where she was looking. "You okay? Something wrong?"

Eve looked back at Parker. "The rose, it means something. I know it does."

He didn't answer her.

"There are roses in Bonner's backyard."

"And how would you know that?" he asked with a smirk.

"Why don't you dig up the rose garden in his backyard? Something might be buried there. Or *somebody*."

"I can't get a backhoe there without DeMarco's permission."

Eve just stared at him.

"No, Eve. Don't. You've done enough already. I don't need you implicating yourself any more than you already have."

Eve still didn't say anything.

"Just cool your jets for a minute, Eve. Okay? Let me see what I can do. Promise me you won't do anything stupid."

She gave him a curt nod.

"I know this is difficult for you, but we can't trample over our own evidence and screw this whole thing up. I want to catch Tightrope, or this copycat, both of them, just as badly as you do."

Eve doubted that. "There's another possibility."

"What's that?"

"Maybe Tightrope was at Bonner's house. Maybe Tightrope made Bonner kill himself. You didn't see Bonner's face when I told him I'd gotten an email from Tightrope, and when I asked him about North Star. Bonner told me there was nothing I could do to him that would be as bad as what they could do. And he implied that either he or they had his mother killed. I know Bonner benefited from his mother's death, and maybe there was some satisfaction on his part, but maybe there's more to his mother's death."

"Eve," Parker said, putting his hands out in a placating gesture. "Just let me see what I can do. I know things are going too slow for you, but we have to do things right. Okay? Just let me work on some things. Can you do that for me, please?"

Eve nodded, closing her eyes for a second and sighing.

"Okay," he breathed out. And he seemed relieved . . . a little, anyway.

THIRTY-FOUR

"Where the hell have you been for the last two hours?" Martinez asked as Parker walked up to him. "Oh wait, don't tell me . . . I think I already know."

Parker had gone back to the field office after his meeting with Eve to get Martinez. He asked Martinez to come along with him. He told him he had a lead on the Brady case. For a moment it seemed like Martinez was going to resist, but then he walked with Parker to the car.

"You were with your girl," Martinez said after he and Parker left the parking lot and pulled out onto the road. "Am I right?"

Parker didn't answer. He slowed down and took a left turn at the next stop sign.

Martinez didn't bother pressing—he tried a different approach. "What about your little meeting with DeMarco earlier at Bonner's house? The meeting I wasn't *allowed* to attend. What did you guys need to talk about that was such a secret?"

Parker knew Martinez didn't like DeMarco, didn't trust him. Martinez believed DeMarco hated him, and he was sure DeMarco was a racist. Parker had tried to defend DeMarco before, but now he was beginning to believe that Martinez had DeMarco pegged all along. He told Martinez everything he and DeMarco had talked about in Bonner's mother's bedroom, telling him about DeMarco's theory that Bonner was the Copycat and that the case was over now.

Martinez wasn't buying DeMarco's theory, either.

Parker left out the part about DeMarco's veiled threat for him to drop anything about North Star.

"That guy's a dick," Martinez grumbled as he looked out the passenger window.

Parker wasn't going to argue or try to defend DeMarco, not this time, not anymore.

"Where are we going, anyway?"

"Bonner's house," Parker said. It was late in the afternoon, but there was still at least an hour of daylight left. They should still be able to get this done.

"Why?"

"I want to check on something."

"The lead?" He said it like he didn't believe a word of it.

Parker nodded.

"You clear this with your new bestie DeMarco?"

Parker didn't answer.

Martinez smirked. "Yeah, I didn't think so."

Parker drove down Bonner's street, then pulled into his driveway, parking in front of the white Honda backed up in front of the free-standing garage. The FBI techs, M.E. and local cops were all gone. There was no yellow crime scene tape, just a notice pasted to the front and back doors warning people that this house was the location of a crime scene investigation and that it was a felony to trespass. The notices on the doors were the only signs that any police had been at Bonner's house this morning. Now all the evidence collected from Bonner's home had been taken back to labs. Bonner's body was now resting in a large metal drawer at the morgue. The house would now sit empty until the case was filed with the court and a decision made about beneficiaries of Richard Bonner, if there were any. If not, the property would be seized by the county and eventually sold at an auction.

Parker got out of the car and popped the trunk. He met Martinez at the trunk, handing him a folded plastic tarp—brand new and still encased in the plastic wrap—and a new shovel. Parker grabbed the other tarp and the other shovel and shut the trunk.

"I guess we're doing some digging," Martinez said. He didn't sound too excited about the idea of it.

"Yep."

Parker could have done this tomorrow, but he was too afraid of Eve coming by later tonight and doing a little excavation work of her own.

They walked around the back corner of the house and entered the fenced-in backyard.

Martinez stopped in his tracks, the shovel clenched in one hand, the new tarp tucked under his other arm. "Roses," he said, spotting the line of spindly rose bushes at the far end of the yard in front of the old wooden fence. Now he knew why they were here.

Parker unfolded his plastic tarp in front of the rose bed, laying it down on the grass. Martinez did the same. Parker slipped on a pair of nitrile gloves and handed a pair to Martinez.

"You think that rose on Bonner's lap was from one of these bushes?" Martinez asked.

"Look at this," Parker said, pointing to where a rose had been recently cut away.

Martinez just stared, pulling his gloves on, smoothing them out on his hands.

"We'll dig this one up," Parker said.

"You really think something's under here?"

"Just a loose end I want to tie up," Parker said as he sank his shovel down into the dirt next to the base of the rose bush.

"Why didn't you tell your buddy DeMarco about this?" Martinez still hadn't started digging.

"He seems dead-set on the idea that Bonner is the Copycat, or maybe even Tightrope."

"But you don't think Bonner is the Copycat. Or Tightrope."

"Not really," Parker said as he dropped another shovelful of dirt onto the spread-out tarp, the dirt slapping the plastic with a solid thump. "It just feels . . . too easy. Too much of a coincidence."

Martinez leaned on his shovel, watching Parker work.

Parker could imagine the wheels turning in Martinez's mind. Martinez had already guessed about Parker meeting with Eve earlier. Martinez knew Eve had something to do with all of this, more than just getting an email from Tightrope. Parker wished he could tell Martinez more, but he didn't dare.

At least Martinez didn't push it. Not yet, at least.

"Besides," Parker said as he dug up another shovelful of dirt and dumped it on the tarp. "It's not like we've been batting a thousand with DeMarco and the search warrants. I figured we'd look here on our own. If this turns out to be nothing, then fine, nobody needs to know."

Another shovelful of dirt. The dirt hit the tarp.

"But if it turns out to be something," Martinez said, "then you look like a hero to DeMarco."

Parker let the jab from Martinez go. He dug up another shovelful of dirt.

"You think a body's under here? That's what you think? That missing woman from ten years ago?"

Parker just shrugged. "Jennifer Watson? Maybe."

Martinez still hadn't started digging, still leaning on his shovel.

"Could be Jennifer Watson," Parker continued. *Or it could be something worse,* he thought. *Like Maddie Townsend's bones.* But he didn't want to say that, didn't even want to think about that just yet. And if the worst happened, if Maddie—or parts of her—were under here somewhere, then he damn well didn't want Eve coming here tonight and finding it.

Parker stopped digging for a moment. He looked at Martinez. "You going to help dig or stand there all day like a government worker?"

"We *are* government workers," Martinez reminded him with a tight smile. He picked up his shovel from the ground, but he didn't shove it into the rose bed just yet. "You know if you find a bone or something, we're going to have to stop and call the techs in."

Parker sank his shovel down into the hole he was digging, the large rose bush already leaning, almost falling all the way over. The tip of his shovel struck something hard under the dirt.

"Rock?" Martinez asked.

Parker dug a little more with his shovel, a little faster, pushing the dirt out of the way. He got down on his knees and moved the dirt away with his gloved hands, revealing a rectangular object buried in the ground. He got his fingers underneath the object, loosening it from the soil, lifting it up.

"Holy shit," Martinez whispered. "We got something."

THIRTY-FIVE

Parker carried the dirt-crusted metal box and laid it down on Martinez's clean tarp. The box was about the size of a large hardcover book. A small padlock kept the clasp locked.

"This is something," Martinez said. "People don't bury metal boxes in their backyard for the hell of it."

Parker brushed the dirt away from the box with his gloved fingers, cleaning it up as best he could. He picked it up, inspecting it.

"Maybe it's cash," Martinez said. "We'll split it fifty-fifty," he joked.

"Sixty-forty," Parker said. "I did all the work." He picked up the box and gave it a slight shake. Something rattled around inside.

"Not cash," Martinez said, feigning disappointment.

Parker set the box back down on the tarp and inspected the padlock. It was small, the metal loop threaded through the clasp was thin, but it was still locked in place. He stood up and walked over to get his shovel. It only took two sharp whacks with the blade of his shovel to break the lock and clasp apart. He laid his shovel aside and got down on his knees, pulled the pieces of the lock away. He opened the box. The hinges of the lid made a gritty sound.

Martinez was right next to Parker, down on his knees too, staring into the box. "Holy shit," he whispered. "It's a key."

Parker plucked the key out of the box, holding it in his gloved fingers, looking at it closely. The only other thing inside the box was a folded slip of paper. He picked it up, looked at it, and handed it to Martinez.

"Storage," Martinez said, reading the word on the piece of paper. "And a four-digit code."

"A key and a four-digit code," Parker said. "Storage. A storage unit."

"A key to something pretty valuable," Martinez said. "I'm guessing that's why it was buried."

"I have a storage unit," Parker said. "You need a code to get in. And a key to unlock the padlock unless you use a combination lock."

Parker got to his feet and grabbed his shovel. He shoveled the dirt from the tarp back into the hole he'd made next to the rose bush.

Martinez didn't bother asking why Parker was righting the rose bush and filling the hole back in, packing the dirt in around the roots of the plant. He set the metal box with the key and piece of paper inside on the grass and refolded his new tarp back into a neat little square.

When Parker was done filling the hole back up and spreading the dirt around, trying to make it look similar to what it had looked like before, he shook the dirt off his tarp over the rose bed, then folded his tarp back up.

With their folded tarps, shovels, and the metal box they had unearthed, Parker and Martinez walked back to the car. Parker popped the trunk and they loaded the tools and the box back inside.

For just a second Parker felt like someone was watching him. He glanced around at the front yard of Bonner's home, the street down below, the houses across the street. He didn't see anyone.

"You just buy these shovels?" Martinez asked.

"Yeah. Earlier today."

"You should go get your money back."

Parker closed the trunk—he had no intention of going back to the hardware store to get money back for the shovels.

"What about the rest of the rose garden?" Martinez asked as he sat down in the passenger seat.

Parker got in the driver's side, sitting down and slamming the door shut. He started the car.

"Might be more stuff under those roses," Martinez said. "Maybe even under the lawn. Watson's body. Other bodies."

Parker backed down into the street, backing out into the street after making sure the road was clear of traffic. "I'll tell DeMarco about it. See if he wants to send an excavation crew. X-ray crew. Cadaver dogs. But first I want to go back and see what we can find out about storage unit facilities."

*

When Parker and Martinez got back to the station, Parker found Angie in the tech lab. She perked up when she saw him coming.

"You think you could get me a list of storage unit facilities in the area?" he asked.

"How big of an area?"

"At least fifty miles from Richard Bonner's house." He wrote the address down for her on a Post-It note that she was already sliding toward him for that purpose. "Start with the ones closest to Bonner's house and then work your way out."

"Anything particular I'm looking for?"

"Just a list of the storage unit businesses. The addresses. Phone numbers."

Angie nodded, eager to get started.

Parker walked away. He knew it wouldn't take Angie long to get the list printed out for him, but it would probably be too late to check them today—most of the offices would be closed by now.

Martinez was at his desk, his feet up as usual, in his "deep thought" position.

"What is it?" Parker asked as he sat down at his own desk—he knew something was bothering Martinez.

"How could Bonner have had a storage unit? He's been in a psych ward for the last nine years. How did he pay for it?"

"Maybe he just got one."

"That box looked like it was buried under those roses for quite a while."

"Maybe he got one before he got arrested. Before he went to Cedar Haven."

"Then who was paying for it all these years?"

Parker stared at Martinez. He saw the answer in his partner's eyes as soon as he spoke the words.

"His mother," they said in unison.

It made sense. The house belonged to Bonner's mother, Gloria Bonner. That box might not even belong to Richard Bonner—it might belong to Bonner's mother. A sinking feeling dropped in his stomach as he realized that they might have just dug up something that wouldn't mean anything. All of the leads in the Tightrope case came back to him, one lead after another that went nowhere. Would this be one of those same leads?

But no . . . the box had to lead to something. Bonner was murdered; Parker was sure of that. And Eve was sure, too. The rose had been cut from the bushes in the backyard and laid onto Bonner's lap after he was dead. Someone wanted that box under the rosebush found.

The conversation he'd had with Eve only hours ago came back to him. He heard Eve's voice in his mind like a ghost. She said that Bonner's mother may have been murdered. For retaliation for turning against Bonner in court, testifying against him? Or no . . . maybe there was another reason; maybe she had been involved with all of this.

THIRTY-SIX

It finally came—another email from Tightrope.

Earlier, after talking to Parker, Eve left the park and come straight home. Parker had not been happy with her; that was for sure. She'd been careful, but she'd been at Bonner's house twice now, once illegally. She knew she hadn't left any fingerprints behind, but there was always the chance a stray hair could be found, or fibers that matched her clothing or her car interior, or, even more likely, a neighbor saw her car parked at Bonner's house, or someone saw her jogging by last night. All were longshots, but all were possible.

She couldn't worry about it now. She'd gone to Bonner's house. She'd broken in. She'd seen his dead body slumped in the chair. It was over now. If she needed the defense attorney Harold had recommended, then she would call him. Until then, worrying about it was a waste of time.

Her mind drifted back to the park, to Agent Parker and how upset he'd been. He just wanted her to be patient, but it wasn't easy to sit back and wait when she felt like she was already so close . . . and running out of time.

And now she'd gotten another email from Tightrope, another cryptic message.

There was another thing that bothered her on the drive home: at the park, it felt like someone had been watching her and Parker. She'd looked around, but she hadn't seen anyone. But she had *felt* them. She wasn't a believer in any kind of psychic phenomena, but she was a believer in instinct, a believer in intuition, a believer in a kind of sixth sense that warned you when something wasn't quite right. She'd read it somewhere described as God whispering in your ear, and that's what it had felt like at the park, a warning whispered into her ear, deep into her mind, her skin crawling, stomach tightening, heart beating faster—the same sensations she'd had when she had rushed down Bonner's basement steps last night, a feeling that everything was about to go very wrong . . .

. . . or maybe click into place.

She'd still felt jittery on the drive home, still restless, like she should've done something.

But what?

She hadn't eaten much all day, so she made a quick dinner when she got home: a chicken breast, steamed broccoli and carrots, and bottled water. The food was bland, just fuel for energy.

She ate in silence. She didn't turn on the TV or the radio—she hardly ever watched TV or listened to music; it seemed so much of her time was devoted to checking the internet for new crimes, new suspects, new serial killers. She did research, printing out anything she found, filling up the folders in her filing cabinets with possible cases or evidence, looking for clues of Tightrope, and others like him.

She'd already put files together of the two murdered families, looking for any connections between the cases, any clues that could help her figure out who the copycat was. The similarities were pretty obvious: the red rope, the torture, the strangulation, using one family member (the father in the Brady family, like he had used her parents and Michael to torture in front of her ten years ago) as the tortured, trying to get the others to struggle so they would strangle themselves. Both families were upper middleclass, both lived in the same area of the county, both families lived on large pieces of land—at least five acres. Neither family had dogs or guns or security systems. The killer had done his research on his victims. Both families had been drugged in their sleep, the same type of animal tranquilizer Tightrope had used on her and her family. Then both families had awakened to a nightmare, like she had ten years ago.

All of that seemed similar to Tightrope's methods, but for some reason it *felt* different to her.

Maybe this really was Tightrope killing again. She hadn't let herself even ponder that possibility. But what if it was? Maybe he had lied in his email about a copycat mimicking his crimes. She remembered Parker asking her why she would trust Tightrope. He was a sick and twisted killer; surely, he wasn't above telling a lie.

Parker had said that Tightrope was still torturing her. After all these years, he was still doing it.

Eve cleaned up the dishes after she ate. Her kitchen was immaculate, everything put away. It didn't even look like anyone used this kitchen or lived in this house. Her décor and furniture were beyond minimalist, the bare necessities that served a function. Her home looked like a place staged for sale, lacking that "lived in" look.

Was this what she had become? A nonperson obsessed with finding the monster who had killed her family and taken her sister? A robot who chased leads as life passed her by? She had no room in her life for relationships, family, kids, art, fun. Nothing.

If she could just find Tightrope, she would change—she swore she would. Everything would change. Even if Maddie was dead, knowing would be so much better than not knowing what had happened to her. It was that hope of Maddie being alive that scared her the most. If she found out Maddie had been dead all these years, it would be like Maddie was taken from her all over again; she would go through all that pain and grief once again. But not knowing, imagining Maddie still alive and suffering, that was worse. The not knowing was killing her, breaking down her mind inch by inch. She'd trained herself to be strong and tough, but she wasn't sure if she could handle this much longer. What if Tightrope slipped back into the shadows and she never heard from him again? What if she lived the rest of her life never knowing, never finding out what happened to her sister? She was afraid it would drive her insane.

Was it already driving her insane?

She didn't want to think about that.

While eating dinner and then cleaning the kitchen, she felt the pull of the emails on her phone—she hadn't checked them for almost an hour.

She checked her phone and froze.

The email address was different this time, a string of what seemed like random letters and numbers, but then there was the subject heading: From Tightrope.

Her legs went weak, but at the same time adrenaline coursed through her. She took her cell phone with her as she bolted to her office. She sat down in front of her bank of monitors, pulling up her email service on the middle monitor, opening up Tightrope's message, reading it.

Eve,

I'm afraid the copycat has struck again. He needs to be stopped before he kills another family. I suspect he already has another family targeted. I hope we can help each other. The closer you get to the copycat, the closer you will get to me. When you find him near the North Star, there will be a clue with him. I'm sure he will want to open his mouth and tell you all about it.

And remember: A man's abodes is his castle.

Just you, Eve.

TR

Eve only read the strange email once, then she hit REPLY, typing as quickly as she could.

Tell me what happened to Maddie. Where's my sister?

She hit SEND and read Tightrope's email two more times before her reply was sent back to her as undeliverable. She replied again, but she knew it was going to bounce right back to her.

"Shit!" Eve yelled and jumped up from her office chair, the chair rolling back and almost tipping over. It took everything she had to keep herself from going on a rampage in her office, smashing everything in sight, shoving everything onto the floor.

She made herself freeze, made herself breathe, made herself calm down.

She needed to think about this.

After grabbing her chair and rolling it back in place in front of the computer monitors, she sat back down and studied Tightrope's email. There had been clues in the last one, so there had to be clues in this one.

He's playing a big game with you . . . still torturing you after all these years.

Maybe Parker was right, maybe this was all a big game, but she couldn't take the chance that it wasn't a game. If there was the smallest chance she could get to Tightrope, and then to Maddie, she was going to take it. If that meant finding this copycat, then she would do it. She didn't understand why Tightrope didn't go after the copycat himself, especially when he seemed to already knew who it was. He wanted *her* to find the copycat. But why?

She didn't care. If it brought her to the next clue, if it brought her closer to finding Tightrope and the answers, then she would figure out who the copycat was. She would stop the copycat, kill him if she had to.

"I'll find you," Eve whispered to the computer screen where Tightrope's email was still displayed.

She grabbed her burner phone from the desktop and dialed Benji's number.

He answered on the second ring. "What's up, Eve?"

"I've got another email for you to trace."

THIRTY-SEVEN

It was seven o'clock when Parker and Martinez got to the first storage unit business on the list that Angie had compiled. Parker had asked Angie to narrow the list of storage unit facilities down to businesses that had been open for at least ten years, which knocked several of them off the list. Parker and Martinez tried the storage business closest to Bonner's home first.

"Could we ask you a few questions?" Parker asked the woman behind the counter in the office. He flashed his ID and badge. Martinez did the same.

"Uh . . . sure," the woman said. She was older and slightly stooped, wearing jeans and a flower-print shirt, a lot of silver and turquoise jewelry. It looked like she'd just gotten to work; her purse and a tall takeout coffee were on the counter behind her, the computer to her left booting up. A heater vent in the ceiling blasted out warm, stale air into the cold lobby.

"Are you the owner here?"

"Part owner. Me and my sister. Used to be my dad's business, but . . ." She let her words trail off, like she didn't need to state the obvious.

"We're working on a case and we were wondering if you could help us with something."

"I'll certainly try."

Parker found that most people were more than willing to help when he asked. They didn't legally have to answer questions, but most understood that they were there looking for a bad guy and they wanted to do their best to help.

"Could you tell me if a man named Richard Michael Bonner rented a storage unit here?"

The name seemed to ring a bell with the woman, but she didn't say anything. She went to work on the computer behind the counter, then she shook her head. "Sorry. No."

"How about a Gloria Bonner?"

"No one named Bonner. Sorry."

There was a possibility that the unit could have been rented using a different name, but that would take a lot of time to figure out. For now, they'd keep looking for storage units rented under the name Bonner.

"Thank you, ma'am."

"Sorry. I wish I could've been more help."

They left the office, walking to Parker's car. Maybe they would get lucky with the next storage unit business.

Parker's phone rang on his belt. He grabbed it and looked at the screen, then answered it. He got into his car and started it, still on the phone. "Thanks, Angie. Could you text the directions to Martinez's phone? Thanks." He hung up.

"She found it?" Martinez asked, getting his phone out, ready for the text.

"A unit rented under a Marge Bonner, Gloria Bonner's middle name. About ten miles from here. Angie's calling them now and letting them know we're on the way."

*

The owner of the storage unit facility was waiting in the office for Parker and Martinez when they got there. He was a short and heavy man who looked nervous, but he pretended to be eager to help.

"Name's Jeff McClintock," the man said, thrusting out a sweaty hand in greeting. "I understand you're looking for some information about one of our customers."

"Yes, sir," Parker answered, declining the handshake, showing his badge and ID instead. Martinez flashed his badge too.

Jeff retracted his hand, his face flushing red, smiling.

"We just wanted to know if a Gloria Margery Bonner has a storage unit rented here."

Jeff glanced at his employee, who sat next to the computer and the phone. He looked back at Parker with the nervous smile still on his face. "I think you already know that."

"We're doing an investigation into her son," Martinez said. He hadn't removed his mirrored sunglasses, staring right at Jeff. "There may be something in her unit we need to see."

"I'm afraid I'm going to need Ms. Bonner's permission first before I can open her unit."

"She's dead," Martinez said. "Been dead for almost a year now."

"Oh. A warrant then?"

"On the way," Parker said.

Jeff nodded, swallowed hard.

"How long has Ms. Bonner had a unit here?" Parker asked.

Jeff looked at his employee. She looked up the information on the computer.

"A little over ten years," the employee said after a moment.

"Could you give me a more exact time?"

"Uh . . ." the employee studied the computer screen. "Ten years and three months."

So, a few months before Bonner was caught killing the three women at Blount Creek, Parker thought.

"Has Ms. Bonner ever been late with her payments?" Parker asked the employee.

"Not in the last three years."

"Same unit all these years?" Martinez asked.

The employee checked. "Yes. Same one. 510."

"How does she make her monthly payments?"

"Uh . . . pays yearly. Direct transfer from a checking account."

"When did she renew?" Parker asked.

"Uh . . . looks like last month."

"Did you know Ms. Bonner has been dead for the last six months?" Parker asked, turning his attention to Jeff.

Jeff's face reddened even more, his ears almost turning purple. "No. Why would I know that? If someone dies, we don't know unless someone from their family notifies us. If someone stops paying and we can't get a hold of them for three months, we auction their possessions off. It's in the contract they sign."

"Her son, Richard Bonner, took over her accounts after her death," Parker informed Jeff.

Jeff shrugged, his neck a fiery red like his face. "The yearly contract was renewed. Paid in full. That's all I know from my end."

"Mr. Bonner is dead now too. Just died."

"Okay. I didn't know that." Jeff seemed like he was about to demand a lawyer.

"Like we said, a warrant's on the way. So could we see Ms. Bonner's unit?"

"Sure."

Parker and Martinez followed Jeff through a side door that led outside. They followed him to a golf cart. They all got in. Jeff drove them down a wide ribbon of paved asphalt, the main aisle through the storage units. They turned a corner at the end of the line of units, entering a maze of narrow streets through different sized storage units. They turned another corner, passed eight units, and then Jeff stopped, pointing at the unit.

"It's a ten-by-fifteen-foot unit," Jeff said. "Our most popular size."

Parker pulled the key he'd found in the metal box buried in the rose garden behind Bonner's house out of his pocket; it was sealed in a plastic baggy. He slipped on a pair of nitrile gloves and then pulled the key out of the bag.

"What are you doing?" Jeff asked, but he didn't step in to stop Parker.

Parker didn't answer. He checked to see if the key fit the lock.

It didn't.

The padlock on the storage unit door looked newer, bright silver glinting in the sun. He wondered if Bonner had replaced the lock . . . or if someone else had.

Martinez took out his penlight and shined the beam around the edges of the garage-style rollup metal door. He got close to it, sniffing.

"You have security cameras here?" Parker asked, glancing up at one of the cameras attached to a wooden streetlight pole. "How far back do you keep the video?"

"A few months. Usually no longer than ninety days."

"If we need to see what you have for this area here, you'd be able to give it to us?"

"Yeah, sure. Of course. Whatever I can do to help."

Martinez's phone vibrated on his belt. He grabbed it. "Agent Martinez." He listened for a moment and then looked at Parker. "The other agents are here with the warrant."

They looked at Jeff.

Jeff stared back at them with a blank expression.

"Could you let them inside?" Parker asked Jeff patiently.

"Oh." Jeff fumbled with his cell phone, pushed a couple of buttons. "I'll have Gina buzz them in."

"Thanks," Martinez said with a sneer.

"Wait," Parker said.

Jeff froze, ready to make the phone call to Gina.

Parker looked at Martinez. "Call them back. Tell them to punch in the four-digit code we have on this paper. See if it works."

Martinez dialed the number on his phone, waiting a moment, walking away with the paper in his hand Parker had given to him, reading the numbers to the agent on the phone.

"Look," Jeff said to Parker, stepping closer to him. "If there's something bad in that unit—"

"Bad?"

"Illegal. If there's something illegal in there, that doesn't have anything to do with me. I give all the customers a long list of items they're not allowed to store here. They sign the paper. They take all the responsibility."

Parker just nodded at Jeff.

Jeff didn't look relieved at all.

Martinez was back, his phone back on his belt. He handed the paper inside the plastic baggie back to Parker.

Moments later, two black SUVs turned the corner and drove toward them, one parking behind the other alongside the line of storage units. Four agents got out of the vehicles, all dressed in dark suits, sunglasses, and FBI windbreakers.

"DeMarco isn't exactly happy about this surprise," Agent Evans said as she walked up to them with a folded wad of papers in her hand.

Martinez gestured at Jeff, and Evans handed the warrant to Jeff without a word in greeting.

"Thanks," Jeff muttered.

"That's enough to take a peek inside the unit," Parker informed Jeff, nodding down at the papers in his hand.

"You got some bolt cutters to get that lock off?" Martinez asked Jeff.

"We actually use a grinder."

"Well?"

"I'll go get it." Jeff was off and hurrying to his golf cart.

"What've you got here?" Evans asked Parker in a low voice.

"I don't know yet."

"But you've got something, right?" She looked worried.

"Maybe."

Evans nodded. "DeMarco said he'll be here soon."

Great. "You brought along your dog?"

She nodded.

A few minutes later Jeff was back. He drove his golf cart past the two SUVs and parked right in front of Gloria Bonner's storage unit. He had a battery-operated grinder with him. It took him roughly thirty seconds to cut through the lock. He stepped back after letting the pieces of the lock fall to the ground, like he didn't want to touch the lock or the door of the unit.

"You'll need to drive your golf cart away from here," Parker told Jeff. "Get a safe distance away while we inspect it."

Jeff didn't argue; he got into the golf cart and set his grinder down on the passenger seat. He looked relieved to be driving away.

Parker instructed the other agents to stand back. Two of the agents waited behind the open doors of their vehicles. Parker didn't think the unit was rigged to explode, or some other kind of booby trap had been set, but you never knew.

Martinez was beside Parker as he lifted the garage door up, the metal rumbling in the tracks. Stale air hit him in the face—he imagined this was what the air rushing out of sealed tomb might feel like that. The faint sickly-sweet odor of rot came from inside.

The unit was full of furniture. Cardboard boxes, plastic tubs, and other kinds of containers were stacked up on top of a couch, a recliner, several tables and wooden chairs.

And at the back of the storage unit, a row of people stood.

THIRTY-EIGHT

Parker and Martinez drew their guns, aiming them at the back of the storage unit.

A second later Parker relaxed and lowered his weapon. It wasn't people standing along the back wall of the storage unit behind the boxes and plastic tubs—it was a row of mannequins, only their heads and shoulders visible above the collection of junk in front of them.

Martinez let out a dejected sigh as he holstered his weapon.

Parker had an idea of what Martinez might be thinking as they all stared at the storage unit filled with junk—they'd gotten another warrant for nothing.

But that smell . . . something wasn't right about the storage unit. Parker was sure of that.

"Will you get the dog?" Parker asked Agent Evans.

Agent Evans went to the back of the second SUV and got the cadaver dog out. She led the dog on a leash to the open unit.

The dog went nuts, pulling against her leash, whining.

"There's something in there," Evans said, pulling the dog back a little.

The dog shrank back when Evans pulled on the leash, like she was suddenly afraid of what was inside the unit.

Evans crouched down beside the dog and petted her, whispering to her: "It's okay, girl." She gave the dog a treat from a pouch on her belt and then led her back to the SUV.

Parker still had his nitrile gloves on. "Let's get to work."

The other agents helped Parker and Martinez pull boxes, tubs, and containers from the unit, stacking them up far enough away so they could pull the furniture out.

In the boxes they found tools, moldy books and magazines, papers that looked like business and tax records with little insect turd pellets all over them.

As they got deeper into the unit, they found boxes and tubs with men's and women's clothes inside: dresses, suits, skirts, shirts. Maybe some of the clothes were meant for the mannequins in the back. Now that some of the furniture was out of the way, Parker could see that all of the mannequins were full-body mannequins, no partials, some propped up on thick bases with metal bars. It was like a row of people watching them from the back of the unit. Only one of the mannequins was fully clothed, the largest of them, a male mannequin in the middle of the row, but the mannequin was dressed in women's clothing, a short skirt and a white off-the-shoulder blouse.

"I'm not seeing anything here," Martinez said while standing over another open plastic tub. He wasn't trying to hide his frustration. "Nothing here but a bunch of junk." He looked at Agent Evans who pulled papers out of another tub, sifting through them carefully, letting the insect turds spill off them, rattling down into the bottom of the tub. "Why was your mutt going crazy?"

"Uh . . . because she smelled something."

"False alarm," Martinez mumbled. "Probably smelled rat shit."

"She doesn't give false alarms, "Evans said.

Parker stood up, stretching a little. They had cleared out more than half the unit now, but there were no signs of bodies, blood, bones, skulls. Nothing.

Could this be a false alarm like Martinez thought?

But the rose had led to the flower garden, which had led to the metal box with the key and code to the storage unit facility inside, which had led here to this storage unit. Parker was beginning to get a sinking feeling in his gut that he had missed something. Maybe the key went to something else.

He thought of his words to Eve, how he'd told her that Tightrope was still torturing her after ten years. Many people wondered why Eve had been left alive by Tightrope. Could this be the reason? So she could live in misery, searching for answers that she couldn't ever possibly find?

And was he being used as a part of it, used by Tightrope to torture Eve? Was he unwittingly helping Tightrope torture her?

Every lead in the Tightrope case had led to dead ends ten years ago, and now it seemed like the same nightmare was happening again—dead ends. With Tightrope laughing at them, orchestrating all of this like he was moving pieces around on a game board.

DeMarco's words from yesterday entered Parker's mind: *Let it go. Stop chasing this. Stop chasing North Star. You've got a great career going. I think you're going to move up, get that position in D.C. you've been gunning for. I can feel it.*

Parker had taken DeMarco's words as a veiled threat, a warning to stop chasing these leads. But maybe DeMarco had truly been concerned for him, for his career at the Bureau, maybe even his safety.

Sometimes life gave you presents wrapped up with neat little bows, DeMarco had said, and DeMarco believed you had to accept those presents when they were handed to you, because they were few and far between.

"Wait a minute," Agent Evans said. She was seated on the pavement next to a big cardboard box, a stack of folders and papers beside the box that she had already removed, many of them brittle with age and dotted with roach droppings and insect eggs. She had a metal box in her hands, a box similar to the one Parker had dug up in Bonner's backyard, only this one was at least twice as big.

"What is it?" Parker asked, hurrying over to her.

"This box was mostly just old papers, but about halfway down, buried under the papers, was this metal box, right at the bottom. Like it was hidden there." She still held the metal box in her gloved hands, hefting it. "Doesn't seem too heavy." She frowned at the small padlock on the clasp. "It's locked."

"Let me try something," Parker said. "Set it down on the ground."

Evans bent down and set the box on the pavement, backing up a step.

Parker pulled the plastic baggy out of his pants pocket with the key and piece of paper inside. He took the key out and tried it on the lock. The key slid easily into the small padlock, unlocking it.

"How do you have the key?" she whispered.

"Found it buried in a box in Bonner's backyard."

"Shit," Evans breathed out, watching Parker open the rusty metal box, the hinges squeaking just a bit.

Martinez was right beside them. "What did you find?"

Parker pulled out a driver's license, holding it in his gloved fingers. He handed it to Martinez.

"Jennifer Watson," Martinez whispered in amazement. "This is her driver's license from ten years ago." He looked at Parker. "What else is in that box?"

The other agents gathered around them.

"Some jewelry," Parker said. "Some odds and ends. Like stuff from someone's pockets or purse."

"I bet some of these clothes in these tubs are hers," Martinez said. "And maybe some of these clothes are from the other three women he killed. Their IDs, their jewelry, stuff from their purses."

The bodies of the three women Bonner killed at the creek were naked and washed when found, their clothes and shoes never recovered. Parker thought Martinez was right; they'd found the victims' clothing.

Parker looked at the line of mannequins at the back of the unit again. He could see them easily now that most of the boxes and furniture had been taken out of the storage unit. He wondered if the mannequins were Richard Bonner's. Or maybe they were his mother's mannequins. They were all naked except the one in the middle of the row—the male mannequin dressed in the short skirt and skimpy top, the clothes a little too small for the mannequin, stretched tight across the hard plastic, forced onto it. Had Bonner been dressing these mannequins up in his dead victims' clothing? Playing with them. Fantasizing about being with his victims again?

Something bothered Parker about the male mannequin dressed in the women's clothes. There were female mannequins among the row, why dress the male in the women's clothes? That mannequin also seemed different, a little taller than the others, a little larger, with a thicker base, metal rods holding it in place. The arms were down at its sides instead of bent slightly, the head facing straight forward instead of turned a little to the side. There was some kind of metal tabs on each side of the mannequin's head, just above the ears.

Parker ventured deeper into the unit, moving the last few tubs and a table out of the way so he could get closer to the mannequin in the middle. Now that he was closer, he saw what the metal pieces on the sides of the mannequin's head were: two small hinges on the right side and a metal clasp on the other side—similar to a clasp on a briefcase. And there was a thin line all the way around the head of the mannequin, down into the neck on each side. The whole front of the face could be opened up, unclipped and swung open on the small hinges.

Parker looked down at the mannequin's arms, the legs, the feet spread apart, flat-footed. There were more lines down the arms, down the side of the torso, down the legs. The whole front half could be removed from the back half of the body, but those lines were different, they looked smeared, almost melted, like a clear glue had been used to seal the two halves back together.

"Oh God," Parker whispered, his stomach sinking, the coffee and donuts he'd downed earlier sitting like a rock in his gut, gurgling, threatening to come back up.

He looked closer at the face of the mannequin—there were holes drilled into the nostrils, and the faint smell of rot came from those holes.

"What's up, Parker?" Martinez called from the front of the storage unit.

Parker didn't answer. He looked at the next two closest mannequins, seeing if they had the same kind of clasp and hinges on the sides of their heads, the same lines that showed that the halves could come apart. They didn't.

He looked back at the mannequin in front of him and pushed on it a little. Heavy. Sturdy. He wasn't a mannequin expert, but he was pretty sure they should be lighter than this.

Too heavy . . .

Like there was something inside of it . . .

With trembling gloved fingers, Parker unhooked the silver clasp—it made a loud metal-on-plastic snapping sound.

"Parker." Martinez was closer. Almost right behind him now.

Parker still didn't answer, still didn't turn around to look at his partner—he held his breath and pulled on the face plate, the front of the face and neck sticking a little for a moment on the seams. He pulled harder and the face and neck broke free with a sucking sound, swinging open on the stainless-steel hinges.

A mummified face stared back at Parker, long brown hair matted to the sides of the papery skin, lips dried and pulled back from the teeth in a grimace, eyeholes sunken beneath closed eyelids.

"Holy fucking shit," Martinez whispered from right behind Parker.

THIRTY-NINE

It had to be Jennifer Watson inside the mannequin—that's what Parker kept telling himself. It made the most sense. Jennifer Watson's driver's license was found inside the storage unit, probably her jewelry too. These were probably her clothes dressed on the mannequin.

But Parker's thoughts turned to Maddie Townsend. He knew it probably wasn't Maddie inside there, but he couldn't help thinking about it. Maybe it didn't make much sense, but nothing made much sense anymore.

Could Maddie's body be in one of the other mannequins? She'd been young at the time of her abduction, smaller, able to fit inside one of the other smaller mannequins.

Thoughts streaked through Parker's mind. Why would Bonner put Jennifer Watson inside a mannequin when his other three victims had been found on the shore of Blount Creek? Why change the way he had killed Jennifer Watson? Why change his M.O. so radically? Could that mean Bonner had changed his M.O. at different times—a chameleon serial killer? Could it mean that Bonner was the copycat, like DeMarco seemed so sure of?

Or was there another killer linked with Bonner? Maybe *he* was the copycat mimicking Tightrope's murders right now. Had this copycat hooked up with Bonner ten years ago, and now he was mimicking Tightrope's crimes?

Or was Tightrope involved with this? Sealing a person inside a mannequin seemed like something sadistic and spectacular that Tightrope might do. If Tightrope was involved with this ten years ago, and now, and he was the one who had taken Maddie, then there was a possibility that the woman inside this mannequin could be Maddie.

Don't be Maddie . . . please don't let it be her.

He didn't want to have to tell Eve that Maddie had died this way, sealed inside a plastic tomb and locked away inside a dark storage unit.

It had to be Jennifer Watson . . . had to be.

*

The next few hours went by in a blur for Parker. Other agents showed up at the storage center, which had been shut down temporarily while the FBI investigated. Forensics techs had come, roping off the area, setting up lights. The M.E. was there—he joked that Parker was keeping him very busy these days.

And then DeMarco showed up.

DeMarco didn't say anything about Parker finding the body in Bonner's storage unit, but Parker could feel the man's dissatisfaction coming off him like heat from a radiator.

You just couldn't let it go, could you? he could imagine DeMarco saying. *You just had to keep on digging.*

As neat as DeMarco wanted this to be, as much as he wanted Bonner to be the Copycat, there were still other questions. Like Gloria Bonner. Could she have been involved? This was her storage unit, one she had paid for during the nine years her son had been at Cedar Haven.

Parker pulled out his phone and walked away to be by himself. He called Angie at the station.

"I need you to find out anything you can about Gloria Margery Bonner, specifically if she was ever in the clothing business, or any business where she would work with mannequins."

"Of course. I'm on it."

Angie hung up and Parker paced in front of the open storage unit, thinking.

*

Thirty minutes later Angie called Parker back.

"What have you got, Angie?"

"Nothing about Gloria Margery Bonner working in the clothing business. She was an insurance agent most of her life. Her husband died young from a heart attack twelve years ago."

"Okay." Parker nodded.

"But guess what?" Angie said.

"What?" Parker asked. His voice sounded tired to his own ears.

"There was a pretty large life insurance policy on him."

"No doubt suggested and set up by Gloria before her husband died," Parker said more to himself than Angie. "Okay, Angie. Thanks. That's a lot of help." He hung up the phone.

Could Gloria Bonner be involved with this? A mother-and-son serial killer team? Or at least a mother covering her son's sins.

Parker was back with Martinez and DeMarco when the M.E. approached them, his face droopy with weariness, maybe from the shock of what he'd just examined. He had stripped off his gloves, but he kept wiping his hands more and more vigorously, without seeming to notice, like he was trying to rid himself of some invisible material on them.

"Just when I think I've seen the worst humans can do to each other," the M.E. muttered.

"Cause of death?" DeMarco asked, ignoring the M.E.'s musings.

"Not sure yet. We'll have to get her back to the lab."

DeMarco stared at the M.E.

"Best guesses?" the M.E. said. "Dehydration. Shock. Cardiac arrest."

"Whoever put her in that mannequin—" Parker began.

"It was Bonner," DeMarco snapped. "I think that's kind of obvious."

"—they must've drugged her first," Parker continued, finishing his sentence. "No way you could stuff someone into a mannequin like that without that person putting up a hell of a fight. Maybe there are scratch marks on the mannequin. On the inside of it. Her fingernails broken off."

DeMarco stared at Parker with a what's-your-point look on his face.

"Tightrope drugged his victims before he placed them exactly how and where he wanted them."

DeMarco looked away, shaking his head.

"We'll check for drugs in the system," the M.E. said. "But if she's really been there for ten years, I don't know if we'll pick anything up."

"Why a male mannequin?" Martinez asked. "You think there's any significance to that?"

DeMarco turned his dagger-stare at Martinez. "What the hell does it matter? You're starting to sound like Parker."

"It's a little bigger than a female mannequin," Parker said to Martinez, answering his question. "Maybe it was easier to fit her body inside after they cut it open."

"They?" DeMarco said, shaking his head again. "Sheesh, for fuck's sake."

"Cut it open how?" Martinez said, ignoring DeMarco.

Parker swore he saw the slightest look of satisfaction on Martinez's face because the two of them were ignoring DeMarco.

"Some kind of machine?" Martinez suggested.

"Maybe," Parker answered, but he looked at the lead tech for an answer.

"Could've been a small handheld power saw," the tech said. "They would've had to have been pretty careful to make sure they were getting both sides pretty close to even, but I think that's how it was done. Then it was sealed back together with some kind of industrial glue, possibly also heated and melted together."

Parker turned his attention back to the M.E. "Holes in the nostrils. You see those?"

The M.E. nodded. He looked sick. "So she could breathe. The killer didn't want her to suffocate. Maybe so she wouldn't die too quickly. The face and neck opened up, so maybe they even stuck an IV into her neck to keep her hydrated. We'll check the skin for a port mark."

Parker's stomach swam. They kept the woman alive as long as possible, to prolong her torment, her suffering, her fear. That didn't sound like Bonner, who had cut his victims' throats right away, killing them quickly and then washing their bodies in the river. Had this one been Gloria's to play with? Or Tightrope's? Someone else?

"There's one other thing I found you need to know about," the M.E. said. He swallowed hard like his throat was suddenly dry. "The pupils in the mannequin's eyes are drilled out."

"So she could see," Parker said. "He wanted her to breathe, but he also wanted her to *see*."

"See what?" Martinez asked. "She was in a dark storage unit."

"Maybe not at first," Parker said. "Maybe she'd been moved there after a week or a month. Maybe he wanted her to see the world while she slowly rotted away inside that thing, her last glimpse of the world."

The others were quiet.

A truly disturbing thought came to Parker. "Maybe he held a mirror up to the mannequin's face, or set a full-length mirror in front of the mannequin, so she could see what she was trapped inside of. She might not have known at first."

"And that's why he put the female clothes on the mannequin," Martinez said. "*Her* own clothes. Sick fuck."

"It's over now," DeMarco snapped. "Bonner did this. Bonner's dead. We can't prosecute a dead guy."

"We're going to take the mannequin with her inside to the morgue," the M.E. told Parker. "Easier that way. We'll cut it open there. We've got a flatbed truck and tarps coming soon."

"Fine," DeMarco said, then looked at Parker. "Once he gets that mannequin out of that unit, let's get this mess cleaned up. Get that shit packed up and on the truck—it's all evidence." He gestured at the boxes, tubs, and furniture, and then he walked away, marching back to his SUV.

Parker watched DeMarco walk away.

"This is some strange shit," Martinez said. "And it just keeps getting weirder."

Parker nodded in agreement. "I need to make a phone call."

Martinez smiled and shook his head. He knew who Parker wanted to call—Eve Townsend.

FORTY

It was almost dark when Benji came over to Eve's house.

"This email was a lot harder to track," he told her. He'd come by last night and taken Eve's laptop back with him to his house. She'd called him a few times, but he still hadn't traced the email.

But now he was here.

"You traced it, though. Right?"

"It was bounced around the world about a zillion times, like you would figure it would be. But it seems to have come from Ukraine."

"But it didn't *really* come from there."

"No. Like I told you before, Tightrope could've used a slave account or hacked into an inactive account, changed the address, and then sent it to you."

Eve had a printed copy of the email next to a spiral notebook where she'd been jotting down the words and numbers from the email, trying to come up with possible patterns and meanings.

"Maybe it's nothing," Benji said.

"No, these mean something." Parker's words came back to her about Tightrope playing a big game to torture her, a game he'd been playing for a long time.

Benji just nodded. He seemed antsy, like he'd done his part tracing the email, but deciphering clues from a murderous madman was outside his area of expertise.

"The last one he sent," Eve said. "The numbers in the address, they were the same numbers in my parents' home address. He'd made that one easy, but these numbers have to mean something. The words. They're clues to something."

"I wish I could help more."

"Will you think about the email?" She handed him another printed copy.

He took it, but she was sure he already had one.

"If you think of anything, no matter how strange, just let me know. Would you?"

"Of course." He grabbed his coat from the back of the other chair in her office. "Sorry, but I need to go. The girls are all hopped up about this trip tomorrow."

"Trip?" The word slipped out before Eve could stop it.

Benji stared at her—he knew she'd forgotten about it, like his life was of no consequence to her unless he was helping her.

She smiled. "Sorry, Benji. It's just . . ." She shook her head, her words dying away, not able to come up with a good enough excuse.

"It's okay. I think I told you about it before. Lorie and her class are going on a field trip to the National Forest. Learning about the forest plant life and animals and stuff."

"That's cool."

"Yeah, I think a park ranger's going to be guiding them for the day. My wife is one of the chaperones, so they let Amber go along too. They went to the store the other day, bought new backpacks, and they wanted to wear these certain brand of rubber boots—I guess it's the trend now or something. But anyway, they're excited. I wanted to get back and spend some time with them."

"You're not going with them tomorrow?"

"Nah. Gotta work on some things. I have other clients besides you," he teased. He smiled. "But you're my favorite. You know that."

Eve wasn't sure if that was true, but she probably paid him the most for his services. "Thank you for everything, Benji."

"Of course." He slipped his coat on and headed for the office door.

Eve walked with him to the front door and disarmed the alarm system to let him out. "Tell Tracy and the girls I said hi."

"Sure. If I think of anything, I'll let you know."

Eve nodded, looked down and realized she had the printout of the email still in her hand, walking around with it, like it had become a part of her, like the mystery of it might sink into her skin, seep into her bloodstream.

Benji walked to his car, a sleek black vehicle that was something between a sports car and a family sedan.

Eve closed the door, locked it, armed the alarm system. She went back to her office and plopped down into her chair. She felt bad that she'd forgotten about Benji's daughters' field trip. What else had he told her about his life that she had tuned out because she was so absorbed with this dark obsession of hers?

Benji might be her only true friend. There was Agent Parker, of course, but she wondered if their relationship was bound only by tragedy and Parker's guilt that he was never able to keep his promise to her and catch Tightrope and find her sister.

She knew the two of them loved her in their own way, and she loved them in her own way.

There was Harold Shoemaker, the family lawyer. And Aunt June. A few cousins.

But nobody else.

She brushed aside her moody thoughts—they were just distractions right now. She turned her attention back to the printed email she had carried to the front door, studying it again.

These words and numbers mean something.

She'd written the numbers down, rearranging them into different sequences, but nothing was coming to her. The numbers could mean anything: an address, a phone number, a security code.

Maybe she needed to figure out the meaning of the words first—maybe that would help her figure out the numbers.

Just you, Eve. That's how Tightrope had ended the email.

Just her for what? Was that a warning not to involve the police or FBI? And Agent Parker? Did Tightrope know about Agent Parker?

And then there was the enigmatic short sentence, like some passage of wisdom taken from a book . . . or maybe even a fortune cookie: *A man's abodes is his castle.*

Tightrope had said to remember that. Did the word "remember" have anything to do with it? And abodes was plural, but the verb "is" was singular. Grammar mistake? No. It had to mean something. A castle was an abode. And abode and a castle could both be buildings. They could both be homes of some kind. What was it about buildings or homes? Was this a key to the Copycat's address? The numbers might coordinate with it if she figured out a street name or a city name.

Tightrope said the Copycat Killer needed to be stopped before he killed another family. Tightrope said he believed the killer had already targeted another family. And then he said that he hoped they could help each other. *The closer you get to the copycat, the closer you get to me. When you find him near the North Star, there will be a clue with him. I'm sure he will want to open his mouth and tell you all about it.*

What did that mean, finding him near the North Star? What did North Star mean, and how did Tightrope know where the Copycat was going to be? How did Tightrope know she would catch the Copycat and find the clue?

She set the paper with the email down on her desk. She needed to take a break, rest her mind. Relax, and then maybe the answers would come to her.

Her cell phone buzzed. It was one of her burner phones, the one she used to call Agent Parker. She'd been calling him for the last few hours but the calls had gone to voicemail. Now he was finally calling her back.

"Parker," she practically snapped at him when she answered the phone.

"Hey, Eve. Sorry about missing your calls today. We've been busy with something."

"What's going on? Did something happen?"

Parker was silent for a long moment.

"Parker? What? What's going on?"

"Yeah, I'm here. Okay. I want to talk to you about something. You mind if I come over?"

"No. Come on over. What is it?"

"We found something."

"What?"

"It would probably be better if I spoke to you about it in person."

FORTY-ONE

Eve paced as she waited for Agent Parker to show up at her door, still trying to decipher the mysterious meaning of Tightrope's email, but mostly she wondered what Parker wanted to talk to her about, what he had found. He seemed tense on the phone, so she figured this wasn't going to be good news.

We found something.

Her first thought was the rose garden in Bonner's backyard, where she'd told Parker he should look. Had they looked? Dug it up? They found something there?

A body?

She didn't want to think about it, and she tried to block it out of her mind, but it kept coming back. Maddie's face swam into her mind.

No, it's not Maddie. No way. Tightrope wouldn't be contacting me if this was about Maddie, would he?

Her alarm system buzzed, letting her know that a car had entered and passed the threshold at the beginning of her long, winding driveway through the woods.

Eve wanted to tell Parker about the latest email from Tightrope—she knew she *should* tell him about it, but instead, she hid the printout among some other papers on a shelf above her desk. She logged out of her emails and turned off her computer.

Just you, Eve.

Maybe Tightrope meant that Parker, or anyone else, wasn't supposed to read the email he had sent to her. She couldn't be sure, but she wasn't going to take any chances right now.

She went to the front door, punched in the security code on the keypad next to it, and watched for the doorbell chime. The screen on the keypad lit up when the doorbell rang, showing who was at the door—Parker. He was alone. The image also automatically transferred to her cell phone in case she wasn't home or at the front door.

"Parker," she said, opening the front door for him. "Come on in."

"Thanks," he muttered. He looked exhausted. His suit and shirt were rumpled, his tie loosened. He looked so much older.

Eve closed the door and locked it, resetting the alarm system.

"You want a drink?" she asked as he followed her into the formal living room.

"Yes. Please."

Eve didn't drink anymore, but she always kept some whiskey, vodka, rum, and wine in the house for when people came by—not that company visited very often. She also liked to keep alcohol in the house to prove to herself that her will was strong, that she cold have booze in the kitchen cabinets, mere steps away, and still refuse to give in to it.

"Rum?" she called out from the kitchen. "Whiskey and soda?"

"Whiskey and soda. Thanks."

She made the drink for Parker and brought it to him. He was seated on the white sofa, his suitcoat removed and laid over the back, his sleeves rolled up a few turns on his forearms.

"Thank you," he said after she handed him the drink. He took a big sip.

Eve sat down in the chair across from the sofa. "What's wrong?"

"We found something today."

Yeah, you already said that on the phone. "What?"

"We dug up the rose bushes in Bonner's backyard yesterday afternoon."

She nodded—she knew he would.

"We found a small metal box buried under a rose bush. It was about the size of a book. There was a paper with a four-digit code on it and the word 'storage' written on it."

Eve nodded for him to go on.

"And there was a key inside the box, too. That was it, just the piece of paper and the key. It looked like the box had been buried under the roses for a while."

"What did the key go to? A storage unit?"

He nodded. "We found the business that housed the storage unit."

"The key unlocked the storage unit?"

"No, the key didn't fit the lock on the storage unit."

Eve was quiet for a moment.

"We had the owner of the business cut off the padlock. The key opened a metal box inside the storage unit. The unit was full of boxes, tubs, furniture. We found another metal box hidden down inside a carboard box under some old papers. It was a little larger than the one that was buried under the rosebushes."

Eve waited for him to go on.

"The storage unit was rented under Gloria Margery Bonner's name—Richard Bonner's mother."

Eve nodded impatiently; she knew who Gloria Bonner was.

Parker shook his head and grinned just a little, realizing he was going too slow for Eve; she wanted the information right away. He sipped more of his drink. "She's had the storage unit for ten years."

"Since Bonner started killing."

He nodded. "Timeline, down to the month. She rented the storage unit two months before Bonner's first victim was found at Blount Creek. She died six months ago, but the yearly lease was renewed last month. The owner of the business said the lease renews automatically unless the owner of the unit cancels or there isn't enough money in the account or the credit card is declined."

"And you found something in the unit. In that box."

"Yeah," he said, his voice almost a croak. "There was more, though."

It was something bad—she could see it on his face. A chill danced on little spider legs along her skin, but at the same time she was suddenly flushed with heat. She shook her head slowly. "Not Maddie. Don't tell me you found Maddie." Her world felt like it was spinning suddenly. She almost clutched the arms of the chair just to have something to hold onto. She wasn't ready for this.

"No," Parker said quickly. "But we found a woman inside the storage unit."

"Not Maddie?" Eve breathed out.

"No. We're sure it's not her." He paused for a moment, like he was psyching himself up to say the rest.

"What is it? There's more. Who was the woman in the storage unit? Jennifer Watson?"

"Yes. We think that's who it is. She was put inside a . . . sealed up inside a mannequin."

"A mannequin?"

"A male mannequin. It had been cut apart, cut into two halves, and the woman was placed inside, then it was sealed back together again with some kind of strong glue. But there was a face plate on the mannequin, hinges and a clasp, so the whole face of the mannequin could be swung open."

Eve shook her head just a little. "Bonner did that to her? It doesn't match his earlier crimes."

"I know. We're checking with Cedar Haven to see if Bonner had been diagnosed with any kind of split personality disorders, but right now we believe someone else helped him kill Jennifer Watson. Or maybe someone else did this and Bonner hid it for him."

"You mean like Tightrope?"

Parker shrugged. He sipped more of his drink. Ice clinked in the glass.

"The copycat?" Eve asked.

"Remember when you talked to me about Bonner's mother?"

"Yeah."

"Only you and I know that Bonner told you he believed his mother had been murdered. And she rented this storage unit right before he murdered those three women. Quite a coincidence."

"Someone killed Bonner's mother because she knew too much. Maybe she'd been helping Bonner or covering for him."

"Or helping someone else," Parker said. "Or covering for someone else. There may be someone else involved. After all, if Gloria Bonner was really murdered, then someone other than Richard Bonner had to have done it since he was locked up at Cedar Haven at the time."

Eve stared at Parker, searching his eyes. "How long has this woman been in the storage unit? Inside the mannequin?"

"M.E. thinks it could be ten years. Body was mummified to some degree. That's one of the reasons we believe it's Jennifer Watson. They're running tests right now."

"Ten years," Eve whispered. "But could it be Maddie? You're absolutely sure it's not Maddie?"

"The body was an adult; the M.E. was pretty sure of that. Not Maddie's age or height."

"But Maddie could have been kept somewhere for a few years, and then . . . then sealed in that mannequin . . ."

"No," Parker said, the word a little too sharp. "It's not Maddie. We found Jennifer Watson's driver's license inside the locked metal box in the storage unit. There was some jewelry inside that box that we think might have been hers too. And the mannequin, it was wearing women's clothes, a short skirt, a kind of halter top. I looked it up, same type of clothing Jennifer Watson was reported to be wearing when she disappeared."

Eve breathed out a sigh of relief. Now that she believed the body couldn't have been her sister, she put it out of her mind and focused on other things. "North Star. When I told Bonner about North Star, he got afraid. He said *they*, like it's a group. Like maybe a group or a network of criminals, or killers who work together, maybe providing alibis for each other, or assisting each other in some way. And he was afraid of what they could do to him. He said it was far worse than anything I could do to him."

"Like stuffing a person inside a mannequin to waste away for weeks. Or even months."

Eve stared at him.

"It was bad. The mannequin had nose holes in the nostrils so Jennifer Watson could breathe. Holes drilled out in the eyes so she could see. Like I said, the face plate opened separate from the body. The M.E. suspects that she might have been hydrated with an IV tube in her neck to keep her alive longer. Who knows what else they did to her?"

"Maybe Bonner's mother knew about the three women he killed and covered it up. Maybe the whole story about her abusing him as a child was a distraction, something to help him get an insanity plea."

"Which seemed strange that the judge went along with it. And the jury."

"You think someone got to them? Someone from this North Star network got to the judge? Or the jury members?"

Parker shrugged like it could be a possibility. "That would be a pretty powerful group."

"So, Gloria Bonner wasn't helping her son with the three women he killed, but she might have known what he was doing, covering for him. But not Jennifer Watson. Bonner never admitted to Jennifer Watson's abduction, even though he readily admitted to killing the three women found at Blount Creek. In fact, he adamantly denied having anything to do with Jennifer Watson."

"But her body was in his mother's storage unit."

"Maybe someone else took Jennifer Watson, not Bonner or his mother. Someone else did this to her. Maybe she was somewhere else at first, but then she was delivered to Gloria Bonner's storage unit as a warning, and to always have something on her."

"A constant reminder not to talk," Parker suggested.

"Or not to disturb their plan." Eve shook her head. "Someone else did this to Jennifer Watson, not the Bonners. Someone who might still be out there."

"Like Tightrope?"

"I don't know. Doesn't fit his M.O."

"But I'm guessing he could get creative if he wanted to." Parker finished his drink.

"You want another one?"

"Just half, please."

Eve took Parker's glass to the kitchen and made him another drink, only half filled, as he had asked. She brought it back to him.

"Thank you."

"What about Gloria Bonner? Maybe you could exhume her body. Check for toxins. See if her heart attack was caused by poison."

"Don't think DeMarco would go for that. He wants to believe Bonner and the Copycat are the same. He wants to believe all of this is over. He told me to stop digging, to stop chasing North Star."

"The North Star website is gone now. My computer guy looked for it, but all signs of it are gone from the dark web."

Parker nodded like he already knew that. "I still think Tightrope could be involved with all of this. There's got to be a reason he came out of the shadows to contact you."

"He wanted me to find something at Bonner's house. And now we have."

"So, Tightrope was there," Parker said. "Tightrope paid Bonner a visit. Made him kill himself. It was better to slice his own throat rather than end up inside a mannequin. Or something even worse. And after Bonner was dead, Tightrope cut the rose from the bush in the backyard and laid it on Bonner's lap."

"Because he wanted me . . . *us* . . . to find Jennifer Watson's body, and maybe find out who did this to her." But not the Copycat, she thought. That was something different; that was something just for her. She didn't mention it.

"Why would Tightrope want this exposed? Why put himself at such a risk to expose this?"

Eve didn't have an answer for him.

Parker gulped his drink down and stood up.

Eve took his empty glass from him.

"If Tightrope wants you to find the Copycat, then how is exposing Bonner and his mother helping? Unless Bonner really was the Copycat."

Eve knew he wasn't. She knew the Copycat was still out there. Tightrope had just told her that in the email he'd sent earlier.

Parker grabbed his suitcoat, flipping it over his shoulder. "I need to go. It's been a long day. I just wanted to come by and tell you what we found. And to tell you that it's not Maddie."

"Thank you."

Eve walked with Parker to the front door, disarmed the alarm and unlocked the front door for him.

Parker hesitated before walking outside. He looked at her, locking eyes with her. "You haven't gotten any more emails from Tightrope, have you?"

The question rocked her, and for a moment she almost confessed the truth.

He knows, anyway.

But she shook her head. "No. Nothing yet. I keep checking."

He searched her eyes for a few seconds, then he gave a curt nod and left. Eve closed the front door and locked it. She reset the alarm system.

Just you, Eve—Tightrope's words whispered in her mind.

FORTY-TWO

The killer waited at the national forest for the group of school kids and their chaperones. He'd been following them for over an hour now, but keeping well behind them on the trail. But now he ventured a little closer when they stopped for the park ranger guiding them who gave a little lecture about the trees and plants, asking questions, the girls raising their hands to guess at the answers.

He'd been careful. He hadn't been spotted so far. He was an expert in the woods, able to remain quiet and hunt like a wolf.

The chaperones consisted of one teacher and two mothers. One of the mothers was Tracy Kelso. Her daughter Lorie and her class were on the field trip, but it seemed like little Amber had been allowed to tag along.

He noticed that Lorie hung out with the friends in her class, ignoring Amber. Even Tracy was keeping an eye on the group while Amber wandered away here and there.

A little after noon, while the park ranger was talking about the animals of the forest, Amber wandered away again from the group, following a yellow butterfly floating over the ferns. She followed the trail around the bend, keeping up with the butterfly.

The killer stepped out of the woods on the other side of the trail, watching as Amber entered the woods.

He followed her as she ventured deeper into the woods after the butterfly. Both of them were hidden from the rest of the kids and chaperones by the brush and the trees of the bend.

Amber took another step deeper into the woods with her bright red rubber boots. Her new backpack was slung over her shoulders. The woods were damp, the ground soggy, but it hadn't rained at all so far throughout the morning.

"Beautiful butterfly, isn't it?" the killer said from behind Amber.

She whirled around to face him, freezing when she saw him.

"You're a little far from your group, aren't you?" he said, frowning just a little to show her that he was serious.

She nodded, then looked out at the trail beyond them like she just realized how far she had wandered away, realizing that no one else was around.

"It's okay," the killer said, smiling. "They're right up the trail. I just saw them a few minutes ago. I was walking back down the trail when I saw you go into the woods."

Amber didn't respond. She just stared at him, still frozen in place.

"I think your butterfly is gone now, but there are more. I see them all the time around here."

"You do?"

"I've seen whole families of them. Dozens and dozens of them."

Amber smiled. Giggled.

"You're on a field trip with your school, aren't you?"

"It's my sister's class. But they let me come with them." She frowned. "But she's too busy hanging out with her friends."

"Oh," the killer said, matching her frown. "Yeah. It's tough being the younger sister, isn't it?"

She nodded.

"I bet the butterfly families all hang out together," he said. "I bet they never fight."

She giggled again.

"I like your red boots. Are they new?"

She looked down at her boots, then looked back up at him, nodding, her long hair bouncing just a little. "My mom bought them for me. She said it might be muddy here."

"Yeah, it can be. I'm here all the time."

She just nodded.

"It's beautiful here, but it can also be dangerous," he told her. "There are other animals besides butterflies in the woods, you know."

She nodded, but looked unsure.

"There are wolves in these woods. And bears."

Amber's eyes widened. Her eyes cut to the woods all around her.

"You shouldn't be wandering off. It's easy to get lost out here. You should always stay with your group."

"Amber!"

The killer and Amber looked down the trail at Tracy as she raced toward them, her frown of fear turning to relief when she saw Amber.

"That's my mom," Amber said. "I gotta go."

"Of course," the killer said, stepping aside so Amber could run past him out of the woods and onto the trail to meet her mother.

Tracy crouched down and hugged Amber as she emerged from the woods, then she pushed her back, holding her at arm's length, staring at her like she was checking for cuts and bruises. She was trying to look angry at her daughter, but she still looked scared. "You don't wander off. You hear me?"

"Sorry, Mom. There was this . . . this yellow butterfly . . ."

Tracy stood up as the killer stepped out of the woods. She smiled at him. "Thanks for keeping her company."

"It's partly my fault, ma'am," the killer told her. "I told her she needed to get back with her group, but I got her talking about animals in the forest."

"He said he's seen whole families of butterflies," Amber told her mother.

"He did?" she asked in an exaggerated tone.

Amber nodded.

"What else did I tell you?" the killer asked Amber in his "serious" voice.

She frowned. "You said there are wolves and bears in the woods."

"Which is why you need to stay with your group," he said with mock severity, but he gave Tracy a quick wink when Amber looked down at the toes of her boots, pouting just a little.

"The wolves and the bears never come onto the trails when there are people around," he told Tracy when he saw the concern in her eyes. "I promise . . . you're safe."

"Well, *you* should know," Tracy said. "You're a park ranger."

"Ranger Cassel," he said, gesturing at his nametag. "Todd Cassel."

"Pleased to meet you, Ranger Cassel," she said. "And thanks again. We better get back before we lose the others."

"Ranger Brenda won't let that happen," Todd said. "She'll notice you two are gone soon enough. She's a good one. She's been at this for over twenty years. She's the one who trained me, in fact."

"Yeah, she's great. And thanks again. I'm so glad you were here."

He smiled at them and watched them walk away, down the trail, hand in hand.

When they were almost around the bend, Todd noticed something shiny down on the trail. He bent down to pick it up. A bracelet. Amber must have dropped it and not noticed it. She would probably want it back.

He would bring it back to her later.

I'll be seeing all of you very soon.

FORTY-THREE

Eve woke up in the middle of the night and saw Tightrope standing at the foot of her bed, barely visible in the glow of the nightlight she kept plugged into the wall socket. He was dressed in black clothes, black gloves, and black boots, the same thing he'd been wearing the night he had killed her family and taken her sister. Only now, he wasn't wearing the black hood with holes for his eyes and mouth like he'd worn before; tonight, he wore the mask of a mannequin. A pale, expressionless face floated in the darkness. He held a hunting knife in one hand and Ralph the Rabbit in the other hand.

"Just you, Eve," he whispered from behind the plastic mask.

She lunged for the Glock 19 on the table next to her bed, grabbing it, twisting back around and aiming it at Tightrope, her finger on the trigger.

Tightrope wasn't there.

Eve sat on her bed, breathing hard, heart jackhammering, still aiming the gun at the foot of her bed, her finger still on the trigger.

It was only a nightmare.

She had almost pulled the trigger. She had almost fired her gun inside her house.

Her skin crawled as she lowered her gun, her breathing beginning to slow down a little.

Just a dream . . . that's all. Just a dream.

She set her gun back down on the table and sat on the edge of her bed. She was still groggy, her head a little light. She'd slept a few hours, but it had been a fitful sleep. She never slept well, usually waking up several times a night, sometimes sleep eluding her for hours. Tonight, the sleep she'd gotten had been haunted with visions of words and numbers, combinations of the two, all of them running through her dreams.

After a drink of water, she lay back down on her bed, staring up at the ceiling. It was a little cool in her bedroom; she usually kept it that way.

She closed her eyes and drifted off for a few more hours, or maybe she'd floated somewhere between sleep and consciousness. When the lights of the cold, gray morning invaded her bedroom, she got out of bed. She knew she wouldn't be able to go back to sleep.

She worked out in her gym, punching and kicking the bags, then running on the treadmill for thirty minutes. She took a shower. She ate a breakfast of scrambled eggs, chopped veggies, half a grapefruit, a piece of dry rye toast, and a cup of tea.

After she ate, she paced her home with the email printout and her spiral notebook in her hands, glancing at them every so often, trying to see what she hadn't seen before.

Nothing was coming to her.

She went back to bed and flopped down, the email printout and the notebook on the table. She was tired, but she knew she wouldn't be able to fall back asleep now, not with the Copycat prowling for his next family to kill. She felt helpless. Useless.

Her eyes closed. She almost drifted off to sleep as the words "abodes" and "castle" flashed through her mind. They were similar: both buildings, both homes, both constructions. Both old? Why was one plural and the other one singular?

She sat up in bed. Something was coming to her, but it was still too far away, lost in a sea of fog. But she swore she could just see the outline of it . . . and it was getting closer, getting clearer.

An address. The numbers and words had to be a clue to the Copycat's address. In the last email Tightrope had used her parents' address numbers in his own email address. Abodes and a castle would have an address.

Eve got up and went to her office. She searched her computer for street names in King County and the surrounding counties. First, she used the word "homes" in her search.

Nothing.

Next, she used the word "abodes."

Nothing.

Castle. Some street names and neighborhoods popped up: Castle Street, two Castle Roads, a Castle Court, some other street names with the word Castle in them, one housing development, one apartment complex, three motels. She wrote each of these down, but it felt too easy—too simple.

Homes? Maybe it sounded like Homes. Holmes?

She typed in Holmes and got a few street names. She wrote those down and then began typing numbers from the email address until the computer began auto-filling in the rest.

Twenty minutes later she had four possibilities. One was fifty miles away in another county. She did a reverse search of the address to find out the name of the owner of the property. It still didn't mean anything because the Copycat could be renting one of these places.

She looked up the owner of the next property. This house was a little closer to Seattle.

She froze, staring at the computer screen. The owner's name was Todd Cassel.

Todd Cassel on Holmes Street.

That was him. Had to be.

*

An hour later, Eve drove past Todd Cassel's small house on Holmes Street a few times before parking half a block away.

Todd Cassel's home was a small two-story with an attached garage that looked like it had been added on after the house was built sixty years ago. Gray siding, darker gray trim. A cramped neighborhood of older homes, mature (and somewhat overgrown) landscaping, tall and ancient trees.

The only vehicle in Todd Cassel's driveway was an old 80s Chevy Blazer jacked up on big tires. It was backed in, the rear of the vehicle butting up to the garage door. If there was another vehicle in the one-car garage, the Blazer would have to be moved to get it out. The Blazer was an off-road vehicle, or maybe a project car, not his regular vehicle; he must've had something more dependable than the Blazer—a car that wasn't there right now.

She couldn't break into the DMV website to see what kind of vehicle Todd Cassel owned, but maybe Benji could do it later. Or there was always Agent Parker. But she couldn't involve Parker in this just yet, not until she learned more about Todd Cassel.

Just you, Eve.

She studied Cassel's house from where she was parked down the street. The curtains in the windows were closed, the inside dark. The small front porch was clean and clear of any furniture, just a plain doormat in front of the door, a black metal mailbox attached to the siding near the front door, one porch light above that, the light off.

No one seemed to be home. Maybe Todd Cassel worked during the day. Or maybe he had run, something scaring him. She didn't know—she would have to wait.

She looked up any information she could find online about Todd Cassel while she waited, but Cassel was a pretty common name. She found Twitter and Facebook accounts, but she didn't think any of them were the man she was looking for. He wouldn't have splashed his face and name all over the internet—if he had, he would have used a sock puppet account.

Giving up on the internet search, she looked up information on the house. It had been purchased four years ago. Only one owner. Cassel bought it for a decent price, an average price at the time. The house had probably gone up quite a bit in value.

She watched the neighbors, many of whom also seemed to be gone. To the right of Todd's house, a woman got into her car while talking on the phone, her voice carrying across the street. Eve slouched down a little in the seat, but the woman didn't seem to notice her. The woman got into her car, started it, then backed out of her driveway.

A little while later a man jogged by—he had the emaciated body of a marathon runner.

The day was cold and cloudy; gusts of wind rocked her car slightly every so often. It drizzled for a bit and then stopped.

She didn't want to talk to any of the neighbors just yet, and she really couldn't stay parked her too much longer. Someone would eventually get suspicious—maybe someone was even peeking out their window right now, using a pair of binoculars so they could jot down her license plate numbers. She couldn't bring attention to herself, and there was always the possibility of a patrol car driving by, stopping to ask her why she was parked on the side of the road.

No, she would need to leave soon. Maybe drive by a few more times in the evening and then at night. She would find a place where she could park her car tonight and then she would jog down these streets and enter Todd Cassel's house, just like she'd done at Bonner's house.

FORTY-FOUR

Tracy Kelso jumped when someone knocked at the front door. She'd been back from the national park forest field trip for two hours now, stopping on the way to pick up some McDonald's because the girls had been begging for it. She still had dinner to get ready, something light for her and Benji—he probably wouldn't be home until six, or maybe seven. Or even eight. Who knew these days?

Benji was always working, but it was his "secret client" Tracy worried about the most. She knew Benji's client was Eve Townsend, but he had sworn her to secrecy, and she hadn't told anyone about it. At least Eve paid well—very well, ten to twenty times more than other clients, and Benji promised he was squirrelling the extra money away and making good investments for them.

Still, there was something about Benji's relationship with Eve that she didn't like. Maybe it was the secrecy. They fought about it sometimes. They weren't hurting for money. Benji could pick up a few more new clients to replace Eve, but it was like he didn't want to leave her; it seemed like he enjoyed being around her. The danger of it. The thrill of it.

Normally a knock at the front door wouldn't send a jolt of fear through Tracy, but with Tightrope (the killer who had murdered Eve Townsend's family and taken her sister, by the way) back in the news again, and with two families murdered within a week of each other, she couldn't help being a little paranoid.

Tightrope was probably the first thought in everyone's mind around here.

Of course, the idea of it was irrational. For one thing, it was still daytime. Late afternoon, yes, but still day. Everyone knew Tightrope snuck into people's homes in the middle of the night. Ever since Benji had begun working with Eve (whom Tracy still hadn't been introduced to), Tracy had read two books and watched three documentaries about the Townsend Tragedy. (The Townsend Tragedy was the *actual* title of one of the books).

Also, Tightrope wouldn't knock on the front door, waiting patiently for someone to answer.

Still . . . it wouldn't hurt to peek through the peephole. The door was locked. It was probably just someone selling something.

She approached the front door, trying to be quiet so the visitor wouldn't know she was there. She'd done this before, peering out through the peephole rather than answering the door, or peeking out through the curtains over the front windows—maybe it was wrong, but if it was a salesperson, she didn't feel like saying no three times before they gave up.

At least the girls hadn't come running at the sound of the knocking. She had expected Amber, the nosy one, to race to the door before she could get to it. No matter how many times Tracy had told her not to, Amber would just open the door before Tracy could get there.

Tracy looked through the peephole. She froze, taking a moment to understand what she was seeing. She knew who it was on her front porch; it was the park ranger from the forest, the one who had kept Amber from wandering too far into the woods. But she didn't know why he was there.

"Mrs. Kelso," the ranger said like he knew she was right on the other side of the door watching him. He flashed a boyish grin. "Sorry to bother you, but your daughter lost something on the trail today when she was wandering off. A bracelet."

Tracy remembered Amber saying something on the way home from the forest about losing a bracelet. They had searched the car but never found it.

The park ranger's smile faltered just a bit, like he was suddenly aware of how creepy this looked. "I'm sorry. I'll just leave it out here on the table by the chairs."

Shame bombarded Tracy—she was hiding behind the front door while this park ranger (Cassel . . . she was pretty sure his name was Ranger Cassel) had come all the way here to return the bracelet. She unlocked the door and opened it.

Todd Cassel was caught in the act of stepping toward the metal chairs and glass-topped table on their front porch, a tiny manila envelope in one hand.

"Sorry," Tracy said. "I tried to get to the door as quickly as I could." It felt like her face was flushing with heat from the lie she'd just told.

He smiled like he knew it was a fib, but also like he understood *why* she would lie. "I'm sorry," he said. "I swear I don't usually go to people's houses like this. I just thought your daughter might miss this."

"Thank you . . ."

"Todd. Just call me Todd."

Todd was still dressed in his park ranger uniform: tan pants, bulky green jacket, and waterproof hiking boots. But he didn't have his hat on. He really was a looker, Tracy thought. He was lean and muscular, with blue eyes and sandy-blond hair, perfect white teeth. Tan skin. He even smelled like the outdoors, a fresh piney/leather scent. She would never cheat on Benji—never even think about it—but if she did . . .

"Thank you, Todd."

His smile faltered just a bit again as he took a step closer to her, the small envelope still in his hands. He had large hands. Strong and powerful-looking hands.

Tracy couldn't even imagine which bracelet Amber had lost in the forest today. It wouldn't be valuable, not valuable enough for Ranger Todd to drive all the way here to deliver it in person, but it was valuable enough to Amber, who had pouted all the way home about it.

An uneasy feeling began to crawl through Tracy, a pit forming in her stomach, her muscles beginning to feel a little rubbery and weak. A barely noticeable high-pitched whine sounded in her mind. Something seemed wrong about Ranger Todd's visit. Was he flirting with her? Stalking her? It was just a kid's bracelet. Why not send it in the mail? Or just keep it in a Lost-and-Found box in their office? And even though he did come all the way here, why not just stuff the envelope in their mailbox with a note?

Why knock on their front door? He had knocked, not rang the doorbell.

"How did you get our address?" Tracy asked. The smile plastered on her face felt wrong, it felt silly.

Get back inside! Close the door! Lock it!

But she didn't go back inside. She didn't lock the door. For some reason, some social etiquette pounded into her over the years, she hesitated. She didn't want to seem rude. She waited.

Ranger Todd was right in front of her. She hadn't remembered him moving this close to her.

"Brenda, the ranger who led your group today," he said. "She gave me your address."

The confusion must have shown on her face.

"She's friends with one of the other mothers who was there—the mother gave Brenda your address, and she gave it to me."

Tracy tried to think of which of the other mothers would know where she lived, but other thoughts were competing and buzzing in her mind: Why had Ranger Todd been on the trail in the woods earlier when Amber had wandered off to chase a butterfly? Had he been following them? Watching them?

"Well, thanks," Tracy stammered. "I appreciate you coming by. I need to get back inside. Dinner, you know." She looked at the driveway, but she didn't see Ranger Todd's vehicle.

"You haven't taken your daughter's bracelet yet," Todd said, his voice lower, his smile no longer friendly and disarming—now it was menacing, his blue eyes seemingly darker and twinkling with savagery. He had the manila envelope pinched between his thumb and forefinger, holding it like he might pull it back if she tried to grab it, like a bully taunting another student with his brown-bag lunch.

Tracy reached out and snatched the envelope from Todd. She couldn't hide the trembling of her fingers.

Something was wrong. She knew right away as soon as she had the envelope in her hand—it felt so light. Empty. There was no bracelet rattling around inside.

While concentrating for a second on the envelope, Tracy felt a sharp jab of pain in her upper arm.

He just stabbed me!

Tracy stumbled back in through the doorway, her head suddenly light, her vision blurry.

Todd pushed his way into the house, gently maneuvering Tracy back a few steps so he could close the front door and lock it. He was wearing latex gloves now.

When did he put those gloves on? What was happening?

"Mom!" Amber called from her bedroom. "Who was at the door?"

Tracy wanted to scream at Amber and Lorie to run, to call the police, but her throat felt like it had locked up, her body and muscles turning to mush, the world spinning, the edges of her vision growing dark.

FORTY-FIVE

Benji Kelso pulled into his driveway at 7:30, later than he'd meant to be home. The world had been dark for a while, darker out here where he lived. The porch lights, like twin beacons, guided him up to the front of his home.

Tracy was already upset with him because he hadn't been able to take some time off to be with her and the girls today on their field trip in the forest, and getting home later than he should probably wasn't going to put her in a much better mood. He'd called her several times on the way home, but she wasn't answering her cell phone. And the house phone was unplugged.

She must really be mad at him.

He knew Tracy and the girls had gotten home okay from the field trip because she had resorted to talking to him for a few minutes earlier in the afternoon. She still wasn't over their argument they'd had last night before going to bed, an argument that had carried over to this morning with sullen looks and the silent treatment from Tracy—well, not really the silent treatment, more like one-word answers and grunts to any questions he asked.

And he'd gotten the same one-word answers from Tracy when he'd called earlier in the afternoon, then she had handed the phone off to Lorie and Amber, both of whom were more than willing to talk to him about their field trip in the forest. Amber told him that she had chased after a yellow butterfly and had almost gotten lost in the woods, but a park ranger was there who told her whole families of butterflies lived in the forest, but there were bears and wolves too.

Benji's heart had skipped a beat at the thought of Amber wandering away from the group. It only took a few minutes to lose your way in the woods. Amber could have fallen down a hill or hit her head on a rock.

Thank God that park ranger had been there.

Benji's first thought was to scold Tracy for not watching Amber closely enough, but he didn't say anything about it to Tracy, or to Amber.

Besides, Tracy would probably be angry enough at herself, and she would be stressed out after spending the day with a big group of schoolkids. Amber was okay—she wasn't hurt—no point in dredging up another argument.

And he knew about stress—he'd been working for more clients than he could handle lately, and still jumping at the drop of a hat when Eve called him.

In fact, part of his and Tracy's argument last night had been about Eve. Of course, it was mostly about him working too many hours and not spending enough time with her and the girls, but a lot of it had to do with Eve. Tracy just didn't like Eve; she didn't trust her.

"Don't believe the rumors on the internet," he'd told her last night.

There were cruel rumors online that Eve had been involved with her family's deaths and her sister's disappearance, that she'd had so much to gain from their deaths: her family's fortune. Even though there wasn't any evidence that Eve had had anything to do with the murders and abduction, people still spread rumors about it; people still wanted to believe it.

But there was something else that Tracy didn't like about Eve, and Benji wasn't so sure Tracy could even spell it out if she had to. Eve was an intense person; there was no doubt about that. And Benji had to admit he was drawn to her, not in a sexual way, but there was something fascinating about her that he couldn't put into words. But she also seemed to suck the energy right out of him. He wondered if Eve ever relaxed, or even slept.

He understood the reason for Eve's intensity. If something ever happened to his family like that, he was sure he'd either fall apart or go on the warpath, not stopping until he found the person responsible . . . like Eve was doing. He couldn't turn his back on Eve—she needed his help. He wished Tracy could understand that.

He was sure he would continue working for Eve. He wanted to. But if he was being totally honest with himself, he'd been getting the jitters lately just being around Eve. She could be an intimidating person; she was rich, famous, beautiful, driven, intense. But it was more than that, it was like she was some kind of bad luck charm, a dark cloud that drew evil toward her, a human omen, a tempter of the fates. It felt like just being around her was going to pull him into her world where true monsters existed. Maybe it was getting to be too much, looking things up for her, doing research, tracing emails from Tightrope, or Bonner, or some other psychopath.

Maybe Tracy was right about this. He could admit that it was getting to him a little, and maybe Tracy was just picking up on that. But he couldn't turn his back on Eve right now. It wasn't just about the money she paid him, it was also that he understood her drive to find Tightrope, to expose him to the world and finally bring him to justice.

Just as Benji parked behind his wife's SUV, his cell phone rang.

It was Eve.

He was about to answer the phone; it was an automatic Pavlovian reaction. But he stopped himself. Maybe it was the argument with Tracy—it had been a bad one—but he was going to go inside and spend some time with his wife and girls, at least say hello to them, before he jumped to attention for Eve.

He shut his car off and got out. The only light came from the front porch. The windows of the house were dark, the lights inside off. Maybe the girls were in their bedrooms, or they were all in the family room at the back of the house, snuggled up together with Tracy, watching a movie. The image made him smile even though his skin prickled as he hurried from the car to the porch, his keys in his hand, the door key poking out.

For once he wished he had a gun on him, something to defend himself with if someone (a monster) came rushing out of the darkness at him. Eve had pestered him about getting a gun, but he'd never liked the idea of it. He'd never even shot one, and he didn't want one in the house with his daughters around—they were still too young, and Amber was too curious. He decided on the spot as he walked up the steps of the front porch that he would get a security system installed soon—he could at least do that.

It's just my nerves. Eve's got me spooked, jumping at every shadow.

He got to his front door, relieved but not totally relaxed yet, not until he got inside. He unlocked the door and rushed inside with his laptop tucked in the carrying case, the strap looped over his shoulder.

The house was dark and a little chilly. He wondered for a second if Tracy had gone somewhere with the girls without telling him.

No, the car was still in the driveway.

He shut the front door and flipped the knob above the doorhandle to lock the deadbolt, the thunking of metal in the doorframe slamming home a comforting sound.

"Tracy! I'm home!"

No answer. He flipped the switch on the wall to turn on the foyer lights, but the lights weren't turning on.

Was the electricity out?

No, the front porch lights were on. Then why were the foyer lights out? Why was the house so dark and cold?

"Girls!"

Still no answer. Usually, Amber would come running and jump into his arms when he came home. Not Lorie, though—she was too old for that now.

His eyes were adjusting quickly to the darkness of the house, but he pressed the button on his cell phone to give himself a little more light. He shined the flashlight beam on his cell phone down at the doorhandle of the front door, checking it, making sure it was locked.

He heard a noise from behind him in the darkness, the scuffing of a shoe on the hardwood floor.

Maybe it was Amber sneaking up on him. Her new thing now was to wait behind corners, then jump out and try to scare him. Most of the time he knew she was there, but he had to admit that she'd gotten him a few times. Maybe that's why the lights were off—maybe they were all trying to scare him, Tracy orchestrating it to get back at him for not being around.

"Tracy?" Benji turned with his cell phone in his hand, providing the little light that he had.

A man materialized from the darkness. His pale face had a slight bluish tint to it from the cell phone's light. The man's wicked smile was wide, his eyes like little black rocks set deep under his brows. He had something in one hand, raising it up as he rushed forward.

Benji saw the object in the man's hand just a little too late . . . a claw hammer. His reaction had been too slow. He turned to run, but he also put an arm up to defend himself from the hammer blow, the strap of his laptop carrying case slipping off his shoulder, the case landing on the floor with a thud.

There was another thud at that exact moment, a duller thud, but Benji also heard a sound inside his head like ice cracking on a frozen pond.

A blast of pain created a starburst of lights behind Benji's eyes, and then everything went dark.

FORTY-SIX

Eve went back to Todd Cassel's house later that night, driving past it slowly. The house was still dark, no porch light on. The old Chevy Blazer was still parked in the driveway, no other vehicles there.

Todd still wasn't home, or didn't seem to be.

Fifteen minutes later Eve drove past his house again, this time watching the neighbors' homes, making sure no one was outside. She drove a few streets away to the edge of a parking lot where employees of a small strip plaza parked their cars. A few of the businesses were still open and would be open for the next few hours, a few shoppers drifting in and out.

Eve was dressed as a jogger in clothing similar to what she'd worn when she had broken into Bonner's home. Her clothes were dark, but wouldn't be mistaken for anything other than a runner's outfit. There were a lot of health nuts around the city, and she would fit right in as an early-evening jogger.

She brought the same items she'd brought to Bonner's home in the fanny pack she wore around her waist under the bottom of her sweatshirt:

her .380, her conceal and carry ID, her driver's license, a small flashlight, her cell phone, a canister of pepper spray. The lock-pick kit, two pairs of black nitrile gloves, and the silencer that fit her pistol were stuffed down into her right sock, which was bunched up just above her sneaker.

After stretching for a few minutes next to her car, she pulled out her cell phone and checked it.

No calls from Benji.

She'd been calling Benji for the last few hours, but he hadn't returned her calls. She didn't leave any messages; she didn't need to—Benji would know it was important to get back to her. It wasn't like him not to call back.

But she couldn't have her phone ringing while she was doing this, so she powered it off and stuffed it down into the small pack around her waist, zipping it up, and then pulling the bottom of her large sweatshirt down over it.

It only took ten minutes to jog to Todd's street, then another few minutes to get to his house. These streets were darker than Bonner's streets and not nearly as busy with traffic. The lots were larger, with more shrubs and trees providing better cover than she'd had last time. She slipped in behind a row of bushes and crept across the driveway to the Chevy Blazer parked in front of the garage. She waited in the small space between the rear of the truck and the garage door, listening for a few minutes and waiting for her breathing to slow down.

In her drive-byes and the photos she had studied of Todd's house, she hadn't seen a sign advertising a security system, but that didn't mean he didn't have one. There could also be a dog (or dogs) inside the house. A big dog could attack, but even small dogs could yap, possibly alerting neighbors. She hadn't had the time to do the research she'd needed to do, and she hadn't already visited the house like she had at Bonner's house, so she was going in blind.

Benji could have researched the house for her, but he hadn't gotten back to her yet. And it wasn't like she could call Agent Parker for help; she didn't know enough about Todd Cassel to get Parker involved yet.

After she went inside and found some evidence, once she was sure evidence was there, she would contact Parker.

Maybe.

The truth was that she really didn't want to involve Parker just yet. She wanted the freedom to do things her own way, but the more selfish reason was that Tightrope had promised that the Copycat would have a clue on him—one that he would be more than willing to open his mouth and tell her about.

Another clue.

Just you, Eve. That's what Tightrope had ended the last email with.

It was time to get going. Everything seemed quiet. She crept down the side of the garage, stopping to peek in through a side window.

Too dark to see inside.

She went around to the back of the attached garage, then into the backyard. There was no fence back here, so maybe that meant no dog. There wasn't a doghouse, a dog run, or any dog shit on the ground—all good signs. Even though there wasn't a fence, a line of tall shrubs blocked the view of the backyard from the other neighbors, painting the small yard in darker shadows.

A second later she was beside the back door of the house, crouched down near a window. The windows were dark back here too. She pulled the gloves out of her thick sock and slipped them on and then got the lock-pick kit out.

She had the lock picked in a few seconds, the clicking sounds so loud in the silence of the night. She tested the doorknob, turning it slowly. It was unlocked now. She put her lock-pick kit away and pulled out the silencer, screwing it onto the end of her pistol.

After a deep breath, she turned the doorknob again slowly, then eased the door open. She slipped inside and closed the door gently, but she didn't lock it.

The house was quiet. No dogs barked or moved around in the house.

A sense of déjà vu washed over her—this was like sneaking in through Bonner's back door again. Todd's back door even led to the kitchen, just like Bonner's house.

She waited another two minutes, listening. If there was a dog in the house, she was pretty sure it would have charged her by now, or at least come closer to see who had come into the house, perhaps wagging its tail. But there were still no sounds.

Her body was tense as she waited; she was ready to react if she had to. Her eyes were already well-adjusted to the darkness. She looked around at the kitchen and the small dining room it opened up to on the left. An archway to the right led to what seemed to be the living room at the front of the house. A door on that side of the kitchen must lead to the attached one-car garage.

The place was OCD neat, nearly Spartan in décor. A faint odor of cleaning products lingered in the air. The dishwashing liquid, a sponge, and other items were lined up neatly on the counter behind the sink, all dishes put away, a dishtowel neatly folded up in front of the empty sink.

She'd waited long enough—it was time to search the house. She pulled out her small flashlight, holding it by the end with two fingers, covering most of the end of it to cut down on most of the light.

The first bedroom she came to was a guest bedroom. It was tidy, the bed made, extra storage in the closet. Todd's bedroom was catty-corner from the guest bedroom. His bed was made, the floors swept clean, his bathroom scrubbed, the tub gleaming. She checked in the medicine cabinet—normal stuff. She checked his dresser drawers, carefully sifting through the neatly folded clothes.

No clues.

She checked the closet, where more clothes hung, including a row of park ranger uniforms that looked like they'd been ironed. She stopped for just a moment, staring at the uniforms.

Park ranger. Todd Cassel was a park ranger?

Benji said his girls had gone on a field trip today to the forest.

Was it a coincidence that Todd Cassel was a park ranger?

She had a sinking feeling as she pulled out her cell phone and powered it up, waiting for it to turn on again. Why hadn't she heard from Benji all day?

As she waited for her phone to turn on, she looked through some of the boxes on the top shelf of the closet. There were some older papers, tax returns, bill receipts, photos of Todd and his family. It seemed like Todd had a brother and a sister, both younger than he was. There were photos of him on fishing trips, hunting and camping, posed in front of a log cabin. She flipped the last photo over and saw that Todd had scrawled the words: Windfield, Alaska.

But there wasn't a shred of evidence that Todd was the Copycat, that he was the one who had killed the Krugmans and the Bradys.

The park ranger uniforms were still bothering her.

She checked her phone. No calls from Benji yet. She thought about calling him again, or at least leaving a text. But she didn't want to, not from Todd Cassel's house.

There had to be something in this house—Tightrope wouldn't have sent her the clues in the email if there wasn't something here. Would he?

She checked through the house again, going through boxes a little more carefully. She checked the attached garage; there was no car inside, and one wouldn't have fit with the kayak sitting in the middle of the floor. She'd seen the same kayak in a few of the Alaska photos.

The shelves of the garage had more junk on them: car cleaning stuff, boxes, extra lightbulbs, tools, toolboxes, more outdoor equipment and gear, tents, camping gear, some holiday decorations, a floor jack in the corner of the garage.

Still nothing—nothing she could give to Parker for a warrant.

She was back in the living room, staring at the two bookcases built into the wall flanking a flat-screen TV. Something bothered her about the bookcases, the molding, the color of them. They didn't seem to go with the rest of the house. There was something about the faux antique finish that seemed familiar to her. The books on the shelves were mostly outdoor survival stuff, a few hardback thrillers and mysteries, a few action paperbacks, some knickknacks, more small family photos in frames.

Running a hand along the bookcase to the left she realized that the wall unit seemed built into the wall, but there was the slightest of seams around it. She had one like this in her home disguising the entrance to her basement, although hers was of much higher quality. This bookcase hid the entrance to a room—she was sure of it.

The door would be sealed magnetically. There should be some kind of object that would release the magnetic locks when waved in front of it. She scanned the shelves: books, framed photos of Todd's Alaskan adventures, a ceramic bowl that looked handmade, a stack of ceramic coasters. That was it. She picked up the coasters that were cemented together and waved it in front of the edge of the bookcase until she heard a faint thump from behind the shelves, the whole bookcase bumping open just a bit.

She set the stack of tiles back on the shelf and pulled the door open slowly, her gun in her hand now. It was dark inside the hidden room and Todd could be waiting in there for her.

She stood just to the side of the open bookcase, listening for a moment, trying to pick up the sound of someone breathing.

Nothing.

Relaxing just a little, she fished the small flashlight out of her sweatshirt pocket and turned it on, shining the thin beam of light into the room, sweeping it back and forth slowly.

It was a small room cluttered with furniture against the back wall and a bookcase to the left. A desk, office chair, and a table shoved against the far wall. Posters and paintings hung on the walls.

She found the light switch on the wall to the right and turned on the overhead light.

She'd found the evidence she needed.

FORTY-SEVEN

The bookcases of Todd's hidden room were stuffed with books about serial killers: Ted Bundy, Jack the Ripper, The Green River Killer, The BTK Killer, Jeffrey Dahmer, John Wayne Gasey, and many others. And of course, Tightrope. There were books about martial arts and wilderness survival, books on FBI and police procedures, books about guns, books about computer programming and software design, books about government conspiracies, books about ropes, knot tying, bondage and S&M.

Cardboard boxes on the floor held more books and magazines, all of them stacked up inside. On the walls were crude drawings of sadistic and intricate rope and bondage designs. A large bulletin board had internet printouts and clipped newspaper articles pinned to it.

The table next to the desk was cluttered with two wireless prints with papers and books, pieces of ropes with intricate knots in them. More boxes below the table had ropes and chains, padlocks, a set of knives rolled up in a large piece of canvas. The desk was just as cluttered, the drawers full of notebooks.

There was so much to see, so much to take in at first glance. The walls were painted blood-red, the trim a glossy black. The bookshelves, desk, and table were all mismatched, garage-sale furniture. There was a claustrophobic feel to the room, a musty odor with something worse just under that smell. This small room was the exact opposite of the rest of Todd's neat and organized home.

Eve sat down in the office chair and set her gun and flashlight on the desk top. She went through the first drawer, leafing through the papers inside: drawings of naked women bound in different positions, drawings of different knots and rope configurations. Todd was no master artist, but he was competent enough that Eve could tell exactly what she was looking at. There were also cutout photos from bondage magazines, printouts from the internet. The photos seemed more instructional for Todd rather than for stimulation, like he was studying rope bondage, studying the methods Tightrope might use to tie knots and arrange ropes, to bind his victims.

In the next drawer, among different papers and magazines, Eve found more drawings: re-creations of the Townsend murders, her own family tied to the wooden chairs, schematics of the room with distances measured in feet and inches.

She opened the laptop next to the lamp on the desk, sifting through more papers while it booted up.

The laptop was password protected. She wouldn't be able to break it. Maybe Benji could unlock it. She thought about taking the laptop with her when she left, but she didn't know how she would be able to jog down the street with it. Maybe she could hide it somewhere in the yard and come back for it.

It didn't matter. There was enough here to get Parker involved, for him to try to get a warrant. She thought about calling Parker when she got out of the house and back to her car, but she knew she wouldn't.

Just you, Eve.

She sifted through more papers in the next drawer, which was more of the same as the first drawer. Todd had become a true student of Tightrope's methods. She used her phone to take photos of the papers, the bulletin board of printouts and newspaper articles, the rows of books on the shelves.

She checked the bottom drawer of the desk on the right side, the deepest of the drawers. Her skin pricked at the thought of Todd coming home, sneaking into his house. He would see the bookcase opened, see the light shining out from his secret room. She needed to hurry, but she also needed to find more. There was more here, she could feel it.

Eve tried to be careful as she combed through Todd's stuff—she didn't want him to know that she'd gone through it. But as OCD as Todd seemed to be, she was sure he'd be able to tell if a paper was out of place in this room.

The third drawer had more magazines, file folders with papers inside, spiral notebooks, more photos of him in Alaska, standing in front of the same cabin he'd posed in front of in other Windfield, Alaska photos. Eve took a picture of several of these photos.

At the bottom of the drawer, she found a large notebook. When she pulled it out, she realized it seemed more like a photo album or a scrap book, bound in faux leather. There were pages and pages of notes written in his small and precise handwriting, chronicling the research he'd done on the Krugman family. She took more photos with her phone as she flipped through the pages. Everything was dated and organized, like he was doing research for a book.

The next section was about the Brady family: research about their property and home, Ken and Lucy's occupations, the teenage kids' afterschool activities. There were notes about them not having dogs, guns, or a security alarm at their house. There were photos of their home, the school the kids went to, their vehicles, a blurry photo of Ken at the restaurant he'd managed.

Then there were the photos of the murders, the mutilated body of Ken Brady hanging by his wrists from the ceiling, his pale flesh covered with blood, a small hole in his abdomen, a string of intestines pulled out and piled up on the floor near his dangling feet.

There were other closer photos of Ken's cuts and mutilations: his face, his eyes half-closed, the gag cruelly tight around his mouth, biting into his skin. Ken was in shock, already near death, a glassy and faraway look in his eyes.

More photos of Lucy and the kids, the red ropes lashing them together in an intricate webbing as they stood in a line, the nooses tight around their necks, their eyes bulging from the pressure and fear, tears shiny on their faces, the white rags stuffed into their mouths, white strips of bedsheets tied around their faces.

A flashback of being tied to the wooden chair hit Eve like an electric shock. For just a second, she was back in her home, tied to the chair, watching her father and mother being tortured slowly by Tightrope.

She looked at the photos again in the large notebook. Todd was mimicking Tightrope's crimes, but not exactly—he was building on what Tightrope had begun; Cassel was evolving, raising the bar, his tortures bolder, proving to be Tightrope's superior, improving where he had failed.

And Todd wasn't done—he was just getting started. There would be more families.

Eve turned to the next section of the large book, to the next family Todd had researched.

She froze.

It was the Kelso family.

Todd had written detailed bios of each member of the Kelso family, with photos of their house, their cars, one photo of Tracy taking her daughters to a department store.

Next page: A photo of Tracy and her girls at the national park where Todd must work. Eve remembered Benji telling her last night that he needed to get back home because his girls were taking a field trip the next day to the forest and were excited about it.

Today . . . they had gone to the forest today.

But Benji hadn't said which forest they were going to. He'd just said, "to the forest." She hadn't bothered to ask him, too wrapped up in her own thoughts, her world of catching Tightrope and the Copycat. And the Copycat's next victims had been right under her nose.

Maybe Cassel hadn't finished stalking them yet, hadn't planned it all out yet.

She prayed there was still time.

Benji hadn't called her back tonight. That was strange. That wasn't like him. He always got right back to her.

She checked her phone again, her fingers trembling, her skin flushed with a sudden heat, her heart tap-dancing inside her chest.

No calls from Benji. No texts. No emails. Nothing.

"God, no . . ."

She jumped to her feet, not bothering to put the notebook and other papers back into the bottom drawer—she didn't have time. She left the secret room, shutting off the light and closing the bookcase that served as the secret door.

She still needed to be careful. Cassel could still come home. Maybe tonight wasn't the night he was going to kill Benji and his family.

God, she hoped so.

She slipped her phone into her pack. She got to the back door and peeked out through the curtains at the backyard. The moonlight shined down through a break in the clouds.

No one out there.

She opened the back door, twisted the lock on the doorknob, closed it gently, then bolted for the driveway. She still needed to be cautious; she couldn't blow everything now by letting a neighbor see her prowling through Todd's yard and driveway. As she crept through the deeper shadows created by the back of the house, she pulled off her black nitrile gloves and stuffed them down into her sock.

It took a few minutes to sneak down the driveway, past the bushes, and then out to the sidewalk.

Please be okay, Benji . . . please . . .

FORTY-EIGHT

It took much less time for Eve to get back to her car than it had to get from her car to Todd's house. She'd been trying to pose as a jogger before, running along at a leisurely pace. Now she sprinted back to her car.

She was a little out of breath when she got to her car, scanning the parking lot as she approached, making sure there weren't any vehicles close by . . . and no cops.

After she got into her car and started it, she checked her phone again.

No messages from Benji.

She thought about calling him again, but decided not to. If her worst fears were true and Cassel was at Benji's house, she couldn't take the chance that he had Benji's phone, waiting to see if she would call. She couldn't take the chance of tipping him off in any way.

The minutes ticked by excruciatingly slow as she sped out of the city toward the country, the Cascades a dark wall in the distance, black jagged shapes against the dark blue night sky. Benji lived in a somewhat rural area, maybe not as rural as where the Krugmans and the Bradys had lived, but quite a few miles outside of Seattle.

Why had Cassel chosen Benji and his family for his next victims? It couldn't be a coincidence. Could Cassel have known she was getting close to finding out who he was? Was she—the one Tightrope had let go, the one Tightrope had let live—the ultimate prize for Todd Cassel, the one he was ultimately working toward? Had he been watching her, researching her like he'd researched the Krugmans and the Bradys? Was he trying to take Benji away from her to hinder her, or was he trying to upstage Tightrope? Or was he trying to punish her? If so, who was next? Harold Shoemaker and his wife? Her aunt? Her cousins? Agent Parker? She hadn't seen any research in Todd's papers about her or anyone else close to her (except Benji), but maybe she'd missed it. She hadn't had time to look through every notebook, every scrap of paper, and she couldn't get into his laptop—as soon as she saw that Benji and his family had been targeted, she had left. So maybe there was more in those papers and on those computer files somewhere.

If Benji had been selected purposely, then how had Cassel found out about her and Benji's working relationship? She thought she'd been so careful. Even Agent Parker didn't know about Benji.

Could Tightrope be controlling all of this behind the scenes?

These thoughts raced through Eve's mind as she drove. She needed to push them away. There would be plenty of time later to contemplate the hows and the whys. For now, she needed to focus on getting to Benji's house, making sure he and his family were safe. And if Cassel wasn't there yet, then she would get them to a safe place.

As she rounded the bend that led to Benji's home, she turned off her headlights and shifted into neutral, slowing the car down and easing it onto the grassy shoulder. The cold, dry grass crunched under her tires as she came to a stop. She was still at least twenty-five yards away from the end of Benji's driveway, her car hidden among the darker shadows the trees created.

It would take a few extra minutes to get down Benji's driveway on foot, but if Cassel was here, she didn't want him to hear her car rumbling down the driveway—she wanted to sneak up on the house. She was afraid if he spotted her car, if he knew someone was coming, then he would stop the torture and kill them all. Maybe this way she could still save them . . . or at least some of them . . . even one of them.

She'd already shut off the interior lights in her car, and she got out as quietly as she could, easing the door shut. She still had the fanny pack around her waist tucked under her black sweatshirt, her lock-pick kit still in her sock. She dug her gloves out of her socks and slipped them on to cover up more of her skin. She had a black knit cap on, and her hair was tied up in back, but there wasn't anything she could do to cover her face.

As she hurried through the grass far to the right side of the driveway, closer to the woods, she glanced around, listening. The cold wind whistled down across the plain of grass, rustling the tree branches—it sounded like a thousand death rattles shaking. Somewhere an animal scurried deeper into the brush, startled by her approach.

The nearly full moon shined down between the clouds that raced by in the night sky, giving her just enough light to see, the clouds creating gigantic shadows that swept across the large yard, the driveway, and the house.

The house was dark, few if any lights on—none in the front part of the house. The only lights came from the front porch, lights on each side of the door that looked like shining eyes in the darkness.

Eve slipped past the two vehicles parked in the driveway, Benji's car parked right behind a Soccer Mom SUV that must be Tracy's. No other vehicles around. Maybe that was a good sign, maybe Cassel wasn't here yet. She prayed that she had gotten here in time.

She crept to the back of the house, stopping at the first window she came to. It was too dark to see inside, but she could see muted lights shining out from the sliding glass door at the deck attached to the back of the house. The backyard stretched toward the woods in the distance. Two large sheds in the far corner and the girls' playground set right in the middle of the yard—the structures just dark shadows in the night, black geometric shapes.

A muffled scream sounded from inside the house, a woman or a girl's scream. She'd never been inside Benji's house before, but she guessed the sliding glass doors led to a living room or a family room.

As she stood right next to the house, flush against the siding, she heard a man's voice talking from in the home. She couldn't make out the words. Cassel was in there. He had Benji and his family captive. She couldn't go in through the sliding glass doors. No, she'd go back around to the front door, pick the lock, sneak in that way, take Cassel by surprise.

She needed to hurry—she saw the pictures in her mind of the Bradys, the father hung by his wrists, tortured to death while his family watched.

Moments later Eve was at the front door of the home. It only took her fifteen seconds to pick the lock on the door. She stuffed the lock-pick kit back down into her sock and pulled her gun out of her hoodie pocket. She turned the doorknob slowly and pushed the door open, hoping it wouldn't creak. She slipped in through the half-open door and then eased it closed until she heard it shut with a soft click.

Now that she was inside the house, she could hear Cassel's voice more clearly.

"Hold on," Cassel said casually from the family room beyond the foyer and hallway. "Don't move too much or the ropes will get even tighter."

For just a second Eve froze in the dark hallway, her mind back in her own home. For just a moment she was seventeen years old again, bound to a wooden chair with red ropes, struggling as her mother, father, and brother were cut up and tortured. Maddie's eyes were wide, pleading with her to do something. Tightrope was telling Eve's mother and father not to struggle or the nooses would tighten.

The same thing Tightrope said . . . almost word for word . . .

The choking sounds from the family room brought her back. There were grunting sounds, muffled sobs and cries. They were already choking to death.

Eve bolted down the hallway to the family room.

FORTY-NINE

Like a bull charging a crowd at a rodeo, Eve ran down the front hall toward the family room, her gun in her gloved hand, her finger on the trigger.

When she got to the archway, she froze for just a second . . . maybe a second too long.

Benji hung from the ceiling, just like Ken Brady had hung in the photos she'd seen less than an hour ago in Cassel's secret room. Tracy and her daughters were across from Benji, fifteen feet away, all of them tied to wooden chairs with red ropes, more ropes connecting them to each other, and to the nooses looped around their necks. Cassel stood between Benji's hanging body and the bound family, dressed all in black with a black hood over his head, a hole for his mouth in the mask and holes for his eyes, a hunting knife in his hand.

For just a moment, Eve was seventeen years old again, back home and tied to the chair, staring at Tightrope, a monster dressed in black who had killed her family, the monster who had taken her sister.

She had only hesitated for a few seconds, but those seconds allowed Cassel to bolt to the sliding glass doors. He swatted the plastic vertical blinds out of the way, slid the door open and escaping out onto the wood deck.

Maybe it was the sound of the clattering plastic, the blinds slapping against each other in a whirlwind, a few of the slats falling out of the track. It brought her back. She pulled the trigger, then she pulled it again and again, shooting at the shadowy figure that had escaped out into the night, the glass doors shattering from the bullets.

She wanted to chase Cassel—she wanted that more than anything in the world right now—to run him down like a lioness on the savannah; she wanted to put a bullet in his brain and end his miserable existence. The pull of the chase was almost too strong, but she couldn't do it. Tracy and her daughters were choking to death, their eyes bulging, glassy, staring at her like they didn't dare believe she was really there, like they thought she was a hallucination brought on by a lack of oxygen and the approach of death, like she was an angel, a glimpse of the afterlife they would soon be visiting. They screamed and grunted through their gags, their bodies trembling under the network of ropes.

Eve didn't have a knife, and she didn't have time to look for one. She was behind the youngest daughter first (Amber—Benji had talked about her many times; her name was Amber). She dug her fingers underneath the noose, pulling the rope and loosening the slipknot enough to pull it up over Amber's head.

The other ropes began to slack just a little after that, but the nooses were still tight around Lori and Tracy's necks.

Amber could breathe again, choking into her gag, inhaling huge greedy gulps of air through her nostrils.

Eve loosened Lorie's noose next, then Tracy's, all while keeping an eye on the sliding glass door, waiting for Cassel to pop back in with some kind of gun. All three of them were breathing again, inhaling and exhaling through their noses rapidly. Eve untied the rags around their mouths.

"He's gone," Eve told them, even though she couldn't really be sure of that. She didn't know if Cassel had a gun on him. Maybe he had one in his vehicle, wherever he had parked it. Maybe he had gone for a gun and was coming back. Or maybe he was running . . . getting away.

Eve still had her gun in her hand. She'd had to lay it down while she had loosened the nooses and gags, but she had it again while she ran to the kitchen for a knife. She found a serrated knife in the second drawer she opened.

"I'm going to untie you," Eve told Tracy when she came back.

"Hurry," Tracy grunted. The girls were sobbing, thrashing against the ropes, the wood chairs creaking.

Once again, in a span of seconds, Eve froze when she rushed past Benji on her way back to Tracy and her daughters. She had trained herself through the years for this, training her mind and body to be strong enough for horrors like this. But maybe the training hadn't been enough. Maybe she still wasn't strong enough. She hadn't been ready to see Benji hanging by his wrists, his body mutilated, his eyes closed. Dead.

Maybe she would never be ready for this.

She'd been too late to save Benji, but there was still time to save Tracy and her daughters.

She set her gun on the floor as she sawed at the red ropes binding Tracy's wrists, arms, and torso to her chair, and then she cut the ropes around her ankles and knees. As she worked to free Tracy, she kept an eye on the vertical blinds covering the sliding glass door, a few of the slats fallen, the rest gently swaying back and forth from the violent shove Cassel had given them, the plastic pieces lightly tapping each other. She could imagine Cassel out there, concealed in the darkness beyond the back porch, aiming his gun at the shattered sliding glass doors. The doorway would be lit up out there in the night, so easy for him to see, to pick her off when she came out through the doors. He was a hunter—she'd seen the photos from his Alaska trips. He would be good with a gun. Maybe he'd run back to his truck for a rifle and a night scope. She could imagine seeing a flash of light between those slowly swaying vertical blinds, feeling the thud of a bullet before she even heard the gunshot.

She should have left the back porch light on so she could see him out there.

Too late now.

Concentrate . . . focus on what you're doing.

TIGHTROPE

Tracy squirmed more and more as Eve cut the ropes away, panicky to get free. The girls were still sobbing. Lorie stared at her dead father hanging from the ceiling across the room.

As soon as Tracy was free, Eve picked up her gun. She handed the kitchen knife to Tracy. "Get your daughters loose," she told her. "Then call 911."

Tracy nodded numbly, holding the knife in both hands like she was suddenly unfamiliar with the utensil. She looked unsteady on her feet, like she might pass out at any second.

"Stay with me," Eve told her. "You have to be strong right now."

Tracy nodded, sniffed back tears.

"After you call 911, get to a bedroom. Go in there. Lock the door."

"Wait, where are you going?"

"After him."

"Stay here with us. He could come back. He could be out there right now."

"I have to go."

"Mom," Lorie wailed. "Get me out of here."

Tracy crouched down to cut Lorie's ropes, but her hands were shaking so badly.

Seconds were ticking by too quickly—Cassel was getting away. Eve felt the urge to leave, to track, to hunt. But she ran to the kitchen to get another knife. She ran back and cut Amber free, then she helped Tracy cut the ropes away from Lorie's legs.

"Call the police," Eve told Tracy again. "Get to a room. Lock the door."

Tracy had a cordless phone in her hand, about to dial 911. She looked right at Eve. "It was a park ranger. That . . . that man in here, it was Ranger Cassel. He was . . . he was at our field trip today. In the woods." She started to cry.

"I know," Eve told her. "Tell them who he is when you call 911. You need to call the police."

Tracy nodded and wiped at her tears. She began pressing the buttons on her cordless phone.

Eve didn't wait any longer; she pushed the vertical blinds back on their tracks and stepped out through the shattered sliding glass door, her gun in her hand, her sneakers crunching on broken diamonds of glass all over the wooden deck.

This was the most dangerous moment. If Todd hadn't run, if he waited outside or he had circled back from where his vehicle was parked, she would make a perfect target for him.

It took a few seconds for her eyes to adjust to the darkness again. The moonlight helped.

She didn't see Cassel anywhere.

He had run. Where? Back home? Maybe. But he knew the cops would be called and Tracy knew who he was. But Eve had nowhere else to look, so she would go to Cassel's home first, start from there.

She didn't see any drops of blood on the deck among the pieces of shattered glass, so she probably hadn't hit him with one of her shots.

A moment later she was around the back corner of the house. She raced past Tracy's SUV and Benji's car. She didn't know how far Cassel had to go to get to his vehicle, so she had no idea how big of a head start he had on her.

She sprinted down the long dirt driveway to the road, and then to her car parked in the shadows of the woods. She felt exposed, expecting to hear a gunshot at any moment. Or he could be waiting behind her car, waiting to jump out and shoot her.

As Eve approached her car, the metal and glass gleaming in the cold moonlight, she aimed her .380 at it. This was slowing her down, but she had to be careful.

Cassel wasn't behind her car, or in it. He might be somewhere in the woods, but most likely he'd already gotten back to his car and was on the run.

She got in her car and closed the door, locking it. She started her car, turning the headlights on. She drove forward and backed up into Benji's driveway to turn around, spraying dirt from the back tires of her Audi.

The drive back to the city seemed to take forever. Mixed emotions plagued her even though she tried to push them away. She was happy she had saved Tracy and her daughters, but she was also angry at herself for not saving Benji. Had she missed a clue that could have led her to Cassel sooner? Had she taken too long searching Cassel's home, finding his secret room, going through his papers and notebooks? She should have left as soon as she'd seen the park ranger uniforms. She couldn't be certain at the time that Todd Cassel was the Copycat just because he was also a park ranger; she couldn't have been certain until she found his secret room. But deep down inside she had known, and she hadn't left at that moment. She had searched the rest of Cassel's home, knowing that if Cassel was the killer, then this would be her only chance to search his home, to find the clue that Tightrope had promised was there. Maybe that extra time, those extra minutes, had cost Benji his life while she was pursuing her own selfish goals.

There would be plenty of time later to grieve and to beat herself up with guilt about Benji's death. Right now, she needed to hold on to her anger, let the rage fuel her, let it drive away any fears, doubts, self-pity, and guilt. She was a predator now tracking another predator, and this time she was going to win.

On the drive to Todd's home, she thought about calling Parker and getting him ahead of this. She almost reached for her cell phone.

But she didn't. She still wanted to do this alone. She wanted to end this. She wanted to find Todd Cassel—he might still have the clue on him. Or he might know something. Tightrope had promised her a clue in his email. But then again, Tightrope could have been lying, still torturing her after all these years, just like Agent Parker had suggested.

Fifteen minutes later, when she was only a few blocks away from Cassel's neighborhood, she saw a faint reddish glow in the night sky above the homes.

"No," she breathed out, speeding around a corner, her tires squealing. She sped down the street and turned left onto Cassel's street.

She had to get closer, had to see what she already knew—Todd's house was on fire. She slowed her car down to a crawl as she passed neighbors gathered on their lawns, driveways, and front porches. Some stood at the edge of the street, some huddled together on sidewalks. A few kids sat on bicycles, staring in awe like they were watching fireworks during the Fourth of July.

Todd's house was an inferno. Sirens wailed in the distance.

Had he beaten her here? If he had, he couldn't have beaten her by much? Ten minutes? Fifteen minutes at the most. Not enough time for him to grab his stuff and set his house on fire.

Had someone else done it for him?

Eve drove past Todd's house as a cop car came up behind her quickly, screeching to a stop in front of Todd's house, police lights flashing. She drove to the end of the street and made a left, driving out of Cassel's neighborhood.

But she wasn't going home.

She had other plans.

Whether Cassel had set his own house on fire or someone else had done it, she had an idea of where he was running to.

Windfield, Alaska. To the cabin she'd seen in the photos.

Eve called Angel, her pilot, and asked him to get the jet ready to fly tonight.

FIFTY

It took Eve less than twenty-four hours to find Todd in Alaska. He was at a cabin similar to the one she'd seen in the photos in his home. He had rented the cabin under a fake name. He had also rented an off-road SUV under the same name. But Eve had paid quite a lot of money for some local information, and here she stood now, two and a half hours from sundown, hidden in the woods one hundred yards away from the cabin in the clearing, the rented SUV parked next to it.

Last night, after leaving Todd's neighborhood and his burning home, Eve had checked into a motel while Angel readied her plane.

She'd cried in the shower of the motel room, sobbing for Benji, for his wife and daughters. It had been a long time since she had cried. Everything came out in her sobs: Benji's death; what it had done, and would do, to his family. She knew too well what it would do, and she vowed to take care of Tracy and her daughters in any way she could. Eve would give them enough money so that they could go anywhere in the world they wanted to, do anything they wanted.

Then she remembered freezing at the sight of Benji, and at the sight of Cassel dressed all in black, just like Tightrope had been dressed: the black clothes, gloves, black hiking boots, the hood and mask with holes for the eyes and a small one for his mouth. Todd had looked so much like Tightrope in that moment, similar in height and build; even the tone of his voice had been similar, the way he had taunted and teased, the joy at the misery and pain he wrought. Even the words he'd spoken had been so similar to Tightrope's.

And that moment of paralysis had allowed Cassel to get away.

She even wondered in that moment if she was really looking at Tightrope standing in the middle of Benji's family room. She had wondered in that moment if there was no copycat, had never been one, if Tightrope had been pretending to be a copycat all along, orchestrating this whole thing like it was one big game.

Or could Todd really be Tightrope? He was in his early thirties, that would have made him around his early twenties when her family was killed and Maddie was taken. Too young? She couldn't be sure, but to her at that time Tightrope had seemed much older than that. But she'd been seventeen years old and traumatized at that time. Could she even trust her memories one hundred percent from that night? Had time altered some of her memories?

It still didn't *feel* true to her that Todd Cassel was Tightrope, and she couldn't waste time thinking about it. Cassel had run. She would find him, and she would get answers from him.

After her shower, Eve had gotten dressed in the spare clothes she kept in a duffel bag in the trunk of her car, throwing her old clothes away later in a dumpster. She ate some take-out food, not really tasting it, just eating the food for the calories, to give her energy for what lay ahead.

Agent Parker had called her burner phone while she'd been in the shower. He'd left a message: "Eve, call me. The Copycat struck again. A family. Ben and Tracy Kelso. Their two daughters." There was a pause during the recording. "But you already know that, don't you? Tracy said Eve Townsend saved her life. Saved her daughters' lives." Another pause, this one not as long. "Eve, please call me back. Work with me on this."

She hadn't called him back. Instead, she had called Angel to ask if the plane was ready to leave.

And now she waited in the woods, by a tree where she'd been for the last twenty minutes. She watched the cabin with a pair of small binoculars. No smoke drifted up from the chimney, but there were solar panels on the roof, which probably provided enough electricity for heat in the cabin, lights, a water heater, kitchen appliances. The log cabin was small, maybe four or five rooms at the most. The front door was solid wood and the porch ran the length of the front of the home. A shed was off to the right, beyond where the SUV was parked, the shed almost half the size of the cabin. Piles of chopped firewood were stacked up against the longer side of the cabin, under the eaves of the roof. A thin layer of snow blanketed everything.

The patchy snow on the ground was pristine, no footprints that she could make out; no human footprints, anyway. There were wolf tracks. She heard the wolves howling every so often, and in the last twenty minutes she'd been watching the cabin, it sounded like the wolves had gotten closer, growing bolder.

Eve was dressed in a woodland-pattern camouflage jacket and pants, waterproof hiking boots, a dark skull cap and thin black gloves. She had a camo backpack which contained the supplies she'd brought with her. She had a hunting knife strapped to her belt, and under her jacket she had a shoulder holster with a handgun and silencer tucked down inside. She had her lock-pick kit in her pants pocket, along with a small canister of pepper spray. In her backpack she had an extra jug of water, protein bars, zip ties, a roll of duct tape, lighter fluid.

Tightrope had said in his email that he would leave a clue with Cassel, one that Cassel would be willing to open his mouth and tell her about, a clue that would lead her closer to him.

Was Tightrope in that cabin? Was this as close as she was going to get to Tightrope? Were Cassel and Tightrope working together? It would explain a few things, like how Cassel had mastered Tightrope's skills so well, and how Cassel had gotten back to his house so quickly and burned it down with all the evidence inside.

Her heart thudded in her chest. She was nervous, more afraid of failing than dying. Afraid of never finding out the answers. She needed to be careful, she couldn't get this close just to blow it.

The sun was getting lower, the air colder, the wolves closer.

It was time.

Eve stayed in the woods as much as she could while creeping closer to the shed, then she darted across the field behind the shed, her gun in her hand, her exhales a plume of mist in front of her face, disappearing within seconds in the freezing air.

She waited a few seconds, watching the cabin from the back corner of the shed. There was a door at the back of the cabin with a set of wooden steps coated with snow.

She got to the first window on that side of the cabin; it looked in on a dark bedroom through parted curtains.

No one in the bedroom. She cupped her hands to the sides of her face so she could see the room better. A bed, nightstand, a throw rug, paintings on the walls, a door to a closet, the bedroom door was halfway open, leading to a hallway. A shaft of light came from down the hall, from the front of the cabin where the living room and kitchen must be.

As she made her way down to the next window—the only other window on this side of the cabin—she saw the wash of light coming from that window; it was more noticeable now as the sun dipped lower behind the mountains and the woods grew darker.

A wolf howled.

Another answered.

She got to the next window and peeked in through the bottom corner, her gun ready in her hand. She had the lighter fluid and matches in her backpack; it was enough to soak this log cabin and start a fire, smoke Cassel out if she had to.

When she looked in through the window, Eve froze at what she saw.

FIFTY-ONE

Inside the cabin, in the middle of the large room that was both the living room and the kitchen, a man was bound to a wood chair with red ropes, seemingly miles of red rope securing the man to the chair, his arms wrenched behind his back, wrists lashed together, lengths of gray duct tape wrapped around his head, covering his mouth, his head hung forward, chin on his chest. He was clothed in jeans and a long-sleeved shirt, the front of it stained with blood. His feet were bare, but looked purple and black with rot, both of them staked to the wooden floor with gigantic metal spikes.

It was Todd Cassel. Even with the blood and the tape covering the bottom half of his face, she could tell it was him.

He wasn't moving.

Was he dead?

Oh, God no . . .

You'll find a clue on him that will lead you closer to me. Tightrope's words from his email echoed in her mind.

Eve made herself wait a moment longer. It didn't seem like anyone else was inside the cabin, but she couldn't be sure.

Who had done this to Cassel? Tightrope? Was Tightrope still around? Still close? Setting a trap for her? Using Cassel as bait? Waiting for her to show up?

Another howl from a wolf, this one even closer. It was like the animals could sense the blood from the cabin, the wounded and helpless prey inside.

There wasn't a lot of daylight left now, and she didn't like the idea of making it back to her vehicle through the woods at night.

She ducked under the bottom ledge of the window and hurried to the front porch, slipped under the railing, and crept to the front door. She stood to the side of the door as she tested the doorknob, her gun ready in her other hand. She twisted the doorknob slowly, feeling the cold metal through her glove.

For just a second the doorknob wouldn't budge. She thought it was locked, but then the knob turned and the door opened. She pushed the door open all the way, staying to the side of the door with her gun ready. The hinges creaked and she could feel the warm air coming from the cabin— not real warm, but enough to keep Cassel from freezing to death.

The inside of the cabin was quiet. No sounds from elsewhere in the cabin. No sounds from Cassel. No shifting of ropes and cloth, the creaking of wood. No intake of air through his nostrils, or exhales.

Nothing.

Eve bolted in through the doorway, gun aimed everywhere. The couch and chair were pushed up against the far wall with the dining room table to make more room for the centerpiece: Todd Cassel tied to the chair. The other side of the room had a row of upper and lower cabinets, a sink, a small refrigerator. The windows all had curtains that were open.

He wanted me to see Cassel through the windows.

There was nowhere for anyone to hide inside the living room and kitchen, but Eve remained cautious. She closed the front door and locked it.

She ventured deeper into the cabin, giving Cassel a wide berth. She walked down the hall, flipping on lights as she went. She checked the two bedrooms, the one bathroom, the closets, under the beds.

No one there. No sign of anyone.

She checked the back door at the end of the hall to make sure it was locked, and then she went back to the living room, a little calmer now, but not calm enough.

She ventured closer to Cassel, staring at him as she approached. She could smell the rot of his feet, both swollen and purple, blood crusted where the stakes had been pounded down through his flesh and bones and into the wood flooring, puddles of blood soaked into the wood slats. And there were other smells: piss, shit, body odor . . . the smell of death.

He hadn't moved, his head down, his bald head dull and pale, streaked with dried blood. She checked around the back of him to make sure his hands and arms were still securely bound. His hands hung down from the ropes, lifeless and pale.

Her gun still in her hand, she poked at his shoulder with the barrel, expecting him to jump, to whip his head up, grunting and crying out into the tape that covered his mouth.

He didn't move.

She poked at him again, harder.

Still nothing.

He wasn't breathing. His nose wasn't covered with tape, but the nostrils were covered with blood, the front of his flannel shirt soaked with it.

Was his throat slashed, like Bonner's had been?

Eve dreaded the idea of it, but she pushed her hand against his forehead, pushing his head back up. It stood upright for just one moment, then rolled to the side, his eyes half-open.

She could feel for a pulse in his neck, but she didn't need to. He was dead.

Damn.

Cassel was gone. She wasn't going to get the answers she wanted. The answers she needed.

Tightrope had gotten here first. He had killed Cassel.

Why?

She studied Cassel's face. His eyes were bruised. A small cut marked the bridge of his nose, a small gash in his forehead. He'd been beaten up. Was that what had killed him? Even though there was a lot of blood on the front of his shirt and lap, the blood hadn't come from his throat. It had come from under the tape around his mouth.

How long had he been here? When had he died? Judging from the smell of Cassel and the dried blood, she figured at least twelve hours. Maybe more.

Had Tightrope gotten to Cassel as soon as he had come up here from Washington? Had Tightrope been waiting for him? Had Tightrope burned Cassel's house down?

Questions raced through Eve's mind, questions she doubted she would ever get the answers to.

She stood there a moment longer, staring at Cassel's face. He had wanted to be Tightrope, to commit the same crimes Tightrope had, to become the monster Tightrope was. But in the end, he'd just been another victim of Tightrope's.

Why would Tightrope have told her about Cassel? How did he know so much about him? Why get her up here just to find him dead?

She thought of the email, of his promise that Cassel would have a clue on him.

A clue that he would be wanting to open his mouth and tell you about.

His mouth.

She needed to take the tape off his mouth.

After setting her gun on the counter within reach, she pulled her hunting knife out of the sheath on her belt and cut the tape at the back of his head. She peeled the tape away from his face in one big piece. She dropped the huge wad of tape on the floor and came around to face him. His head had slumped forward again, his mouth open. It looked swollen, like something was stuffed inside. His lips were cut and crusted with dried blood.

He'll have a clue on him, one he'll want to open his mouth and tell you about.

Eve could barely make out what was stuffed inside Cassel's mouth as she pried it open with the blade of her knife. His jaw had stiffened shut. She pried harder and harder until she heard his bones break. His mouth popped open, and she stepped back, breathing hard.

At first, she thought he had deformed teeth, his teeth way too large, but then she realized that the teeth in his mouth were fake, with two long fangs . . . a set of vampire teeth.

She used her knife to pry the fake teeth out of his mouth. They fell into his lap and his head slumped forward again.

Vampire teeth.

She plucked the fake teeth from his lap and brought them to the sink to wash the crusted blood off. She wrapped the teeth in a plastic baggy she found in one of the kitchen drawers and put it in her pack.

He'll have a clue that will lead you closer to me.

Vampire teeth? That was the clue? But what did it mean?

She walked back to Cassel, staring at him. She lifted his head back up and opened his mouth. All his teeth had been pulled out, that's where all the blood had come from. Tightrope had taken Cassel's teeth out and shoved the fake vampire teeth in, then taped his mouth shut.

Why?

Was that what had killed Cassel? Heart attack? Bleeding in his brain from the beating? Poison?

She had no way of knowing.

She thought of the email again. The clues. North Star. She knew that it was a website on the dark web, but did it have anything to do with Cassel, with Tightrope? Was North Star a clue about Alaska? Had Tightrope been steering her here the whole time?

She didn't know.

All she knew was that these teeth meant something, a clue that Tightrope promised would bring her closer to him, to finding him, to finding out what had happened to her sister.

And she would find him. She swore she would.

Eve glanced around at the cabin one last time, then headed for the door. She opened the front door and propped it open with a big rock.

A wolf howled outside. His pack answered. So many of them out there. And so much closer now.

She entered the woods, beginning her three-mile trek back to her Jeep.

FIFTY-TWO

Two days later Eve met with a few agents at the FBI office in Seattle. DeMarco was one of the agents, and Lewis Parker was *not* one of the agents there.

Eve had the lawyer Harold had recommended, Anthony Malone, there with her. He answered most of the questions for her.

"This is supposed to be a friendly meeting," DeMarco told Eve. "We don't need lawyers involved."

Eve didn't answer him.

"Do you have a question for my client?" Malone asked DeMarco.

"You were contacted by Tightrope," DeMarco said to Eve. "He reached out to you. Gave you clues. That's not your fault. It's not your fault you figured out he was going after the Kelso family, an acquaintance of yours, I understand. Ben Kelso used to do some work for you?"

"Ben Kelso helped my client fix her computers when they broke," Malone said. "That was the kind of work he specialized in."

"Benji?" DeMarco said, looking right at Eve. "Isn't that what you called him?"

"I'm told many people called him that," Malone said with a sigh. "It was his nickname."

"You haven't received any more emails from Tightrope?" DeMarco asked Eve, trying his best to ignore the lawyer.

"No, she hasn't," Malone answered for her.

"You would tell us if you have, wouldn't you?"

"Sir, are you going to charge my client with a crime?" Malone asked in a bored voice.

DeMarco sat back in his chair, smirking. He looked at the other two agents on that side of the table. "She wanted to be in the FBI, you know. She wanted to be one of us." He shrugged and looked back at Eve. "Maybe we could still make that happen."

"Is that supposed to be some kind of bribe?" Malone asked.

DeMarco said nothing.

"If there are no further questions," Malone said, already standing up. "I think my client would like to leave."

"No further questions," DeMarco said, leaning forward, his arms on the table, big hands folded together, his dark eyes shiny under the fluorescent lights of the room, a small smile revealing his upper and lower rows of shark's teeth. He looked right at Eve. "Not at this time."

*

When Eve was outside the building, she thanked her lawyer and then walked to her car. She got in and left the parking lot, driving across town to the park where Parker was waiting for her on the bench, not too far away from Ernie's Hot Dog Stand.

"How'd it go?" he asked as she walked up to him.

"As expected." She sat down next to him.

"I heard you donated quite a sum of money to Tracy Kelso and her daughters. I don't think they'll ever have to worry about money again."

He smirked. "I don't think the girls' grandchildren will ever have to worry about money."

"It's not enough," Eve said. "Nothing could ever be enough to replace Benji. But I'm glad she accepted it."

Parker's smile slipped away as he stared at her. "I wanted to let you know that the DNA tests on the body in the mannequin came back. One hundred percent Jennifer Watson. Not Maddie."

Eve nodded, not meeting his eyes. She looked away. She felt tears coming. She didn't want to cry. Not yet. Not in front of Parker.

"DeMarco knows you flew that night up to Alaska. But from there the trail goes cold."

Eve didn't comment.

"These cases have embarrassed DeMarco. He hasn't come out of this looking so competent. Tightrope kills right under his nose. Bonner's mother was involved all along . . . you finding who Tightrope's next targets were before we did . . . I think he's worried about his career. Rumor is heads are going to roll, people are going to be sacrificed, and others are going to move up."

She looked at him. "You?" She knew he was hoping for a promotion to the D.C. office.

"Time will tell. But before DeMarco . . . leaves, *if* he leaves, he's going to come after you. Just be careful."

"I've got the best defense lawyers money can buy."

"I'm sure you do." He chuckled, then became serious. "DeMarco may be pissed about this, but a lot of us in the Bureau think you're a fucking superhero. You saved a woman and her daughters. And for some reason, I don't know why, I just kind of think Tightrope is going to go back into hiding. I don't know if it has to do with Cassel's body being eaten by wolves in Alaska . . ." He let his words die away.

Pieces of Todd Cassel's body had been found beyond the cabin, what was left from the wolves, and then from the birds. No teeth were found at the scene, no fingerprints, only pieces of bone and clothing. Eve had read the report. There was no red rope found among the body parts. No tape. She wondered if Tightrope had gone back to clean up the mess.

"Todd Cassel," Parker said, shaking his head. "The Copycat was a park ranger. Just some guy who was a park ranger." He said it almost like he was amused by it, and in awe, and also horrified by the thought of it.

Eve nodded. "At least it's over. At least Cassel's dead."

"Yeah. Dead. Died in a very strange way."

Eve said nothing.

"Something else is very strange."

She looked at him.

"Mitch Everett."

She watched him.

"I didn't tell you about him. His phone was used to take the photos of the Brady family, used to put them on the internet."

Eve sat up a little straighter. "He's connected to this?"

"We talked to him and his girlfriend a few days ago. His phone had been stolen from his car when he was parked in front of a gas station store. Seemed like a strange coincidence, but we didn't have enough to arrest him."

"Cassel stole this guy's phone?"

Parker shrugged. "Maybe. Makes sense. He couldn't use his own phone."

Eve watched Parker. He was going somewhere with this. "Where's Mitch Everett now?"

"Dead."

Eve felt like she'd been punched in the stomach. For a moment, a brief flicker of hope had ignited, a possible lead, somewhere to start. But it had all been taken away from her within seconds.

"How?" she asked, but she already had a good idea.

"It was strange," he said, staring at her, locking eyes with her. "Like Cassel's death was strange."

She didn't answer him. She didn't look away.

"He died from a botched burglary at his girlfriend's house. They were both killed. Both of them stabbed to death."

Eve remembered reading the story on the internet yesterday when she'd been looking up recent crimes. She had started her search locally, as usual, but then she had fanned out her search across the country, looking for something specific, anything to do with vampire teeth. But the story of a couple being murdered in their own home, stabbed to death, had caught her attention.

"A few things were stolen from the house. Not a lot."

"And no evidence was left behind," Eve said, her stomach sinking. "No fingerprints. No DNA. Nothing."

Parker shook his head. "Nothing."

Tightrope had been here, Eve thought. She shivered, unable to hide it from Parker. Tightrope had been right here in Seattle. So close to her. Watching her as he played his game from the shadows.

And now Tightrope would be gone, back into hiding as Parker had put it. He was somewhere far away now, waiting for her, beckoning for her to follow him, to follow the clue he had left behind for her.

"I'm sorry," Parker said. "I had to tell you."

Eve nodded. She understood.

"Like I said before, be careful around DeMarco. He wants to pin something on you. Some of this doesn't look so good for you."

Eve didn't answer for a moment. Then: "I wish I would've gotten to Benji's house a little sooner. Figured things out a little sooner."

"Believe me, I know the feeling. But there's nothing you can do about the past. Remember, you did a good thing, Eve. You saved some lives."

"He's still out there. Tightrope. He was *here*. And he's not done with all of this."

"You're going after him, I suppose."

Eve didn't respond.

Parker nodded like he was answering his own question, but he didn't bother pressing her about it. "You ever need help, or anything from me, you let me know. Okay?"

She stared at him. "I'll hold you to that. You're a true friend, Agent Parker."

"I hope so. I really do."

They hugged.

Parker stood up and walked away.

Eve sat on the bench a moment longer. She watched two older women walking by on the bike trail, talking to each other, smiling. Having a good time. A man jogged by. Two teenagers rode past on bicycles. In the distance, a ferry floated on the Sound.

Finally, she got up and walked to her car. And then she went home.

She locked her front door as soon as she was inside her house. As usual, she did a quick walk-through of her home with her gun.

After she was satisfied the house was safe, she made some tea and went to her office. She opened one of the file cabinet drawers and pulled out a small padded envelope. She opened it and shook out the vampire teeth onto her desk. She looked up at her computer screen. She had searched the internet over the last few days and found a series of murders in the Cleveland area that had occurred over the last few months—two women dead so far and a third missing. The two dead women had two puncture wounds in the sides of their necks, among other signs of torture. The media was already labeling them the "Vampire Murders."

"You want me to go there," Eve whispered at the computer screen.

When Anthony Malone, her lawyer, had answered DeMarco's question about getting any more emails from Tightrope, he had told DeMarco the truth—Eve hadn't gotten any more emails from him. But the fake vampire teeth she had pulled out of Todd Cassel's mouth was the clue, a piece of the puzzle he wanted her to solve, the puzzle that would eventually get her closer to him.

She got up and shut the computer off. It was time to pack for her trip to Cleveland.

AUTHOR'S NOTE:

Thank you so much for reading my book, the first book in the Eve Townsend series. I hope you'll check out the rest of the books in this series as Eve Townsend makes her way closer and closer to Tightrope, and the awful truth he is hiding. The next book is due out soon.

Being an author is a dream come true for me, but it only happens because of readers like you. I thank you from the bottom of my heart.

Feel free to reach out to me on social media, on Facebook at Mark Lukens Books and @marklukensbooks

ABOUT THE AUTHOR:

Mark Lukens has been writing since the second grade when his teacher scheduled a conference with his parents because the ghost story he'd written had concerned her a little.

Since then, he's had several stories published and four screenplays optioned by producers in Hollywood. He has written almost thirty books, many of them previous bestsellers on Amazon. Some of his books include: the Ancient Enemy series, the Dark Days Series, Sightings, Devil's Island, Sleep Disorders, The Exorcist's Apprentice, Followed, Four Dark Tales, and many more. All of his books can be found on Amazon.

Mark Lukens was raised in Daytona Beach, Florida. But after many travels and adventures, he settled down near Tampa, Florida with his wonderful wife and son, and two stray cats they adopted.

www.marklukensbooks.com

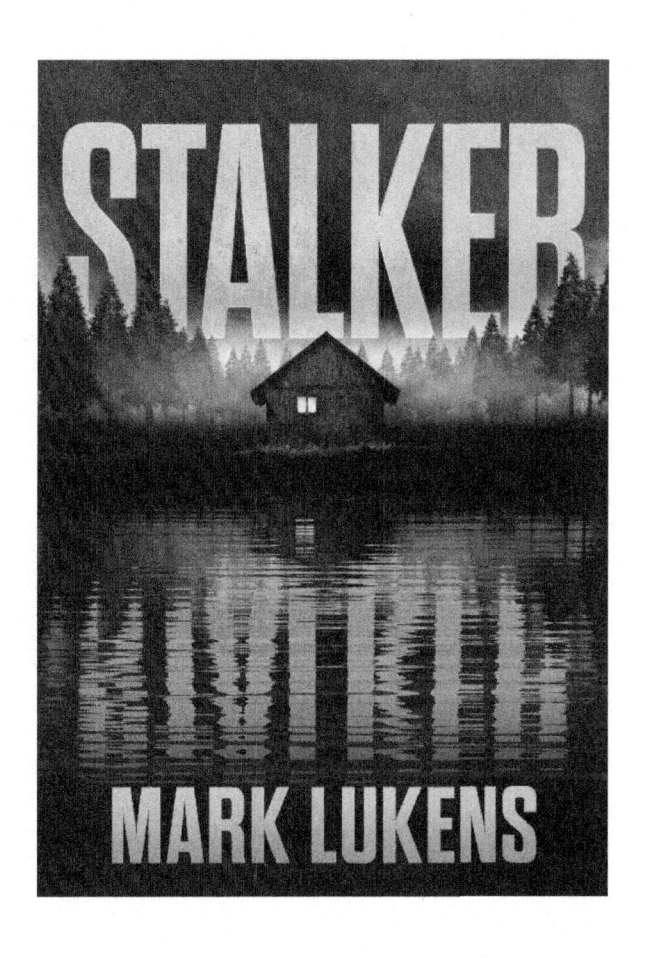

Successful thriller author Teri Holtz just got an email from her biggest fan . . . a man who claims to be a real serial killer.

www.amazon.com/dp/B08WYS731N

As a stalker terrorizes Phil and Cathy, dark secrets from Phil's past emerge that leads Cathy to believe that Phil may know who their stalker is and why he has chosen them.

www.amazon.com/dp/B078WYGMJN

A terrifying secret is trying to surface in Pam's recurring nightmares.

www.amazon.com/dp/B0143LADEY

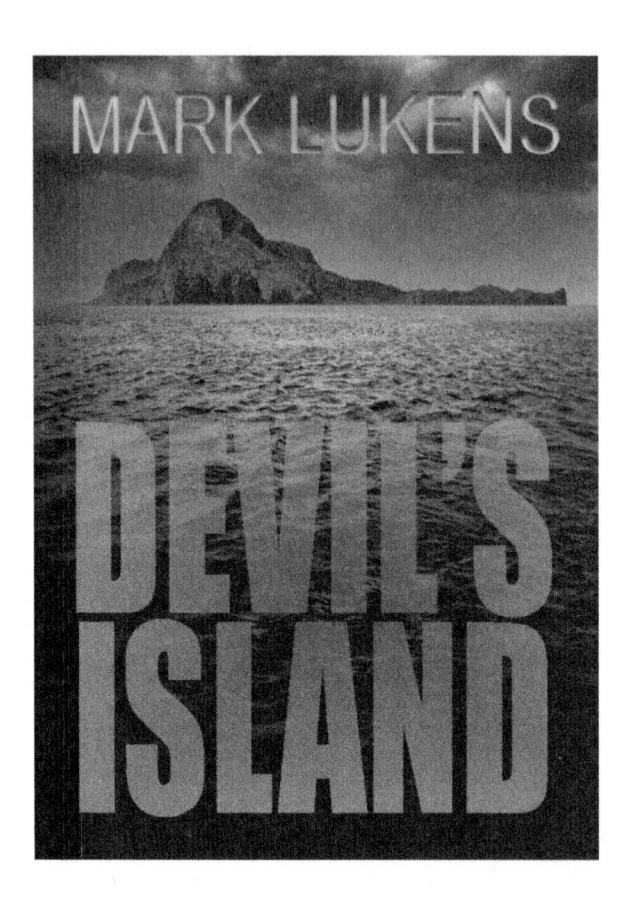

A billionaire leads a team of ghost hunters to an abandoned Caribbean island with a dark and bloody past . . . an island with a terrible secret that could alter all of humanity.

www.amazon.com/dp/B06WWJC6VD

Ancient Enemy . . . it's waiting in the woods. It wants things. You have to give it what it wants or bad things happen. Very bad things.

www.amazon.com/dp/B00FD4SP8M

Printed in Great Britain
by Amazon